THE ARMIES OF ELFLAND

Further Titles by Poul Anderson from Severn House

CONFLICT
KINSHIP WITH THE STARS

THE ARMIES OF ELFLAND

Poul Anderson

This title first published in Great Britain 1994 by
SEVERN HOUSE PUBLISHERS LTD of
9–15 High Street, Sutton, Surrey SM1 1DF.
First published in hardcover format in the USA 1994 by
SEVERN HOUSE PUBLISHERS INC., of
475 Fifth Avenue, New York, NY 10017,
by arrangement with Tom Doherty Associates, Inc.

British Library Cataloguing in Publication Data
Anderson, Poul
Armies of Elfland
I. Title
813.54 [F]

ISBN 0-7278-4574-8

Typeset by Hewer Text Composition Services, Edinburgh.
Printed and bound in Great Britain by
Redwood Books, Trowbridge, Wiltshire.

CONTENTS

Foreword	vii
The Queen of Air and Darkness	1
House Rule	64
The Tale of Hauk	77
Fairy Gold	105
The Valor of Cappen Varra	142
The Gate of the Flying Knives	161
The Barbarian	208
A Feast for the Gods *(with Karen Anderson)*	220

FOREWORD

''Romance'' is one of too many fine old words that in our day have taken on new, usually derogatory meanings. In publishing it denotes a specific, rigidly structured kind of novel, with the implication that this is pap. I don't agree that that is necessarily so. A writer like me can ill afford snobbery while libraries and bookstores shelve ''science fiction'' separately from ''literature.'' But that is beside the point I wish to make, that in the Middle Ages ''romance'' meant a tale full of color and imagination.

Though many early romances were the trash that Cervantes eventually laughed into oblivion, others remain keystone works of our civilization: for example, the Arthurian and Carolingian cycles. Such modern fantasists as James Branch Cabell, Lord Dunsany, E. R. Eddison, and J. R. R. Tolkien were fully in that tradition. Other authors of romances in the same sense, which contain no supernatural elements but nevertheless deal in glamour and adventure, include G. K. Chesterton, Joseph Conrad, W. H. Hudson, Rudyard Kipling, Jack London, and Mary Renault—to pick, almost at random, half a dozen who are well regarded. Clearly, then, this school can evoke beauty and grapple with the eternal questions as well as any other, and better than some.

The adjective ''romantic'' is, likewise, commonly

misused as an antonym of "realistic." Now certainly one can lose one's head in oversimplified, wildly glorified views of the world and of human nature. When believers in these gain power, the result is catastrophe, as witness Nazism and Communism. Yet it would be equally false, or even more so, to deny that heroism and saintliness occur, that wonderful things happen and great things are achieved. For that matter, science, the most powerful examiner of reality that we have ever had, reveals to us a universe of exploding space, coalescing suns, moving continents, quantum leaps, vacuum a-seethe with energies, dinosaurs, Sumeria, rocks brought home from the Moon, machines that think, our kinship with everything alive on Earth, the molecular life-stuff itself—If this isn't sheerly romantic, what is?

Bar occasional poetry, science fiction is virtually the only literary form that celebrates it. Of course, not all science fiction does. Some turns its attention elsewhere, which is good; we need diversity. I simply maintain that romanticism has a legitimate place in the field.

Fantasy too has its stories that concern themselves with the prosaic or the bleak faces of existence. Among them are several of the classics. However, much of it, perhaps most, tries to cast enchantment. Science fiction and fantasy are not the last survivors of romanticism. It flourishes quite lustily in mystery, spy, and historical novels, and sporadically elsewhere. Still, our two kinds may well be its strongest embodiments these days.

Here is a sample of my work in the romantic vein. May you enjoy it. Inevitably, the tales fall short of, but in writing them I always strove for, the ideal that Kipling expressed so well in his long poem "To the True

Romance." I cannot close better than with a stanza from it.

> Time hath no tide but must abide
>   The servant of Thy will;
> Tide hath no time, for to Thy rhyme
>   The ranging stars stand still—
> Regent of spheres that lock our fears,
>   Our hopes invisible,
> Oh, 'twas certes at Thy decrees
>   We fashioned Heaven and Hell!

The Queen of Air and Darkness

Unlike the other stories in the volume on hand, this one is not fantasy but science fiction. In fact, it might be considered "hard" science fiction, for it supposes nothing that a modern scientist would say is outright impossible, such as travel faster than light. (Granted, telepathy is controversial; but if it exists, presumably it operates within the framework of known natural law.) Yet the story embodies immemorial fantasy motifs and seeks to create an atmosphere of faery lands forlorn. I wrote it for a special issue of *The Magazine of Fantasy and Science Fiction* which was to honor me, and naturally wanted it to be something special. Later it won both a Hugo and a Nebula award. You may like to see my notes for the original publication:

"The Queen of Air and Darkness" is a figure of unknown antiquity who continues to haunt the present day. T. H. White, in *The Once and Future King,* identified her with Morgan le Fay. Before him, A. E. Housman had written one of his most enigmatic poems about her. But actually the title—a counterpart to the traditional attributes of Satan—is borne by the demonic female who appears over the centuries in many legends and many guises. She is Lilith of rabbinical lore, who in turn goes back to Babylon; she is the great shejinni of the Arabs; the Persians and Hindus told similar stories; the Japanese were particularly afraid of *kami* who had the form of women; American Indians, especially those of the Athabascan family, dreaded one who went hurrying through the sky at night. In medieval Europe, one of her shapes, among others, is that of the mistress of the elf hill, against whom Scottish and Danish ballads warn the belated traveler, and who reappears in the Tannhäuser story. Her weapon is always the beauty and—in the old sense of the word—the charm by which she lures men away from her enemy God. Certain finds lead me to suspect that they knew about her in the Old Stone Age, and she will surely go on into the future.

The last glow of the last sunset would linger almost until midwinter. But there would be no more day, and the northlands rejoiced. Blossoms opened, flamboyance on firethorn trees, steel-flowers rising blue from the brake and rainplant that cloaked all hills, shy whiteness of kiss-me-never down in the dales. Flitteries darted among them on iridescent wings; a crown buck shook his horns and bugled. Between horizons the sky deepened from purple to sable. Both moons were aloft, nearly full, shining frosty on leaves and molten on waters. The shadows they made were blurred by an aurora, a great blowing curtain of light across half heaven. Behind it the earliest stars had come out.

A boy and a girl sat on Wolund's Barrow just under the dolmen it upbore. Their hair, which streamed halfway down their backs, showed startlingly forth, bleached as it was by summer. Their bodies, still dark from that season, merged with earth and bush and rock, for they wore only garlands. He played on a bone flute and she sang. They had lately become lovers. Their age was about sixteen, but they did not know this, considering themselves Outlings and thus indifferent to time, remembering little or nothing of how they had once dwelt in the lands of men.

His notes piped cold around her voice:

> "Cast a spell,
> weave it well
> of dust and dew
> and night and you."

A brook by the grave mound, carrying moonlight down to a hill-hidden river, answered with its rapids. A flock of hellbats passed black beneath the aurora.

A shape came bounding over Cloudmoor. It had two arms and two legs, but the legs were long and claw-footed and feathers covered it to the end of a tail and broad wings. The face was half human, dominated by its eyes. Had Ayoch been able to stand wholly erect, he would have reached to the boy's shoulder.

The girl rose. "He carries a burden," she said. Her vision was not meant for twilight like that of a north-land creature born, but she had learned how to use every sign her senses gave her. Besides the fact that ordinarily a pook would fly, there was a heaviness to his haste.

"And he comes from the south." Excitement jumped in the boy, sudden as a green flame that went across the constellation Lyrth. He sped down the mound. "Ohoi, Ayoch!" he called. "Me here, Mistherd!"

"And Shadow-of-a-Dream," the girl laughed, following.

The pook halted. He breathed louder than the soughing in the growth around him. A smell of bruised yerba lifted where he stood.

"Well met in winterbirth," he whistled. "You can help me bring this to Carheddin."

He held out what he bore. His eyes were yellow lanterns above. It moved and whimpered.

"Why, a child," Mistherd said.

"Even as you were, my son, even as you were. Ho, ho, what a snatch!" Ayoch boasted. "They were a score in yon camp by Fallowwood, armed, and besides watcher engines they had big ugly dogs aprowl while they slept. I came from above, however, having spied on them till I knew that a handful of dazedust—"

"The poor thing." Shadow-of-a-dream took the boy and held him to her small breasts. "So full of sleep yet, aren't you?" Blindly, he sought a nipple. She smiled through the veil of her hair. "No, I am still too young, and you already too old. But come, when you wake in Carheddin under the mountain, you shall feast."

"Yo-ah," said Ayoch very softly. "She is abroad and has heard and seen. She comes." He crouched down, wings folded. After a moment Mistherd knelt, and then Shadow-of-a-dream, though she did not let go the child.

The Queen's tall form blocked off the moons. For a while she regarded the three and their booty. Hill and moor sounds withdrew from their awareness until it seemed they could hear the northlights hiss.

At last Ayoch whispered, "Have I done well, Starmother?"

"If you stole a babe from the camp full of engines,"

said the beautiful voice, "then they were folk out of the far south who may not endure it as meekly as yeomen."

"But what can they do, Snowmaker?" the pook asked. "How can they track us?"

Mistherd lifted his head and spoke in pride. "Also, now they too have felt the awe of us."

"And he is a cuddly dear," Shadow-of-a-dream said. "And we need more like him, do we not Lady Sky?"

"It had to happen in some twilight," agreed she who stood above. "Take him onward and care for him. By this sign," which she made, "is he claimed for the Dwellers."

Their joy was freed. Ayoch cartwheeled over the ground till he reached a shiverleaf. There he swarmed up the trunk and out on a limb, perched half hidden by unrestful pale foliage, and crowed. Boy and girl bore the child toward Carheddin at an easy distance-devouring lope which let him pipe and her sing:

"Wahaii, wahaii!
Wayala, laii!
Wing on the wind
high over heaven,
shrilly shrieking,
rush with the rainspears,
tumble through tumult,
drift to the moonhoar trees and the dream-
heavy shadows beneath them,
and rock in, be one with the clinking wavelets
of lakes where the starbeams drown."

As she entered, Barbro Cullen felt, through all grief and fury, stabbed by dismay. The room was unkempt. Journals, tapes, reels, codices, file boxes, bescribbled papers were piled on every table. Dust filmed most shelves and corners. Against one wall stood a laboratory setup, microscope and analytical equipment. She recognized it as compact and efficient, but it was not what you would expect in an office, and it gave the air a faint chemical reek. The rug was threadbare, the furniture shabby.

This was her final chance?

Then Eric Sherrinford approached. "Good day, Mrs. Cullen," he said. His tone was crisp, his handclasp firm. His faded gripsuit didn't bother her. She wasn't inclined to fuss about her own appearance except on special occasions. (And would she ever again have one, unless she got back Jimmy?) What she observed was a cat's personal neatness.

A smile radiated in crow's feet from his eyes. "Forgive my bachelor housekeeping. On Beowulf we have—we had, at any rate, machines for that, so I never acquired the habit myself, and I don't want a hireling disarranging my tools. More convenient to work out of my apartment than keep a separate office. Won't you be seated?"

"No, thanks. I couldn't," she mumbled.

"I understand. But if you'll excuse me, I function best in a relaxed position."

He jackknifed into a lounger. One long shank crossed the other knee. He drew forth a pipe and stuffed it from a pouch. Barbro wondered why he took tobacco in so ancient a way. Wasn't Beowulf supposed to have the up-to-date equipment that they still couldn't afford to build on Roland? Well, of course old customs might survive anyhow. They generally did in colonies, she remembered reading. People had moved starward in the hope of preserving such outmoded things as their mother tongues or constitutional government or rational-technological civilization. . . .

Sherrinford pulled her up from the confusion of her weariness: ''You must give me the details of your case, Mrs. Cullen. You've simply told me your son was kidnapped and your local constabulary did nothing. Otherwise, I know just a few obvious facts, such as your being widowed rather than divorced; and you're the daughter of outwayers in Olga Ivanoff Land, who nevertheless kept in close telecommunication with Christmas Landing; and you're trained in one of the biological professions; and you had several years' hiatus in field work until recently you started again.''

She gaped at the high-cheeked, beak-nosed, black-haired and gray-eyed countenance. His lighter made a *scrit* and a flare which seemed to fill the room. Quietness dwelt on this height above the city, and winter dusk was seeping through the windows. ''How in cosmos do you know that?'' she heard herself exclaim.

He shrugged and fell into the lecturer's manner for which he was notorious. ''My work depends on noticing details and fitting them together. In more than a hundred years on Roland, tending to cluster according to their origins and thought-habits, people have developed regional accents. You have a trace of the Olgan burr, but you nasalize your vowels in the style of this area, though you live in Portolondon. That suggests steady childhood exposure to metropolitan speech. You were part of Matsuyama's expedition, you told me, and took your boy along. They wouldn't have allowed any ordinary technician to do that; hence, you had to be valuable enough to get away with it. The team was conducting ecological research: therefore, you must be in the life sciences. For the same reason, you must have had previous field experience. But your skin is fair, showing none of the leatheriness one gets from prolonged exposure to this sun. Accordingly, you must have been mostly indoors for a good while before you went on your ill-fated trip. As for widowhood—you never mentioned a husband to me, but you have had a man whom you thought so highly of that you still wear both the wedding and the engagement ring he gave you."

Her sight blurred and stung. The last of those words had brought Tim back; huge, ruddy, laughterful and gentle. She must turn from this other person and stare outward. "Yes," she achieved saying, "you're right."

The apartment occupied a hilltop above Christmas Landing. Beneath it the city dropped away in walls, roofs, archaistic chimneys and lamplit streets, goblin lights of humanpiloted vehicles, to the harbor, the sweep of Venture Bay, ships bound to and from the Sunward Islands and remoter regions of the Boreal Ocean, which glimmered like mercury in the afterglow of Charlemagne. Oliver was swinging rapidly higher, a mottled orange disc a full degree wide; closer to the zenith which it could never reach, it would shine the color of ice. Alde, half the seeming size, was a thin slow crescent near Sirius, which she remembered was near Sol, but you couldn't see Sol without a telescope—

"Yes," she said around the pain in her throat, "my husband is about four years dead. I was carrying our first child when he was killed by a stampeding monocerus. We'd been married three years before. Met while we were both at the University—casts from School Central can only supply a basic education, you know—We founded our own team to do ecological studies under contract—you know, can a certain area be settled while maintaining a balance of nature, what crops will grow, what hazards, that sort of question—Well, afterward I did lab work for a fisher co-op in Portolondon. But the monotony, the . . . shut-in-ness . . . was eating me away. Professor Matsuyama offered me a position on the team he was organizing to examine Commissioner Hauch Land. I thought, God help me, I thought Jimmy—Tim wanted him named James, once the tests showed it'd be a boy, after his own father and because of 'Timmy and Jimmy' and—oh, I thought Jimmy could safely come along. I couldn't bear to leave him behind for months, not at his age. We could make sure he'd never wander out of camp. What could hurt him inside it? *I* had never believed those stories about the Outlings stealing human children. I supposed parents were trying to hide from themselves the fact they'd been careless, they'd let a kid get lost in the woods or attacked by a pack of satans or—well, I learned better, Mr. Sherrinford. The guard robots were evaded and the dogs were drugged, and when I woke, Jimmy was gone."

He regarded her through the smoke from his pipe. Barbro Engdahl Cullen was a big woman of thirty or so (Rolandic years, he reminded himself, ninety-five percent of Terrestrial, not the same as Beowulfan years), broad-shouldered, long-legged, full-breasted, supple of stride; her face was wide, straight nose, straightforward hazel eyes, heavy but mobile mouth; her hair was reddish brown, cropped below the ears, her voice husky, her garment a plain street robe. To still the writhing of her fingers, he asked skeptically, "Do you now believe in the Outlings?"

"No. I'm just not so sure as I was." She swung about with half a glare for him. "And we have found traces."

"Bits of fossils," he nodded. "A few artifacts of a neolithic sort. But apparently ancient, as if the makers died ages ago. Intensive search has failed to turn up any real evidence for their survival.''

''How intensive can search be, in a summer-stormy, winter-gloomy wilderness around the North Pole?'' she demanded. ''When we are, how many, a million people on an entire planet, half of us crowded into this one city?''

''And the rest crowding this one habitable continent,'' he pointed out.

''Arctica covers five million square kilometers,'' she flung back. ''The Arctic Zone proper covers a fourth of it. We haven't the industrial base to establish satellite monitor stations, build aircraft we can trust in those parts, drive roads through the damned darklands and establish permanent bases and get to know them and tame them. Good Christ, generations of lonely outwaymen told stories about Graymantle, and the beast was never seen by a proper scientist till last year!''

''Still, you continue to doubt the reality of the Outlings?''

''Well, what about a secret cult among humans, born of isolation and ignorance, lairing in the wilderness, stealing children when they can for—'' She swallowed. Her head dropped. ''But you're supposed to be the expert.''

''From what you told me over the visiphone, the Portolondon constabulary questions the accuracy of the report your group made, thinks the lot of you were hysterical, claims you must have omitted a due precaution, and the child toddled away and was lost beyond your finding.''

His dry words pried the horror out of her. Flushing, she snapped, ''Like any settler's kid? No. I didn't simply yell. I consulted Data Retrieval. A few too many such cases are recorded for accident to be a very plausible explanation. And shall we totally ignore the frightened stories about reappearances? But when I went back to the constabulary with my facts, they brushed me off. I suspect that was not entirely because they're undermanned. I think they're afraid too. They're recruited from country boys, and Portolondon lies near the edge of the unknown."

Her energy faded. "Roland hasn't got any central police force," she finished drably. "You're my last hope."

The man puffed smoke into twilight, with which it blent, before he said in a kindlier voice than hitherto: "Please don't make it a high hope, Mrs. Cullen. I'm the solitary private investigator on this world, having no resources beyond myself, and a newcomer to boot."

"How long have you been here?"

"Twelve years. Barely time to get a little familiarity with the relatively civilized coastlands. You settlers of a century or more—what do you, even, know about Arctica's interior?"

Sherrinford sighed. "I'll take the case, charging no more than I must, mainly for the sake of the experience," he said. "But only if you'll be my guide and assistant, however painful it will be for you."

"Of course! I dreaded waiting idle. Why me, though?"

"Hiring someone else as well qualified would be prohibitively expensive on a pioneer planet where every hand has a thousand urgent tasks to do. Besides, you have a motive. And I'll need that. As one who was born on another world altogether strange to this one, itself altogether strange to Mother Earth, I am too dauntingly aware of how handicapped we are."

Night gathered upon Christmas Landing. The air stayed mild, but glimmer-lit tendrils of fog, sneaking through the streets, had a cold look, and colder yet was the aurora where it shuddered between the moons. The woman drew closer to the man in this darkening room, surely not aware that she did, until he switched on a fluoropanel. The same knowledge of Roland's aloneness was in both of them.

One light-year is not much as galactic distances go. You could walk it in about 270 million years, beginning at the middle of the Permian Era, when dinosaurs belonged to the remote future, and continuing to the present day when spaceships cross even greater reaches. But stars in our neighborhood average some nine light-years apart, and barely one percent of them have planets which are man-habitable, and speeds are limited to less than that of radiation. Scant help is given by relativistic time contraction and suspended animation en route. These made the journeys seem short, but history meanwhile does not stop at home.

Thus voyages from sun to sun will always be few. Colonists will be those who have extremely special reasons for going. They will take along germ plasm for exogenetic cultivation of domestic plants and animals—and of human infants, in order that population can grow fast enough to escape death through genetic drift. After all, they cannot rely on further immigration. Two or three times a century, a ship may call from some other colony. (Not from Earth. Earth has long ago sunk into alien concerns.) Its place of origin will be an old settlement. The young ones are in no position to build and man interstellar vessels.

Their very survival, let alone their eventual modernization, is in doubt. The founding fathers have had to take what they could get, in a universe not especially designed for man.

Consider, for example, Roland. It is among the rare happy finds, a world where humans can live, breathe, eat the food, drink the water, walk unclad if they choose, sow their crops, pasture their beasts, dig their mines, erect their homes, raise their children and grandchildren. It is worth crossing three quarters of a light-century to preserve certain dear values and strike new roots into the soil of Roland.

But the star Charlemagne is of type F9, forty percent brighter than Sol, brighter still in the treacherous ultraviolet and wilder still in the wind of charged particles that seethes from it. The planet has an eccentric orbit. In the middle of the short but furious northern summer, which includes periastron, total isolation is more than double what Earth gets; in the depth of the long northern winter, it is barely less than Terrestrial average.

Native life is abundant everywhere. But lacking elaborate machinery, not yet economically possible to construct for more than a few specialists, man can only endure the high latitudes. A ten-degree axial tilt, together with the orbit, means that the northern part of the Arctican continent spends half its year in unbroken sunlessness. Around the South Pole lies an empty ocean.

Other differences from Earth might superficially seem more important, Roland has two moons, small but close, to evoke clashing tides. It rotates once in thirty-two hours, which is endlessly, subtly disturbing to organisms evolved through gigayears of a quicker rhythm. The weather patterns are altogether unterrestrial. The globe is a mere 9,500 kilometers in diameter; its surface gravity is 0.42×980 cm/sec^2; the sea level air pressure is slightly above one Earth atmosphere. (For actually, Earth is the freak, and man exists because a cosmic accident blew away most of the gas that a body its size ought to have kept, as Venus has done.)

However, Homo can truly be called sapiens when he practices his specialty of being unspecialized. His repeated attempts to freeze himself into an all-answering pattern or culture or ideology, or whatever he has named it, have repeatedly brought ruin. Give him the pragmatic business of making his living and he will usually do rather well. He adapts, within broad limits.

These limits are set by such factors as his need for sunlight and his being, necessarily and forever, a part of the life that surrounds him and a creature of the spirit within.

Portolondon thrust docks, boats, machinery, warehouses into the Gulf of Polaris. Behind them huddled the dwellings of its 5,000 permanent inhabitants: concrete walls, storm shutters, high-peaked tile roofs. The gaiety of their paint looked forlorn amidst lamps; this town lay past the Arctic Circle.

Nevertheless Sherrinford remarked, ''Cheerful place, eh? The kind of thing I came to Roland looking for.''

Barbro made no reply. The days in Christmas Landing, while he made his preparations, had drained her. Gazing out the dome of the taxi that was whirring them downtown from the hydrofoil that brought them, she supposed he meant the lushness of forest and meadows along the road, brilliant hues and phosphorescence of flowers in gardens, clamor of wings overhead. Unlike Terrestrial flora in cold climates, Arctican vegetation spends every daylit hour in frantic growth and energy storage. Not till summer's fever gives place to gentle winter does it bloom and fruit; and estivating animals rise from their dens and migratory birds come home.

The view was lovely, she had to admit: beyond the trees, a spaciousness climbing toward remote heights, silvery gray under a moon, an aurora, the diffuse radiance from a sun just below the horizon.

Beautiful as a hunting satan, she thought, and as terrible. That wilderness had stolen Jimmy. She wondered if she would at least be given to find his little bones and take them to his father.

Abruptly she realized that she and Sherrinford were at their hotel and that he had been speaking of the town. Since it was next in size after the capital, he must have visited here often before. The streets were crowded and noisy; signs flickered, music blared from shops, taverns, restaurants, sports centers, dance halls; vehicles were jammed down to molasses speed; the several-stories-high office buildings stood aglow. Portolondon linked an enormous hinterland to the outside world. Down the Gloria River came timber rafts, ores, harvest of farms whose owners were slowly making Rolandic life serve them, meat and ivory and furs gathered by rangers in the mountains beyond Troll Scarp. In from the sea came coastwise freighters, the fishing fleet, produce of the Sunward Islands, plunder of whole continents farther south where bold men adventured. It clanged in Portolondon, laughed, blustered, connived, robbed, preached, guzzled, swilled, toiled, dreamed, lusted, built, destroyed, died, was born, was happy, angry, sorrowful, greedy, vulgar, loving, ambitious, human. Neither the sun's blaze elsewhere nor the half year's twilight here—wholly night around midwinter—was going to stay man's hand.

Or so everybody said.

Everybody except those who had settled in the darklands. Barbro used to take for granted that they were evolving curious customs, legends, and superstitions, which would die when the outway had been completely mapped and controlled. Of late, she had wondered. Perhaps Sherrinford's hints, about a change in his own attitude brought about by his preliminary research, were responsible.

Or perhaps she just needed something to think about besides how Jimmy, the day before he went, when she asked him whether he wanted rye or French bread for a sandwich, answered in great solemnity—he was becoming interested in the alphabet—"I'll have a slice of what we people call the F bread."

She scarcely noticed getting out of the taxi, registering, being conducted to a primitively furnished room. But after she unpacked, she remembered Sherrinford had suggested a confidential conference. She went down the hall and knocked on his door. Her knuckles sounded less loud than her heart.

He opened the door, finger on lips, and gestured her toward a corner. Her temper bristled until she saw the image of Chief Constable Dawson in the visiphone. Sherrinford must have chimed him up and must have a reason to keep her out of scanner range. She found a chair and watched, nails digging into knees.

The detective's lean length refolded itself. "Pardon the interruption," he said. "A man mistook the number. Drunk, by the indications."

Dawson chuckled. "We get plenty of those." Barbro recalled his fondness for gabbing. He tugged the beard which he affected, as if he were an outwayer instead of a townsman. "No harm in them as a rule. They only have a lot of voltage to discharge, after weeks or months in the backlands."

"I've gathered that that environment—foreign in a million major and minor ways to the one that created man—I've gathered that it does do odd things to the personality." Sherrinford tamped his pipe. "Of course, you know my practice has been confined to urban and suburban areas. Isolated garths seldom need private investigators. Now that situation appears to have changed. I called to ask you for advice."

"Glad to help," Dawson said. "I've not forgotten what you did for us in the de Tahoe murder case." Cautiously: "Better explain your problem first."

Sherrinford struck fire. The smoke that followed cut through the green odors—even here, a paved pair of kilometers from the nearest woods—that drifted past traffic rumble through a crepuscular window. "This is more a scientific mission than a search for an absconding debtor or an industrial spy," he drawled. "I'm looking into two possibilities: that an organization, criminal or religious or whatever, has long been active and steals infants; or that the Outlings of folklore are real."

"Huh?" On Dawson's face Barbro read as much dismay as surprise. "You can't be serious!"

"Can't I?" Sherrinford smiled. "Several generations' worth of reports shouldn't be dismissed out of hand. Especially not when they become more frequent and consistent in the course of time, not less. Nor can we ignore the documented loss of babies and small children, amounting by now to over a hundred, and never a trace found afterward. Nor the finds which demonstrate that an intelligent species once inhabited Arctica and may still haunt the interior."

Dawson leaned forward as if to climb out of the screen. "Who engaged you?" he demanded. "That Cullen woman? We were sorry for her, naturally, but she wasn't making sense, and when she got downright abusive—"

"Didn't her companions, reputable scientists, confirm her story?"

"No story to confirm. Look, they had the place ringed with detectors and alarms, and they kept mastiffs. Standard procedure in country where a hungry sauroid or whatever might happen by. Nothing could've entered unbeknownst."

"On the ground. How about a flyer landing in the middle of camp?"

"A man in a copter rig would've roused everybody."

"A winged being might be quieter."

"A living flyer that could lift a three-year-boy? Doesn't exist."

"Isn't in the scientific literature, you mean, Constable. Remember Graymantle; remember how little we know about Roland, a planet, an entire world. Such birds do exist on Beowulf—and on Rustum, I've read. I made a calculation from the local ratio of air density to gravity, and, yes, it's marginally possible here too. The child could have been carried off for a short distance before wing muscles were exhausted and the creature must descend."

Dawson snorted. "First it landed and walked into the tent where mother and boy were asleep. Then it walked away, toting him, after it couldn't fly further. Does that sound like a bird of prey? And the victim didn't cry out, the dogs didn't bark!"

"As a matter of fact," Sherrinford said, "those inconsistencies are the most interesting and convincing features of the whole account. You're right, it's hard to see how a human kidnapper could get in undetected, and an eagle type of creature wouldn't operate in that fashion. But none of this applies to a winged intelligent being. The boy could have been drugged. Certainly the dogs showed signs of having been."

"The dogs showed signs of having overslept. Nothing had disturbed them. The kid wandering by wouldn't do so. We don't need to assume one damn thing except, first, that he got restless and, second, that the alarms were a bit sloppily rigged—seeing as how no danger was expected from inside camp—and let him pass out. And, third, I hate to speak this way, but we must assume the poor tyke starved or was killed."

Dawson paused before adding: "If we had more staff, we could have given the affair more time. And would have, of course. We did make an aerial sweep, which risked the lives of the pilots, using instruments which would've spotted the kid anywhere in a fifty-kilometer radius, unless he was dead. You know how sensitive thermal analyzers are. We drew a complete blank. We have more important jobs than to hunt for the scattered pieces of a corpse."

He finished brusquely. "If Mrs. Cullen's hired you, my advice is you find an excuse to quit. Better for her, too. She's got to come to terms with reality."

Barbro checked a shout by biting her tongue.

"Oh, this is merely the latest disappearance of the series," Sherrinford said. She didn't understand how he could maintain his easy tone when Jimmy was lost. "More thoroughly recorded than any before, thus more suggestive. Usually an outwayer family has given a tearful but undetailed account of their child who vanished and must have been stolen by the Old Folk. Sometimes, years later, they'd tell about glimpses of what they swore must have been the grown child, not really human any longer, flitting past in murk or peering through a window or working mischief upon them. As you say, neither the authorities nor the scientists have had personnel or resources to mount a proper investigation. But as I say, the matter appears to be worth investigating. Maybe a private party like myself can contribute."

"Listen, most of us constables grew up in the outway. We don't just ride patrol and answer emergency calls; we go back there for holidays and reunions. If any gang of . . . of human sacrificers was around, we'd know."

"I realize that. I also realize that the people you came from have a widespread and deep-seated belief in nonhuman beings with supernatural powers. Many actually go through rites and make offerings to propitiate them."

"I know what you're leading up to," Dawson flared. "I've heard it before, from a hundred sensationalists. The aborigines are the Outlings. I thought better of you. Surely you've visited a museum or three, surely you've read literature from planets which do have natives—or damn and blast, haven't you ever applied that logic of yours?"

He wagged a finger. "Think," he said. "What have we in fact discovered? A few pieces of worked stone; a few megaliths that might be artificial; scratchings on rock that seem to show plants and animals, though not the way any human culture would ever have shown them; traces of fires and broken bones; other fragments of bone that seem as if they might've belonged to thinking creatures, as if they might've been inside fingers or around big brains. If so, however, the owners looked nothing like men. Or angels, for that matter. Nothing! The most anthropoid recontruction I've seen shows a kind of two-legged crocagator.

"Wait, let me finish. The stories about the Outlings—oh, I've heard them too, plenty of them. I believed them when I was a kid—the stories tell how there're different kinds, some winged, some not, some half human, some completely human except maybe for being too handsome—It's fairyland from ancient Earth all over again. Isn't it? I got interested once and dug into the Heritage Library microfiles, and be damned if I didn't find almost the identical yarns, told by peasants centuries before spaceflight.

"None of it squares with the scanty relics we have, if they are relics, or with the fact that no area the size of Arctica could spawn a dozen different intelligent species, or . . . hellfire, man, with the way your common sense tells you aborigines would behave when humans arrived!"

Sherrinford nodded. "Yes, yes," he said. "I'm less sure than you that the common sense of nonhuman beings is precisely like our own. I've seen so much variation within mankind. But, granted, your arguments are strong. Roland's too few scientists have more pressing tasks than tracking down the origins of what is, as you put it, a revived medieval superstition."

He cradled his pipe bowl in both hands and peered into the tiny hearth of it. "Perhaps what interests me most," he said softly, "is why—across that gap of centuries, across a barrier of machine civilization and its utterly antagonistic world view—no continuity of tradition whatsoever—why have hard-headed, technologically organized, reasonably well-educated colonists here brought back from its grave a belief in the Old Folk?"

"I suppose eventually, if the University ever does develop the psychology department they keep talking about, I suppose eventually somebody will get a thesis out of your question." Dawson spoke in a jagged voice, and he gulped when Sherrinford replied:

"I propose to begin now. In Commissioner Hauch Land, since that's where the latest incident occurred. Where can I rent a vehicle?"

"Uh, might be hard to do—"

"Come, come. Tenderfoot or not, I know better. In an economy of scarcity, few people own heavy equipment. But since it's needed, it can always be rented. I want a camper bus with a ground-effect drive suitable for every kind of terrain. And I want certain equipment installed which I've brought along, and the top canopy section replaced by a gun turret controllable from the driver's seat. But I'll supply the weapons. Besides rifles and pistols of my own, I've arranged to borrow some artillery from Christmas Landing's police arsenal."

"Hoy? Are you genuinely intending to make ready for . . . a war . . . against a myth?"

"Let's say I'm taking out insurance, which isn't terribly expensive, against a remote possibility. Now, besides the bus, what about a light aircraft carried piggyback for use in surveys?"

"No." Dawson sounded more positive than hitherto. "That's asking for disaster. We can have you flown to a base camp in a large plane when the weather report's exactly right. But the pilot will have to fly back at once, before the weather turns wrong again. Meteorology's underdeveloped on Roland; the air's especially treacherous this time of year, and we're not tooled up to produce aircraft than can outlive every surprise." He drew breath. "Have you no idea of how fast a whirly-whirly can hit, or what size hailstones might strike from a clear sky, or—? Once you're there, man, you stick to the ground." He hesitated. "That's an important reason our information is so scanty about the outway, and its settlers are so isolated."

Sherrinford laughed ruefully. "Well, I suppose if details are what I'm after, I must creep along anyway."

"You'll waste a lot of time," Dawson said. "Not to mention your client's money. Listen, I can't forbid you to chase shadows, but—"

The discussion went on for almost an hour. When the screen finally blanked, Sherrinford rose, stretched, and walked toward Barbro. She noticed anew his pecular gait. He had come from a planet with a fourth again of Earth's gravitational drag, to one where weight was less than half Terrestrial. She wondered if he had flying dreams.

"I apologize for shuffling you off like that," he said. "I didn't expect to reach him at once. He was quite truthful about how busy he is. But having made contact, I didn't want to remind him overmuch of you. He can dismiss my project as a futile fantasy which I'll soon give up. But he might have frozen completely, might even have put up obstacles before us, if he'd realized through you how determined we are."

"Why should he care?" she asked in her bitterness.

"Fear of consequences, the worse because it is unadmitted—fear of consequences, the more terrifying because they are unguessable." Sherrinford's gaze went to the screen, and thence out the window to the aurora pulsing in glacial blue and white immensely far overhead. "I suppose you saw I was talking to a frightened man. Down underneath his conventionality and scoffing, he believes in the Outlings—oh, yes, he believes."

The feet of Mistherd flew over yerba and outpaced windblown driftwood. Beside him, black and misshapen, hulked Nagrim the nicor, whose earthquake weight left a swath of crushed plants. Behind, luminous blossoms of a firethorn shone through the twining, trailing outlines of Morgarel the wraith.

Here Cloudmoor rose in a surf of hills and thickets. The air lay quiet, now and then carrying the distance-muted howl of a beast. It was darker than usual at winterbirth, the moons being down and aurora a wan flicker above mountains on the northern world-edge. But this made the stars keen, and their numbers crowded heaven, and Ghost Road shone among them as if it, like the leafage beneath, were paved with dew.

"Yonder!" bawled Nagrim. All four of his arms pointed. The party had topped a ridge. Far off glimmered a spark. "Hoah, hoah! Ull we right off stamp dem flat, or pluck dem apart slow?"

We shall do nothing of the sort, bonebrain, Morgarel's answer slid through their heads. *Not unless they attack us, and they will not unless we make them aware of us, and her command is that we spy out their purposes.*

"Gr-r-rum-m-m. I know deir aim. Cut down trees, stick plows in land, sow deir cursed seed in de clods and in deir shes. 'Less we drive dem into de bitterwater, and soon, soon, dey'll wax too strong for us."

"Not too strong for the Queen!" Mistherd protested, shocked.

Yet they do have new powers, it seems, Morgarel reminded him. *Carefully must we probe them.*

"Den carefully can we step on dem?" asked Nagrim.

The question woke a grin out of Mistherd's own uneasiness. He slapped the scaly back. "Don't talk, you," he said. "It hurts my ears. Nor think; that hurts your head. Come, run!"

Ease yourself, Morgarel scolded. *You have too much life in you, human-born*

Mistherd made a face at the wraith, but obeyed to the extent of slowing down and picking his way through what cover the country afforded. For he traveled on behalf of the Fairest, to learn what had brought a pair of mortals questing hither.

Did they seek that boy whom Ayoch stole? (He continued to weep for his mother, though less and less often as the marvels of Carheddin entered him.) Perhaps. A birdcraft had left them and their car at the now-abandoned campsite, from which they had followed an outward spiral. But when no trace of the cub had appeared inside a reasonable distance, they did not call to be flown home. And this wasn't because weather forbade the farspeaker waves to travel, as was frequently the case. No, instead the couple set off toward the mountains of Moonhorn. Their course would take them past a few outlying invader steadings and on into realms untrodden by their race.

So this was no ordinary survey. Then what was it?

Mistherd understood now why she who reigned had made her adopted mortal children learn, or retain, the clumsy language of their forebears. He had hated that drill, wholly foreign to Dweller ways. Of course, you obeyed her, and in time you saw how wise she had been. . . .

Presently he left Nagrim behind a rock—the nicor would only be useful in a fight—and crawled from bush to bush until he lay within man-lengths of the humans. A rainplant drooped over him, leaves soft on his bare skin, and clothed him in darkness. Morgarel floated to the crown of a shiverleaf, whose unrest would better conceal his flimsy shape. He'd not be much help either. And that was the most troublous, the almost appalling thing here. Wraiths were among those who could not just sense and send thought, but cast illusions. Morgarel had reported that this time his power seemed to rebound off an invisible cold wall around the car.

Otherwise the male and female had set up no guardian engines and kept no dogs. Belike they supposed none would be needed, since they slept in the long vehicle which bore them. But such contempt of the Queen's strength could not be tolerated, could it?

Metal sheened faintly by the light of their campfire. They sat on either side, wrapped in coats against a coolness that Mistherd, naked, found mild. The male drank smoke. The female stared past him into a dusk which her flame-dazzled eyes must see as thick gloom. The dancing glow brought her vividly forth. Yes, to judge from Ayoch's tale, she was the dam of the new cub.

Ayoch had wanted to come too, but the Wonderful One forbade. Pooks couldn't hold still long enough for such a mission.

The man sucked on his pipe. His cheeks thus pulled into shadow while the light flickered across nose and brow, he looked disquietingly like a shearbill about to stoop on prey.

"—No, I tell you again, Barbro, I have no theories," he was saying. "When facts are insufficient, theorizing is ridiculous at best, misleading at worst."

"Still, you must have some idea of what you're doing," she said. It was plain that they had threshed this out often before. No Dweller could be as persistent as she or as patient as he. "That gear you packed—that generator you keep running—"

"I have a working hypothesis or two, which suggested what equipment I ought to take."

"Why won't you tell me what the hypotheses are?"

"They themselves indicate that that might be inadvisable at the present time. I'm still feeling my way into the labyrinth. And I haven't had a chance yet to hook everything up. In fact, we're really only protected against so-called telepathic influence—"

"What?" She started. "Do you mean . . . those legends about how they can read minds too—" Her words trailed off and her gaze sought the darkness beyond his shoulders.

He leaned forward. His tone lost its clipped rapidity, grew earnest and soft. "Barbro, you're racking yourself to pieces. Which is no help to Jimmy if he's alive, the more so when you may well be badly needed later on. We've a long trek before us, and you'd better settle into it."

She nodded jerkily and caught her lip between her teeth for a moment before she answered, "I'm trying."

He smiled around his pipe. "I expect you'll succeed. You don't strike me as a quitter or a whiner or an enjoyer of misery."

She dropped a hand to the pistol at her belt. Her voice changed; it came out of her throat like knife from sheath. "When we find them, they'll know what I am. What humans are."

"Put anger aside also," the man urged. "We can't afford emotions. If the Outlings are real, as I told you I'm provisionally assuming, they're fighting for their homes." After a short stillness he added: "I like to think that if the first explorers had found live natives, men would not have colonized Roland. But it's too late now. We can't go back if we wanted to. It's a bitter-end struggle, against an enemy so crafty that he's even hidden from us the fact that he is waging war."

"Is he? I mean, skulking, kidnapping an occasional child—"

"That's part of my hypothesis. I suspect those aren't

harassments; they're tactics employed in a chillingly subtle strategy."

The fire sputtered and sparked. The man smoked awhile, brooding, until he went on:

"I didn't want to raise your hopes or excite you unduly while you had to wait on me, first in Christmas Landing, then in Portolondon. Afterward we were busy satisfying ourselves that Jimmy had been taken farther from camp than he could have wandered before collapsing. So I'm only now telling you how thoroughly I studied available material on the . . . Old Folk. Besides, at first I did it on the principle of eliminating every imaginable possibility, however absurd. I expected no result other than final disproof. But I went through everything, relics, analyses, histories, journalistic accounts, monographs; I talked to outwayers who happened to be in town and to what scientists we have who've taken any interest in the matter. I'm a quick study. I flatter myself I became as expert as anyone—though God knows there's little to be expert on. Furthermore, I, a comparative stranger to Roland, maybe looked on the problem with fresh eyes. And a pattern emerged for me.

"If the aborigines had become extinct, why hadn't they left more remnants? Arctica isn't enormous, and it's fertile for Rolandic life. It ought to have supported a population whose artifacts ought to have accumulated over millennia. I've read that on Earth, literally tens of thousands of paleolithic hand axes were found, more by chance than archeology.

"Very well. Suppose the relics and fossils were deliberately removed, between the time the last survey party left and the first colonizing ships arrived. I did find some support for that idea in the diaries of the original explorers. They were too preoccupied with checking the habitability of the planet to make catalogues of primitive monuments. However, the remarks they wrote down indicate they saw much more than later arrivals did. Suppose what we have found is just what the removers overlooked or didn't get around to.

"That argues a sophisticated mentality, thinking in long-range terms, doesn't it? Which in turn argues that the Old Folk were not mere hunters or neolithic farmers."

"But nobody ever saw buildings or machines or any such thing," Barbro objected.

"No. Most likely the natives didn't go through our kind of metallurgic-industrial evolution. I can conceive of other paths to take. Their full-fledged civilization might have begun, rather than ended, in biological science and technology. It might have developed potentialities of the nervous system, which might be greater in their species than in man. We have those abilities to some degree ourselves, you realize. A dowser, for instance, actually senses variations in the local magnetic field caused by a water table. However, in us, these talents are maddeningly rare and tricky. So we took our business elsewhere. Who needs to be a telepath, say, when he has a visiphone? The Old Folk may have seen it the other way around. The artifacts of their civilization may have been, may still be unrecognizable to men."

"They could have identified themselves to the men, though," Barbro said. "Why didn't they?"

"I can imagine any number of reasons. As, they could have had a bad experience with interstellar visitors earlier in their history. Ours is scarcely the sole race that has spaceships. However, I told you I don't theorize in advance of the facts. Let's say no more than that the Old Folk, if they exist, are alien to us."

"For a rigorous thinker, you're spinning a mighty thin thread."

"I've admitted this is entirely provisional." He squinted at her through a roil of campfire smoke. "You came to me, Barbro, insisting in the teeth of officialdom that your boy had been stolen, but your own talk about cultist kidnappers was ridiculous. Why are you reluctant to admit the reality of nonhumans?"

"In spite of the fact that Jimmy's being alive probably depends on it," she sighed. "I don't know."

A shudder. "Maybe I don't dare admit it."

"I've said nothing thus far that hasn't been speculated about in print," he told her. "A disreputable speculation, true. In a hundred years, nobody has found valid evidence for the Outlings being more than a superstition. Still, a few people have declared it's at least possible that intelligent natives are at large in the wilderness."

"I know," she repeated. "I'm not sure, though, what has made you, overnight, take those arguments seriously."

"Well, once you got me started thinking, it occurred to me that Roland's outwayers are not utterly isolated medieval crofters. They have books, telecommunications, power tools, motor vehicles; above all, they have a modern science-oriented education. Why *should* they turn superstitious? Something must be causing it." He stopped. "I'd better not continue. My ideas go further than this; but if they're correct, it's dangerous to speak them aloud."

Mistherd's belly muscles tensed. There was danger for fair, in that shearbill head. The Garland bearer must be warned. For a minute he wondered about summoning Nagrim to kill these two. If the nicor jumped them fast, their firearms might avail them naught. But no.

They might have left word at home, or—He came back to his ears. The talk had changed course. Barbro was murmuring, "—why you stayed on Roland."

The man smiled his gaunt smile. "Well, life on Beowulf held no challenge for me. Heorot is—or was; this was decades past, remember—Heorot was densely populated, smoothly organized, boringly uniform. That was partly due to the lowland frontier, a safety valve that bled off the dissatisfied. But I lack the carbon dioxide tolerance necessary to live healthily down there. An expedition was being readied to make a swing around a number of colony worlds, especially those which didn't have the equipment to keep in laser contact. You'll recall its announced purpose, to seek out new ideas in science, arts, sociology, philosophy, whatever might prove valuable. I'm afraid they found little on Roland relevant to Beowulf. But I, who had wangled a berth, I saw opportunities for myself and decided to make my home here."

"Were you a detective back there, too?"

"Yes, in the official police. We had a tradition of such work in our family. Some of that may have come for the Cherokee side of it, if the name means anything to you. However, we also claimed collateral descent from one of the first private inquiry agents on record, back on Earth before spaceflight. Regardless of how true that may be, I found him a useful model. You see, an archetype—"

The man broke off. Unease crossed his features. "Best we go to sleep," he said. "We've a long distance to cover in the morning."

She looked outward. "Here is no morning."

They retired. Mistherd rose and cautiously flexed limberness back into his muscles. Before returning to the Sister of Lyrth, he risked a glance through a pane in the car. Bunks were made up, side by side, and the humans lay in them. Yet the man had not touched her, though hers was a bonny body, and nothing that had passed between them suggested he meant to do so.

Eldritch, humans. Cold and claylike. And they would overrun the beautiful wild world? Mistherd spat in disgust. It must not happen. It would not happen. She who reigned had vowed that.

The lands of William Irons were immense. But this was because a barony was required to support him, his kin and cattle, on native crops whose cultivation was still poorly understood. He raised some Terrestrial plants as well, by summer-light and in conservatories. However, these were a luxury. The true conquest of northern Arctica lay in yerba hay, in bathyrhiza wood, in pericoup and glycophyllon, and eventually, when the market had expanded with population and industry, in chalcanthemum for city florists and pelts of cage-bred rover for city furriers.

That was in a tomorrow Irons did not expect that he would live to see. Sherrinford wondered if the man really expected anyone ever would.

The room was warm and bright. Cheerfulness crackled in the fireplace. Light from fluoropanels gleamed off hand-carven chests and chairs and tables, off colorful draperies and shelved dishes. The outwayer sat solid in his high seat, stoutly clad, beard flowing down his chest. His wife and daughters brought coffee, whose fragrance joined the remnant odors of a hearty supper, to him, his guests, and his sons.

But outside, wind hooted, lightning flared, thunder bawled, rain crashed on roof and walls and roared down to swirl among the courtyard cobblestones. Sheds and barns crouched against hugeness beyond.

Trees groaned, and did a wicked undertone of laughter run beneath the lowing of a frightened cow? A burst of hailstones hit the tiles like knocking knuckles.

You could feel how distant your neighbors were, Sherrinford thought. And nonetheless they were the people whom you saw oftenest, did daily business with by visiphone (when a solar storm didn't make gibberish of their voices and chaos of their faces) or in the flesh, partied with, gossiped and intrigued with, intermarried with; in the end, they were the people who would bury you. The lights of the coastal towns were monstrously farther away.

William Irons was a strong man. Yet when now he spoke, fear was in his tone. "You'd truly go over Troll Scarp?"

"Do you mean Hanstein Palisades?" Sherrinford responded, more challenge than question.

"No outwayer calls it anything but Troll Scarp," Barbro said.

And how had a name like that been reborn, light-years and centuries from Earth's Dark Ages?

"Hunters, trappers, prospectors—rangers, you call them—travel in those mountains," Sherrinford declared.

"In certain parts," Irons said. "That's allowed, by a pact once made 'tween a man and the Queen after he'd done well by a jack-o'-the-hill that a satan had hurt. Wherever the plumablanca grows, men may fare, if they leave man-goods on the altar boulders in payment for what they take out of the land. Elsewhere— " one fist clenched on a chair arm and went slack again— " 's not wise to go."

"It's been done, hasn't it?"

"Oh, yes. And some came back all right, or so they claimed, though I've heard they were never lucky afterward. And some didn't; they vanished. And some who returned babbled of wonders and horrors, and stayed witlings the rest of their lives. Not for a long time has anybody been rash enough to break the pact and overtread the bounds." Irons looked at Barbro almost entreatingly. His woman and children stared likewise, grown still. Wind hooted beyond the walls and rattled the storm shutters. "Don't you."

"I've reason to believe my son is there," she answered.

"Yes, yes, you've told and I'm sorry. Maybe something can be done. I don't know what, but I'd be glad to, oh, lay a double offering on Unvar's Barrow this midwinter, and a prayer drawn in the turf by a flint knife. Maybe they'll return him." Irons sighed. "They've not done such a thing in man's memory, though. And he could have a worse lot. I've glimpsed them myself, speeding madcap through twilight. They seem happier than we are. Might be no kindness, sending your boy home again."

"Like in the Arvid song," said his wife.

Irons nodded. "M-hm. Or others, come to think of it."

"What's this?" Sherrinford asked. More sharply than before, he felt himself a stranger. He was a child of cities and technics, above all a child of the skeptical intelligence. This family *believed*. It was disquieting to see more than a touch of their acceptance in Barbro's slow nod.

"We have the same ballad in Olga Ivanoff Land," she told him, her voice less calm than the words. "It's one of the traditional ones—nobody knows who composed them—that are sung to set the measure of a ring-dance in a meadow."

"I noticed a multilyre in your baggage, Mrs. Cullen," said the wife of Irons. She was obviously eager to get off the explosive topic of a venture in defiance of the Old Folk. A songfest could help. "Would you like to entertain us?"

Barbro shook her head, white around the nostrils. The oldest boy said quickly, rather importantly, "Well, sure, I can, if our guests would like to hear."

"I'd enjoy that, thank you." Sherrinford leaned back in his seat and stoked his pipe. If this had not happened spontaneously, he would have guided the conversation toward a similar outcome.

In the past he had had no incentive to study the folklore of the outway, and not much chance to read the scanty references on it since Barbro brought him her trouble. Yet more and more he was becoming convinced that he must get an understanding—not an anthropological study, but a feel from the inside out—of the relationship between Roland's frontiersmen and those beings which haunted them.

A bustling followed, rearrangement, settling down to listen, coffee cups refilled and brandy offered on the side. The boy explained, "The last line is the chorus. Everybody join in, right?" Clearly he too hoped thus to bleed off some of the tension. Catharsis through music? Sherrinford wondered, and added to himself: No; exorcism.

A girl strummed a guitar. The boy sang, to a melody which beat across the storm noise:

"It was the ranger Arvid
rode homeward through the hills
among the shadowy shiverleafs,
along the chiming rills.
The dance weaves under the firethorn.

"The night wind whispered around him
with scent of brok and rue.
Both moons rose high above him
and hills aflash with dew.
The dance weaves under the firethron.

"And dreaming of that woman
who waited in the sun,
he stopped, amazed by starlight,
and so he was undone.
The dance weaves under the firethorn.

"For there beneath a barrow
that bulked athwart a moon,
the Outling folk were dancing
in glass and golden shoon.
The dance weaves under the firethorn.

"The Outling folk were dancing
like water, wind, and fire
to frosty-ringing harpstrings,
and never did they tire.
The dance weaves under the firethorn.

"To Arvid came she striding
from whence she watched the dance,
the Queen of Air and Darkness,
with starlight in her glance.
The dance weaves under the firethorn.

"With starlight, love, and terror
in her immortal eye,
the Queen of Air and Darkness—"

"No!" Barbro leaped from her chair. Her fists w
clenched and tears flogged her cheekbones. "You can
pretend that—about the things that stole Jimmy!"

She fled from the chamber, upstairs to her guest be
room.

But she finished the song herself. That was abou
seventy hours later, camped in the steeps where rangers dared not fare.

She and Sherrinford had not said much to the Irons family, after refusing repeated pleas to leave the forbidden country alone. Nor had they exchanged many remarks at first as they drove north. Slowly, however, he began to draw her out about her own life. After a while she almost forgot to mourn, in her remembering of home and old neighbors. Somehow this led to discoveries—that he, beneath his professorial manner, was a gourmet and a lover of opera and appreciated her femaleness; that she could still laugh and find beauty in the wild land around her—and she realized, half guiltily, that life held more hopes than even the recovery of the son Tim gave her.

"I've convinced myself he's alive," the detective said. He scowled. "Frankly, it makes me regret having taken you along, I expected this would be only a fact-gathering trip, but it's turning out to be more. If we're dealing with real creatures who stole him, they can do real harm. I ought to turn back to the nearest garth and call for a plane to fetch you."

"Like bottommost hell you will, mister," she said. "You need somebody who knows outway conditions, and I'm a better shot than average."

"M-m-m . . . it would involve considerable delay too, wouldn't it? Besides the added distance, I can't put a signal through to any airport before this current burst of solar interference has calmed down."

:xt "night" he broke out his remaining equipment set it up. She recognized some of it, such as the rmal detector. Other items were strange to her, cop- l to his order from the advanced apparatus of his rthworld. He would tell her little about them. "I've xplained my suspicion that the ones we're after have elepathic capabilities," he said in apology.

Her eyes widened. "You mean it could be true, the Queen and her people can read minds?"

"That's part of the dread which surrounds their legend, isn't it? Actually there's nothing spooky about the phenomenon. It was studied and fairly well defined centuries ago, on Earth. I dare say the facts are available in the scientific microfiles at Christmas Landing. You Rolanders have simply had no occasion to seek them out, any more than you've yet had occasion to look up how to build power-beamcasters or spacecraft."

"Well, how does telepathy work, then?"

Sherrinford recognized that her query asked for comfort as much as it did for facts, and he spoke with deliberate dryness: "The organism generates extremely long-wave radiation which can, in principle, be modulated by the nervous system. In practice, the feebleness of the signals and their low rate of information transmission make them elusive, hard to detect and measure. Our prehuman ancestors went in for more reliable senses, like vision and hearing. What telepathic transceiving we do is marginal at best. But explorers have found extraterrestrial species that got an evolutionary advantage from developing the system further, in their particular environments. I imagine such species could include one which gets comparatively little direct sunlight—in fact, appears to hide from broad day. It could even become so able in this regard that, at short range, it can pick up man's weak emissions and make man's primitive sensitivities resonate to its own strong sendings."

"That would account for a lot, wouldn't it?" Barbro said faintly.

"I've now screened our car by a jamming field," Sherrinford told her, "but it reaches only a few meters past the chassis. Beyond, a scout of theirs might get a warning from your thoughts, if you knew precisely what I'm trying to do. I have a well-trained subconscious which sees to it that I think about this in French when I'm outside. Communication has to be structured to be intelligible, you see, and that's a different enough structure from English. But English is the only human language on Roland, and surely the Old Folk have learned it."

She nodded. He had told her his general plan, which was too obvious to conceal. The problem was to make contact with the aliens, if they existed. Hitherto, they had only revealed themselves, at rare intervals, to one or a few backwoodsmen at a time. An ability to generate hallucinations would help them in that. They would stay clear of any large, perhaps unmanageable expedition which might pass through their territory. But two people, braving all prohibitions, shouldn't look too formidable to approach. And . . . this would be the first human team which not only worked on the assumption that the Outlings were real, but possessed the resources of modern, off-planet police technology.

Nothing happened at that camp. Sherrinford said he hadn't expected it would. The Old Folk seemed cautious this near to any settlement. In their own lands they must be bolder.

And by the following "night," the vehicle had gone well into yonder country. When Sherrinford stopped the engine in a meadow and the car settled down, silence rolled in like a wave.

They stepped out. She cooked a meal on the glower while he gathered wood, that they might later cheer themselves with a campfire. Frequently he glanced at his wrist. It bore no watch—instead, a radio-controlled dial, to tell what the instruments in the bus might register.

Who needed a watch here? Slow constellations wheeled beyond glimmering aurora. The moon Alde stood above a snowpeak, turning it argent, though this place lay at a goodly height. The rest of the mountains were hidden by the forest that crowded around. Its trees were mostly shiverleaf and feathery white plumablanca, ghostly amidst their shadows. A few firethorns glowed, clustered dim lanterns, and the underbrush was heavy and smelled sweet. You could see surprisingly far through the blue dusk. Somewhere nearby, a brook sang and a bird fluted.

''Lovely here,'' Sherrinford said. They had risen from their supper and not yet sat down again or kindled their fire.

''But strange,'' Barbro answered as low. ''I wonder if it's really meant for us. If we can really hope to possess it.''

His pipestem gestured at the stars. ''Man's gone to stranger places than this.''

''Has he? I . . . oh, I suppose it's just something left over from my outway childhood, but do you know, when I'm under them I can't think of the stars as balls of gas, whose energies have been measured, whose planets have been walked on by prosaic feet. No, they're small and cold and magical; our lives are bound to them; after we die, they whisper to us in our graves." Barbro glanced downward. "I realize that's nonsense."

She could see in the twilight how his face grew tight. "Not at all," he said. "Emotionally, physics may be a worse nonsense. And in the end, you know, after a sufficient number of generations, thought fellows feeling. Man is not at heart rational. He could stop believing the stories of science if those no longer felt right."

He paused. "That ballad which didn't get finished in the house," he said, not looking at her. "Why did it affect you so?"

"I couldn't stand hearing *them*, well, praised. Or that's how it seemed. Sorry for the fuss."

"I gather the ballad is typical of a large class."

"Well, I never thought to add them up. Cultural anthropology is something we don't have time for on Roland, or more likely it hasn't occurred to us, with everything else there is to do. But—now you mention it, yes, I'm surprised at how many songs and stories have the Arvid motif in them."

"Could you bear to recite it?"

She mustered the will to laugh. "Why, I can do better than that if you want. Let me get my multilyre and I'll perform."

She omitted the hypnotic chorus line, though, when the notes rang out, except at the end. He watched her where she stood against moon and aurora.

> "—the Queen of Air and Darkness
> cried softly under sky:
>
> " 'Light down, you ranger Arvid,
> and join the Outling folk.

You need no more be human,
which is a heavy yoke.'

"He dared to give her answer:
'I may do naught but run.
A maiden waits me, dreaming
in lands beneath the sun.

" 'And likewise wait me comrades
and tasks I would not shirk,
for what is ranger Arvid
if he lays down his work?

" 'So wreck your spells you Outling,
and cast your wrath on me.
Though maybe you can slay me,
you'll not make me unfree.'

"The Queen of Air and Darkness
stood wrapped about with fear
and northlight-flares and beauty
he dared not look too near.

"Until she laughed like harpsong
and said to him in scorn:
'I do not need a magic
to make you always mourn.

" 'I send you home with nothing
except your memory
of moonlight, Outling music,
night breezes, dew, and me.

" 'And that will run behind you,
a shadow on the sun,

and that will lie beside you
when every day is done.

" 'In work and play and friendship
your grief will strike you dumb
for thinking what you are—and—
what you might have become.

" 'Your dull and foolish woman
treat kindly as you can.
Go home now, ranger Arvid,
set free to be a man!' "

"In flickering and laughter
the Outling folk were gone.
He stood alone by moonlight
and wept until the dawn.
The dance weaves under the firethorn."

She laid the lyre aside. A wind rustled leaves. After a long quietness Sherrinford said, "And tales of this kind are part of everyone's life in the outway?"

"Well, you could put it thus," Barbro replied. "Though they're not all full of supernatural doings. Some are about love or heroism. Traditional themes."

"I don't think your particular tradition has arisen of itself." His tone was bleak. "In fact, I think many of your songs and stories were not composed by human beings."

He snapped his lips shut and would say no more on the subject. They went early to bed.

Hours later, an alarm roused them.

The buzzing was soft, but it brought them instantly alert. They slept in gripsuits, to be prepared for emergencies. Skyglow lit them through the canopy. Sherrinford swung out of his bunk, slipped shoes on feet, and clipped gun holster to belt. "Stay inside," he commanded.

"What's here?" Her pulse thuttered.

He squinted at the dials of his instruments and checked them against the luminous telltale on his wrist. "Three animals," he counted. "Not wild ones happening by. A large one, homeothermic, to judge from the infrared, holding still a short ways off. Another . . . hm, low temperature, diffuse and unstable emission, as if it were more like a . . . a swarm of cells coordinated somehow . . . pheromonally? . . . hovering, also at a distance. But the third's practically next to us, moving around in the brush; and that pattern looks human."

She saw him quiver with eagerness, no longer seeming a professor. "I'm going to try to make a capture," he said. "When we have a subject for interrogation—Stand ready to let me back in again fast. But don't risk yourself, whatever happens. And keep this cocked." He handed her a loaded big game rifle.

His tall frame poised by the door, opened it a crack. Air blew in, cool, damp, full of fragrances and murmurings. The moon Oliver was now also aloft, the radiance of both unreally brilliant, and the aurora seethed in whiteness and ice-blue.

Sherrinford peered afresh at his telltale. It must indicate the directions of the watchers, among those dappled leaves. Abruptly he sprang out. He sprinted past the ashes of the campfire and vanished under trees. Barbro's hand strained on the butt of her weapon.

Racket exploded. Two in combat burst onto the meadow. Sherrinford had clapped a grip on a smaller human figure. She could make out by streaming silver and rainbow flicker that the other was nude, male, long haired, lithe, and young. He fought demoniacally, seeking to use teeth and feet and raking nails, and meanwhile he ululated like a satan.

The identification shot through her: A changeling, stolen in babyhood and raised by the Old Folk. This creature was what they would make Jimmy into.

"Ha!" Sherrinford forced his opponent around and drove stiffened fingers into the solar plexus. The boy gasped and sagged: Sherrinford manhandled him toward the car.

Out from the woods came a giant. It might itself have been a tree, black and rugose, bearing four great gnarly boughs; but earth quivered and boomed beneath its leg-roots, and its hoarse bellowing filled sky and skulls.

Barbro shrieked. Sherrinford whirled. He yanked out his pistol, fired and fired, flat whip-cracks through the half-light. His free arm kept a lock on the youth. The troll shape lurched under those blows. It recovered and came on, more slowly, more carefully, circling around to cut him off from the bus. He couldn't move fast enough to evade it unless he released his prisoner—who was his sole possible guide to Jimmy—

Barbro leaped forth. "Don't!" Sherrinford shouted. "For God's sake, stay inside!" The monster rumbled and made snatching motions at her. She pulled the trigger. Recoil slammed her in the shoulder. The colossus rocked and fell. Somehow it got its feet back and lumbered toward her. She retreated. Again she shot, and again. The creature snarled. Blood began to drip from it and gleam oilily amidst dewdrops. It turned and went off, breaking branches, into the darkness that laired beneath the woods.

"Get to shelter!" Sherrinford yelled. "You're out of the jammer field!"

A mistiness drifted by overhead. She barely glimpsed

it before she saw the new shape at the meadow edge. "Jimmy!" tore from her.

"Mother." He held out his arms. Moonlight coursed in his tears. She dropped her weapon and ran to him.

Sherrinford plunged in pursuit. Jimmy flitted away into the brush. Barbro crashed after her, through clawing twigs. Then she was seized and borne away.

Standing over his captive, Sherrinford strengthened the fluoro output until vision of the wilderness was blocked off from within the bus. The boy squirmed beneath that colorless glare.

"You are going to talk," the man said. Despite the haggardness in his features, he spoke quietly.

The boy glared through tangled locks. A bruise was purpling on his jaw. He'd almost recovered ability to flee while Sherrinford chased and lost the woman. Returning, the detective had barely caught him. Time was lacking to be gentle, when Outling reinforcements might arrive at any moment. Sherrinford had knocked him out and dragged him inside. He sat lashed into a swivel seat.

He spat. "Talk to you, manclod?" But sweat stood on his skin, and his eyes flickered unceasingly around the metal which caged him.

"Give me a name to call you by."

"And have you work a spell on me?"

"Mine's Eric. If you don't give me another choice, I'll have to call you . . . m-m-m . . . Wuddikins."

"What?" However eldritch, the bound one remained a human adolescent. "Mistherd, then." The lilting accent of his English somehow emphasized its sullenness. "That's not the sound, only what it means. Anyway, it's my spoken name, naught else."

"Ah, you keep a secret name you consider to be real?"

"She does. I don't know myself what it is. She knows the real names of everybody."

Sherrinford raised his brows. "She?"

"Who reigns. May she forgive me, I can't make the reverent sign when my arms are tied. Some invaders call her the Queen of Air and Darkness."

"So." Sherrinford got pipe and tobacco. He let silence wax while he started the fire. At length he said:

"I'll confess the Old Folk took me by surprise. I didn't expect so formidable a member of your gang. Everything I could learn had seemed to show they work on my race—and yours, lad—by stealth, trickery, and illusion."

Mistherd jerked a truculent nod. "She created the first nicors not long ago. Don't think she has naught but dazzlements at her beck."

"I don't. However, a steel-jacketed bullet works pretty well too, doesn't it?"

Sherrinford talked on, softly, mostly to himself: "I do still believe the, ah, nicors—all your half-humanlike breeds—are intended in the main to be seen, not used. The power of projecting mirages must surely be quite limited in range and scope as well as the number of individuals who possess it. Otherwise she wouldn't have needed to work as slowly and craftily as she has. Even outside our mindshield, Barbro—my companion—could have resisted, could have remained aware that whatever she saw was unreal . . . if she'd been less shaken, less frantic, less driven by need."

Sherrinford wreathed his head in smoke. "Never mind what I experienced," he said. "It couldn't have been the same as for her. I think the command was simply given us, 'You will see what you most desire in the world, running away from you into the forest.' Of course, she didn't travel many meters before the nicor waylaid her. I'd no hope of trailing them; I'm no Arctican woodsman, and besides, it'd have been too easy to ambush me. I came back to you." Grimly: "You're my link to your overlady."

"You think I'll guide you to Starhaven or Carheddin? Try making me, clod-man."

"I want to bargain."

"I s'pect you intend more'n that." Mistherd's answer held surprising shrewdness. "What'll you tell after you come home?"

"Yes, that does pose a problem, doesn't it? Barbro Cullen and I are not terrified outwayers. We're of the city. We brought recording instruments. We'd be the first of our kind to report an encounter with the Old Folk, and that report would be detailed and plausible. It would produce action."

"So you see I'm not afraid to die," Mistherd declared, though his lips trembled a bit. "If I let you come in and do your manthings to my people, I'd have naught left worth living for."

"Have no immediate fears," Sherrinford said. "You're merely bait." He sat down and regarded the boy through a visor of calm. (Within, it wept in him: *Barbro, Barbro!*) "Consider. Your Queen can't very well let me go back, bringing my prisoner and telling about hers. She has to stop that somehow. I could try fighting my way through—this car is better armed than you know—but that wouldn't free anybody. Instead, I'm staying put. New forces of hers will get here as fast as they can. I assume they won't blindly throw themselves against a machine gun, a howitzer, a fulgurator. They'll parley first, whether their intentions are honest or not. Thus I make the contact I'm after."

''What d'you plan?'' The mumble held anguish.

''First, this, as a sort of invitation.'' Sherrinford reached out to flick a switch. ''There. I've lowered my shield against mind-reading and shape-casting. I dare-say the leaders, at least, will be able to sense that it's gone. That should give them confidence.''

''And next?''

''Next we wait. Would you like something to eat or drink?''

During the time which followed, Sherrinford tried to jolly Mistherd along, find out something of his life. What answers he got were curt. He dimmed the interior lights and settled down to peer outward. That was a long few hours.

They ended at a shout of gladness, half a sob, from the boy. Out of the woods came a band of the Old Folk.

Some of them stood forth more clearly than moons and stars and northlights should have caused. He in the van rode a white crownbuck whose horns were garlanded. His form was manlike but unearthly beautiful, silver blond hair falling from beneath the antlered helmet, around the proud cold face. The cloak fluttered off his back like living wings. His frost-colored mail rang as he fared.

Behind him, to right and left, rode two who bore swords whereon small flames gleamed and flickered. Above, a flying flock laughed and trilled and tumbled in the breezes. Near them drifted a half-transparent mistiness. Those others who passed among trees after their chieftain were harder to make out. But they moved in quicksilver grace and as it were to a sound of harps and trumpets.

''Lord Luighaid.'' Glory overflowed in Mistherd's tone. ''Her master Knower—himself.''

Sherrinford had never done a harder thing than to sit at the main control panel, finger near the button of the shield generator, and not touch it. He rolled down a section of canopy to let voices travel. A gust of wind struck him in the face, bearing odors of the roses in his mother's garden. At his back, in the main body of the vehicle, Mistherd strained against his bonds till he could see the oncoming troop.

"Call to them," Sherrinford said. "Ask if they will talk with me."

Unknown, flutingly sweet words flew back and forth. "Yes," the boy interpreted. "He will, the Lord Luighaid. But I can tell you, you'll never be let go. Don't fight them. Yield. Come away. You don't know what 'tis to be alive till you've dwelt in Carheddin under the mountain."

The Outlings drew nigh.

Jimmy glimmered and was gone. Barbro lay in strong arms, against a broad breast, and felt the horse move beneath her. It had to be a horse, though only a few were kept any longer on the steadings, and they only for special uses or love. She could feel the rippling beneath its hide, hear a rush of parted leafage and the thud when a hoof struck stone; warmth and living scent welled up around her through the darkness.

He who carried her said mildly, "Don't be afraid, darling. It was a vision. But he's waiting for us, and we're bound for him."

She was aware in a vague way that she ought to feel terror or despair or something. But her memories lay behind her—she wasn't sure just how she had come to be here—she was borne along in a knowledge of being loved. At peace, at peace, rest in the calm expectation of joy . . .

After a while the forest opened. They crossed a lea where boulders stood gray white under the moons, their shadows shifting in the dim hues which the aurora threw across them. Flitteries danced, tiny comets, above the flowers between. Ahead gleamed a peak whose top was crowned in clouds.

Barbro's eyes happened to be turned forward. She saw the horse's head and thought, with quiet surprise: "Why, this is Sambo, who was mine when I was a girl." She looked upward at the man. He wore a black tunic and a cowled cape, which made his face hard to see. She could not cry aloud, here. "Tim," she whispered.

"Yes, Barbro."

"I buried you—"

His smile was endlessly tender. "Did you think we're no more than what's laid back into the ground? Poor torn sweetheart. She who's called us is the All Healer. Now rest and dream."

"Dream," she said, and for a space she struggled to rouse herself. But the effort was weak. Why should she believe ashen tales about . . . atoms and energies, nothing else to fill a gape of emptiness . . . tales she could not bring to mind . . . when Tim and the horse her father gave her carried her on to Jimmy? Had the other thing not been the evil dream, and this her first drowsy awakening from it?

As if he heard her thoughts, he murmured, "They have a song in Outling lands. The Song of the Men:

"The world sails
to an unseen wind.
Light swirls by the bows.
The wake is night.
But the Dwellers have no such sadness."

"I don't understand," she said.

He nodded. "There's much you'll have to understand, darling, and I can't see you again until you've learned those truths. But meanwhile you'll be with our son."

She tried to lift her head and kiss him. He held her down. "Not yet," he said. "You've not been received among the Queen's people. I shouldn't have come for you, except that she was too merciful to forbid. Lie back, lie back."

Time flew past. The horse galloped tireless, never stumbling, up the mountain. Once she glimpsed a troop riding down it and thought they were bound for a last weird battle in the west against . . . who? . . . one who lay cased in iron and sorrow—Later she would ask herself the name of him who had brought her into the land of the Old Truth.

Finally spires lifted splendid among the stars, which are small and magical and whose whisperings comfort us after we are dead. They rode into a courtyard where candles burned unwavering, fountains splashed and birds sang. The air bore fragrance of brok and pericoup, of rue and roses, for not everything that man brought was horrible. The Dwellers waited in beauty to welcome her. Beyond their stateliness, pooks cavorted through the gloaming; among the trees darted children; merriment caroled across music more solemn.

"We have come—" Tim's voice was suddenly, inexplicably, a croak. Barbro was not sure how he dismounted, bearing her. She stood before him and saw him sway on his feet.

Fear caught her. "Are you well?" She seized both his hands. They felt cold and rough. Where had Sambo gone? Her eyes searched beneath the cowl. In this brighter illumination, she ought to have seen her man's face clearly. But it was blurred, it kept changing. ''What's wrong, oh, what's happened?''

He smiled. Was that the smile she had cherished? She couldn't completely remember. ''I, I must go,'' he stammered, so low she could scarcely hear. ''Our time is not ready.'' He drew free of her grasp and leaned on a robed form which had appeared at his side. A haziness swirled over both their heads. ''Don't watch me go . . . back into the earth,'' he pleaded. ''That's death for you. Till our time returns—There, our son!''

She had to fling her gaze around. Kneeling, she spread wide her arms. Jimmy struck her like a warm, solid cannonball. She rumpled his hair; she kissed the hollow of his neck; she laughed and wept and babbled foolishness; and this was no ghost, no memory that had stolen off when she wasn't looking. Now and again, as she turned her attention to yet another hurt which might have come upon him—hunger, sickness, fear—and found none, she would glimpse their surroundings. The gardens were gone. It didn't matter.

''I missed you so, Mother. Stay?''

''I'll take you home, dearest.''

''Stay. Here's fun. I'll show. But you stay.''

A sighing went through the twilight. Barbro rose. Jimmy clung to her hand. They confronted the Queen.

Very tall she was in her robes woven of northlights, and her starry crown and her garlands of kiss-me-never. Her countenance recalled Aphrodite of Milos, whose picture Barbro had often seen in the realms of men, save that the Queen's was more fair and more majesty dwelt upon it and in the night-blue eyes. Around her the gardens woke to new reality, the court of the Dwellers and the heaven-climbing spires.

''Be welcome,'' she spoke, her speaking a song, ''forever.''

Against the awe of her, Barbro said, "Moonmother, let us go home."

"That may not be."

"To our world, little and beloved," Barbro dreamed she begged, "which we build for ourselves and cherish for our children."

"To prison days, angry nights, works that crumble in the fingers, loves that turn to rot or stone or driftweed, loss, grief, and the only sureness that of the final nothingness. No. You too, Wanderfoot who is to be, will jubilate when the banners of the Outworld come flying into the last of the cities and man is made wholly alive. Now go with those who will teach you."

The Queen of Air and Darkness lifted an arm in summons. It halted, and none came to answer.

For over the fountains and melodies lifted a gruesome growling. Fires leaped, thunders crashed. Her hosts scattered screaming before the steel thing which boomed up the mountainside. The pooks were gone in a whirl of frightened wings. The nicors flung their bodies against the unalive invader and were consumed, until their Mother cried to them to retreat.

Barbro cast Jimmy down and herself over him. Towers wavered and smoked away. The mountain stood bare under icy moons, save for rocks, crags, and farther off a glacier in whose depths the auroral light pulsed blue. A cave mouth darkened a cliff. Thither folk streamed, seeking refuge underground. Some were human of blood, some grotesques like the pooks and nicors and wraiths; but most were lean, scaly, long-tailed, long-beaked, not remotely men or Outlings.

For an instant, even as Jimmy wailed at her breast—perhaps as much because the enchantment had been wrecked as because he was afraid—Barbro pitied the

Queen who stood alone in her nakedness. Then that one also had fled, and Barbro's world shivered apart.

The guns fell silent; the vehicle whirred to a halt. From it sprang a boy who called wildly, "Shadow-of-a-Dream, where are you? It's me, Mistherd, oh, come, come!"—before he remembered that the language they had been raised in was not man's. He shouted in that until a girl crept out of a thicket where she had hidden. They stared at each other through dust, smoke, and moonglow. She ran to him.

A new voice barked from the car, "Barbro, hurry!"

Christmas Landing knew day: short at this time of year, but sunlight, blue skies, white clouds, glittering water, salt breezes in busy streets, and the sane disorder of Eric Sherrinford's living room.

He crossed and uncrossed his legs where he sat, puffed on his pipes as if to make a veil, and said, "Are you certain you're recovered? You mustn't risk overstrain."

"I'm fine," Barbro Cullen replied, though her tone was flat. "Still tired, yes, and showing it, no doubt. One doesn't go through such an experience and bounce back in a week. But I'm up and about. And to be frank, I must know what's happened, what's going on, before I can settle down to regain my full strength. Not a word of news anywhere."

"Have you spoken to others about the matter?"

"No. I've simply told visitors I was too exhausted to talk. Not much of a lie. I assumed there's a reason for censorship."

Sherrinford looked relieved. "Good girl. It's at my urging. You can imagine the sensation when this is made public. The authorities agreed they need time to study the facts, think and debate in a calm atmosphere, have a decent policy ready to offer voters who're bound to become rather hysterical at first.'' His mouth quirked slightly upward. ''Furthermore, your nerves and Jimmy's get their chance to heal before the journalistic storm breaks over you. How is he?''

''Quite well. He continues pestering me for leave to go play with his friends in the Wonderful Place. But at his age, he'll recover—he'll forget.''

''He may meet them later anyhow.''

''What? We didn't—'' Barbro shifted in her chair. ''I've forgotten too. I hardly recall a thing from our last hours. Did you bring back any kidnapped humans?''

''No. The shock was savage as it was, without throwing them straight into an . . . an institution. Mistherd, who's basically a sensible young fellow, assured me they'd get along, at any rate as regards survival necessities, till arrangements can be made.'' Sherrinford hesitated. ''I'm not sure what the arrangements will be. Nobody is, at our present stage. But obviously they include those people—or many of them, especially those who aren't fullgrown—rejoining the human race. Though they may never feel at home in civilization. Perhaps in a way that's best, since we will need some kind of mutually acceptable liaison with the Dwellers.''

His impersonality soothed them both. Barbro became able to say, ''Was I too big a fool? I do remember how I yowled and beat my head on the floor.''

''Why, no.'' He considered the big woman and her pride for a few seconds before he rose, walked over and laid a hand on her shoulder. ''You'd been lured and trapped by a skillful play on your deepest instincts, at a moment of sheer nightmare. Afterward, as that wounded monster carried you off, evidently another type of being came along, one that could saturate you with close-range neuropsychic forces. On top of this, my arrival, the sudden brutal abolishment of every hallucination, must have been shattering. No wonder if you cried out in pain. Before you did, you competently got Jimmy and yourself into the bus, and you never interfered with me.''

''What did you do?''

''Why, I drove off as fast as possible. After several hours, the atmospherics let up sufficiently for me to call Portolondon and insist on an emergency airlift. Not that that was vital. What chance had the enemy to stop us? They didn't even try—But quick transportation was certainly helpful.''

''I figured that's what must have gone on,'' Barbro caught his glance. ''No, what I meant was, how did you find us in the backlands?''

Sherrinford moved a little off from her. ''My prisoner was my guide. I don't think I actually killed any of the Dwellers who'd come to deal with me. I hope not. The car simply broke through them, after a couple of warning shots, and afterward outpaced them. Steel and fuel against flesh wasn't really fair. At the cave entrance, I did have to shoot down a few of those troll creatures. I'm not proud of it.''

He stood silent. Presently: ''But you were a captive,'' he said. ''I couldn't be sure what they might do to you, who had first claim on me.'' After another pause: ''I don't look for any more violence.''

''How did you make . . . the boy . . . co-operate?''

Sherrinford paced from her to the window, where he stood staring out at the Boreal Ocean. ''I turned off the mindshield,'' he said. ''I let their band get close, in full splendor of illusion. Then I turned the shield back on, and we both saw them in their true shapes. As we went northward, I explained to Mistherd how he and his kind had been hoodwinked, used, made to live in a world that was never really there. I asked him if he wanted himself and whomever he cared about to go on till they died as domestic animals—yes, running in limited freedom on solid hills, but always called back to the dream-kennel.'' His pipe fumed furiously. ''May I never see such bitterness again. He had been taught to believe he was free.''

Quiet returned, above the hectic traffic. Charlemagne drew nearer to setting; already the east darkened.

Finally Barbro asked, ''Do you know why?''

''Why children were taken and raised like that? Partly because it was in the pattern the Dwellers were creating; partly in order to study and experiment on members of our species—minds, that is, not bodies; partly because humans have special strengths which are helpful, like being able to endure full daylight.''

''But what was the final purpose of it all?''

Sherrinford paced the floor. ''Well,'' he said, ''of course the ultimate motives of the aborigines are obscure. We can't do more than guess at how they think, let alone how they feel. But our ideas do seem to fit the data.

''Why did they hide from man? I suspect they, or rather their ancestors—for they aren't glittering elves, you know; they're mortal and fallible too—I suspect the natives were only being cautious at first, more cautious than human primitives, though certain of those on Earth were also slow to reveal themselves to strangers. Spying, mentally eavesdropping, Roland's Dwellers must have picked up enough language to get some idea of how different man was from them, and how powerful; and they gathered that more ships would be arriving, bringing settlers. It didn't occur to them that they might be conceded the right to keep their lands. Perhaps they're still more fiercely territorial than we. They determined to fight, in their own way. I dare say, once we begin to get insight into that mentality, our psychological science will go through its Copernican revolution."

Enthusiasm kindled in him. "That's not the sole thing we'll learn, either," he went on. "They must have science of their own, a nonhuman science born on a planet that isn't Earth. Because they did observe us as profoundly as we've ever observed ourselves; they did mount a plan against us, one that would have taken another century or more to complete. Well, what else do they know? How do they support their civilization without visible agriculture or aboveground buildings or mines or anything? How can they breed whole new intelligent species to order? A million questions, ten million answers!"

"*Can* we learn from them?" Barbro asked softly. "Or can we only overrun them as you say they fear?"

Sherrinford halted, leaned elbow on mantel, hugged his pipe and replied, "I hope we'll show more charity than that to a defeated enemy. It's what they are. They tried to conquer us and failed, and now in a sense we are bound to conquer them, since they'll have to make their peace with the civilization of the machine rather than see it rust away as they strove for. Still, they never did us any harm as atrocious as what we've inflicted on our fellow men in the past. And I repeat, they could teach us marvelous things; and we could teach them, too, once they've learned to be less intolerant of a different way of life."

"I suppose we can give them a reservation," she said, and didn't know why he grimaced and answered so roughly:

"Let's leave them the honor they've earned! They fought to save the world they'd always known from that—" he made a chopping gesture at the city— "and just possibly we'd be better off ourselves with less of it."

He sagged a trifle and sighed, "However, I suppose if Elfland had won, man on Roland would at last—peacefully, even happily—have died away. We live with our archetypes but can we live in them?"

Barbro shook her head. "Sorry, I don't understand."

"What?" He looked at her in a surprise that drove out melancholy. After a laugh: "Stupid of me. I've explained this to so many politicians and scientists and commissioners and Lord knows what, these past days, I forgot I'd never explained to you. It was a rather vague idea of mine, most of the time we were traveling, and I don't like to discuss ideas prematurely. Now that we've met the Outlings and watched how they work, I do feel sure."

He tamped down his tobacco. "In limited measure," he said, "I've used an archetype throughout my own working life. The rational detective. It hasn't been a conscious pose—much—it's simply been an image which fitted my personality and professional style. But it draws an appropriate response from most people, whether or not they've ever heard of the original. The phenomenon is not uncommon. We meet persons who, in varying degrees, suggest Christ or Buddha or the Earth Mother, or say, on a less exalted plane, Hamlet or d'Artagnan. Historical, fictional, and mythical, such figures crystallize basic aspects of the human psyche, and when we meet them in our real experience, our reaction goes deeper than consciousness."

He grew grave again: "Man also creates archetypes

that are not individuals. The Anima, the Shadow—and, it seems, the Outworld. The world of magic, or glamour—which originally mean enchantment—of half-human beings, some like Ariel and some like Caliban, but each free of mortal frailties and sorrows—therefore, perhaps, a little carelessly cruel, more than a little tricksy; dwellers in dusk and moonlight, not truly gods but obedient to rulers who are enigmatic and powerful enough to be—Yes, our Queen of Air and Darkness knew well what sights to let lonely people see, what illusions to spin around them from time to time, what songs and legends to set going among them. I wonder how much she and her underlings gleaned from human fairy tales, how much they made up themselves, and how much men created all over again, all unwittingly, as the sense of living on the edge of the world entered them.''

Shadows stole across the room. It grew cooler and the traffic noises dwindled. Barbro asked mutedly, ''But what could this do?''

''In many ways,'' Sherrinford answered, ''the outwayer *is* back in the Dark Ages. He has few neighbors, hears scanty news from beyond his horizon, toils to survive in a land he only partly understands, that may any night raise unforeseeable disasters against him, and is bounded by enormous wildernesses. The machine civilization which brought his ancestors here is frail at best. He could lose it as the Dark Ages nations had lost Greece and Rome, as the whole of Earth seems to have lost it. Let him be worked on, long, strongly, cunningly, by the archetypical Outworld, until he has come to believe in his bones that the magic of the Queen of Air and Darkness is greater than the energy of engines; and first his faith, finally his deeds will follow her. Oh, it wouldn't happen fast. Ideally, it would happen too slowly to be noticed, especially by self-satisfied city people. But when in the end a hinterland gone back to the ancient way turned from them, how could they keep alive?"

Barbro breathed, "She said to me, when their banners flew in the last of our cities, we would rejoice."

"I think we would have, by then," Sherrinford admitted. "Nevertheless, I believe in choosing one's destiny."

He shook himself, as if casting off a burden. He knocked the dottle from his pipe and stretched, muscle by muscle. "Well," he said, "it isn't going to happen."

She looked straight at him. "Thanks to you."

A flush went up his thin cheeks. "In time, I'm sure, somebody else would have—What matters is what we do next, and that's too big a decision for one individual or one generation to make."

She rose. "Unless the decision is personal, Eric," she suggested, feeling heat in her own face.

It was curious to see him shy. "I was hoping we might meet again."

"We will."

Ayoch sat on Wolund's Barrow. Aurora shuddered so brilliant, in such vast sheafs of light, as almost to hide the waning moons. Firethorn blooms had fallen; a few still glowed around the tree roots, amidst dry brok which crackled underfoot and smelled like woodsmoke. The air remained warm, but no gleam was left on the sunset horizon.

"Farewell, fare lucky," the pook called. Mistherd and Shadow-of-a-Dream never looked back. It was as if they didn't dare. They trudged on out of sight, toward the human camp whose lights made a harsh new star in the south.

Ayoch lingered. He felt he should also offer goodbye to her who had lately joined him that slept in the dolmen. Likely none would meet here again for loving or magic. But he could only think of one old verse that might do. He stood and trilled:

"Out of her breast
a blossom ascended.
The summer burned it.
The song is ended."

Then he spread his wings for the long flight away.

House Rule

That inn beyond every world, the Old Phoenix, first appeared in my Shakespearean fantasy novel *A Midsummer Tempest*. Elsewhere I have acknowledged "its relationship to works by John Kendrick Bangs, Charles Erskine Scott Wood, Hendrik Willem van Loon, Lord Dunsany, Edmond Hamilton, and others, as well as the origin of all in a common daydream." It also commemorates certain cheerful pubs, here and there around the globe. Still, to the best of my knowledge, nothing else is quite like this place, where you may meet anybody whatsoever. I have returned to it a couple of times and hope to do so again.

Look for it anywhere, anytime, by day, by dusk, by night, up an ancient alley or out on an empty heath or in a forest where hunters whose eyes no spoor can escape nonetheless pass it by unseeing. Myself, I found its doorhandle under my fingers and its signboard creaking over my head when I was about to enter the saloon of a ship far at sea. You cannot really seek this house; it will seek you. But you must be alert for its fleeting presence, bright or curious or adventurous or desperate enough to enter, the first time. Thereafter, if you do not abuse its hospitality, you will be allowed to come back every once in a while.

The odds are all against you, of course. Few ever get this chance. Yet, since nobody knows what basis the landlord has for admitting his guests, and when asked he says merely that they are those who have good stories wherewith to pay him, you too may someday be favored. So keep yourself open to everything, and perhaps, just perhaps, you will have the great luck of joining us in that tavern called the Old Phoenix.

I'm not quite sure why the innkeeper and his wife the barmaid think I deserve it. There are countless others more worthy, throughout the countless dimensional sheaves, whom I have never met. When I suggest such a person, mine host shrugs, smiles, and amiably evades the question, a tactic in which he is skilled. Doubtless I've simply not happened on some of them. After all, a guest may only stay till the following dawn. Then the house won't reappear to him for a stretch which in my case has always been at least a month. Furthermore, I suspect that besides being at a nexus of universes, the hostel exists on several different space-time levels of its own.

Well, let's not speculate about the unanswerable. I want to tell of an incident I can't get out of my mind.

That evening would have been spectacular aplenty had nothing else gone on than my conversation with Leonardo da Vinci. I recognized that tall, golden-bearded man the instant he stepped into the taproom and shook raindrops off his cloak, and ventured to introduce myself. By and large, we're a friendly, informal bunch at the Old Phoenix. We come mainly to meet people. Besides, of the few who were already present, nobody but landlord, barmaid, and I knew Italian. Oh, Leonardo could have used Latin or French with the nun who sat offside and quietly listened to us. However, their accents would have made talk a struggle.

The goodwife was busy, pumping out beer for Erik the Red, Sancho Panza, and Nicholas van Rijn, interpreting and chattering away in early Norse, a peasant dialect of Spanish, and the argot of a spacefaring future, while now and then she helped herself to a tankardful. Mine host, among whose multiple names I generally choose Taverner, was off in a dim corner with beings I couldn't see very well, except that they were shadowy and full of small starlike sparkles. His round face was more solemn than usual, he often ran a hand across his bald pate, and the sounds that came from his mouth, answering those guests, were a ripple of trills and purrs.

Thus Leonardo and I were alone, until the nun entered and shyly settled down at our table. I include medieval varieties of French in my languages; being an habitue of the Old Phoenix mightily encourages such studies. But by then we two were so excited that, while we greeted her as courteously as Taverner expects, neither of us caught her name, and I barely noticed that within its coif her face was quite lovely. I did gather that she was from a convent at Argenteuil in the twelfth century. But she was content to sit and try to follow our discourse. Renaissance Florentinian was not hopelessly alien to her mother tongue.

The talk was mainly Leonardo's. Given a couple of goblets of wine to relax him, his mind soared and ranged like an eagle in a high wind. Tonight was his second time, and the first had naturally been such a stunning experience that he was still assimilating it. But the drink at our inn, like the food, is unearthly superb. (It should be; Taverner can ransack all the worlds, all the ages of a hyper-cosmos which, perhaps, is infinitely branched in its possibility-lines.) Leonardo soon felt at ease. In answer to a question, he told me that he was living in Milan in the year 1493 and was forty-one years old. This squared with what I recollected; so quite likely he was the same Leonardo as existed in my continuum. Certainly, from what he said, he was at the height of his fame, brilliance, powers, and longings.

"But why, Messer, why may you not say more?" he asked. His voice was deep and musical.

"Maybe I could," I replied. "None has ever given me a hard and fast catalogue of commandments. I imagine they judge each case singly. But . . . would *you* risk being forever barred from this place?"

His big body, richly clad though in hues that my era of synthetic dyes would have found subdued, twisted around in his chair. As his glance traveled over the taproom, I caught the nun admiring his profile—the least bit wistfully? She was indeed beautiful, I admitted to myself. A shapeless dark habit of rather smelly, surely heavy and scratchy wool could not altogether hide a slim young figure; her countenance was pale, delicately sculptured, huge-eyed. I wondered why, even in her milieu, she had taken vows.

The room enclosed us in cheer, long, wide, wainscotted in carven oak, ceiling massively beamed. A handsome stone fireplace held a blaze of well-scented logs, whose leap and crackle gave more warmth than you'd expect, just as the sconced candles gave more light. That light fell on straight chairs around small tables, armchairs by themselves, benches flanking the great central board, laid out ideally for fellowship. Along the walls, it touched books, pictures, and souvenirs from afar. At one end, after glowing across the bar where my lady hostess stood between the beer pumps and the racked bottles and vessels, it lost itself beyond an open doorway; but I made out a stair going up to clean, unpretentious chambers where you can sleep if you like. (People seldom do. The company is too good, the hours too precious.) Windows are always shuttered, I suppose because they would not look out over any of the worlds on which the front door opens, but onto something quite peculiar. That thought makes the inside feel still more snug.

"No," Leonardo sighed, "I daresay I too will grow careful. And yet . . .'tis hard to understand . . . if we are mainly here for colloquy, that Messer Albergatore may enjoy the spectacle and the tales, why does he set bounds on our speech? I assure you, for instance, I do not fear your telling me the date and manner of my death, if you know them. God will call me when He chooses."

"You utter a deep truth there," I said. "For I am not necessarily from your future. For all we can tell, I may be from the future of another Leonardo da Vinci, whose destiny is, or was, not yours. Hence 'twould be a pointless unpleasantness to discuss certain matters."

"But what of the rest?" he protested. "You bespeak flying machines, automatons, elixirs injected into the flesh which prevent illness—oh, endless wonders—Why must you merely hint?"

I said into his intensity: "Messer, you have the intellect to see the reason. If I gave you over-much knowledge or foresight, what might ensue? We lack wisdom and restraint, we mortals. Taverner has a—a license?—to entertain certain among us. But it must strictly be entertainment. Nothing decisive may happen here. We meet and part as in dreams, we at the Old Phoenix."

"What then can we do?" he demanded.

"Why, there are all the arts, there are stories real and imaginary, there are the eternal riddles of our nature and purpose and meaning, there are songs and games and jests and simply being together—But it is wrong that I act pompous toward you. I feel most honored and humble, and would like naught better than to hear whatever you wish to say."

Humanly pleased, he answered, "Well, if you'll not tell me how the flying machine works—and, indeed, I can understand that if you did, 'twould avail me little, who lack the hoarded lore and instrumentalities of four or five hundred years—pray continue as you were when I interrupted. Finish relating your adventure."

I reminisced about a flight which had been forced down above the Arctic Circle, and how some Eskimos had helped us. His inquiries concerning them were keen, and led him on to experiences of his own, and to remarks about the variety and strangeness of man—As I said, had nothing else happened, this would still have been among the memorable evenings of my life.

The door opened and closed. We heard a footfall, caught a whiff of city streets which also served as garbage dumps and sewers, glimpsed crowded wooden houses on a cloudy day. The man who had appeared was rather short by my standards or against Leonardo, and middle-aged to gauge by features deeply lined though still sharply cut. Grizzled brown hair fell past his ears from under a flat velvet cap. He wore a monastic robe, with rosary and crucifix, but shoes and hose rather than sandals. His form was slender and straight, his gaze extraordinarily vivid.

Taverner excused himself from his conversation and

hurried across the floor to give greeting. "Ah, welcome, welcome anew," he said in Old French—*langue d'oïl,* to be exact. "At yonder table sit two gentlemen whose companionship will surely pleasure you." He took the monk's arm. "Come, let me introduce you, my learned Master Abélard—"

The nun's voice cut through his. She surged to her feet; the chair clattered behind her. "Pier!" she cried. "O Jésu, O Maria, Pier!"

And he stood where he was for an instant as if a sword in his guts had stopped him. Then: "Héloise," cracked out his throat. "But thou art dead." He crossed himself, over and over. "Hast thou, thou, thou come back to comfort me, Héloise?"

Taverner looked disconcerted. He must have forgotten her presence. The noise and dice-casting at the bar died away. The starry gray ones became still. Alone the hearthfire spoke.

"No, what art thou saying, I, I am alive, Pier," the nun stammered. "But thou, my poor hurt darling—" She stumbled toward him. I saw how he half flinched, before he gathered courage and held out his arms.

They met, and embraced, and stood like that: until our plump, motherly barmaid suddenly shouted, "Well, good for you, dears!" They didn't notice, they had nobody but each other.

The rest of us eased a trifle. Evidently this wasn't a bad event. Erik lifted his drinking horn, Sancho guffawed at such behavior of ecclesiastics, van Rijn held out his mug for a refill, the strangers in the corner rustled and twinkled, Taverner wryly shrugged.

Leonardo leaned across the table and whispered to me, "Did I hear aright? Are those in truth Héloise and Abélard?"

"They must be," I answered, and knew not what to feel. "Belike not from your history or mine, however."

He had grasped the idea of universes parallel in multi-dimensional reality, in some of which magic worked, in some of which it did not, in some of which King Arthur or Orlando Furioso had actually lived, in some of which he himself had not. Now he murmured, "Well, quickly, lest we say unwitting a harmful thing, let's compare what our chronicles tell about them."

"Peter Abélard was the greatest Scholastic of his century," ran from me, while I tried to take my eyes off the weeping pair and could not. "He was in his forties when he met Héloise, a girl in her twenties. She was the niece and ward of a powerful, high-born canon. They fell in love, had a child, couldn't marry because of his career in the Church but—Anyway, her uncle found out and was enraged. He hired a gang of bullies to waylay Abélard and castrate him. After that, Héloise entered a convent—against her uncle's wish, I believe—and never saw her lover again. But the bond that held them was unchanged—the world will always remember the letters that passed between them—and in my day they lie buried together."

Leonardo nodded. "Yes, that sounds like what I read. I seem to recall that they did marry, albeit secretly."

"Perhaps my memory is at fault."

"Or mine. It was long ago. For us. God in Heaven, though, they two yonder—!"

Maybe they consciously recalled this was the single place they could meet; or maybe they, like most people in their age, had scant notion of privacy; or maybe they didn't give a damn. I heard what they blurted forth through their tears.

They were from separate time-lines. She might belong to Leonardo's or mine, if ours were the same; her story was familiar to us both. But he, he was still a whole man. For him, three years before, she had died in childbirth.

Meanwhile Taverner led them to an offside couch; and the barmaid fetched refreshments, which they didn't see; and host and hostess breathed to them what no one else could hear. Not that anybody wanted to. As if half ashamed, they at the bar returned to their boozing, Leonardo and I to our talk; they in the corner waited silent.

My companion soon lost his embarrassment. Tenderheartedness is not notably a Renaissance trait. Since we knew equally little about the branchings of existence, we were free to wonder aloud about them. He got onto constructing such a world-of-if (suppose Antony had triumphed at Actium, because the library at Alexandria had not caught fire when Julius Caesar laid siege, and in it were Heron's plans for a submersible warcraft . . . well, conceivably, somewhere among the dimensions it *did* happen) that I too, chiming in here and there, well-nigh lost awareness of the nun and her Schoolman.

Again the door interrupted us—half an hour later, an hour, I'm not sure. This time I spied a lawn, trees, ivy-covered red brick buildings, before it shut. The man who had arrived was old but stood tall, and much robustness remained to him. He wore an open-necked shirt, fuzzy sweater, faded slacks, battered sneakers. A glory of white hair framed the kind of plain, gentle, but thoughtful and characterful Jewish face that Rembrandt liked to portray.

He saw Héloise and Abélard together, and smiled uncertainly. "*Guten Abend,*" he ventured; and in English: "Good evening. Maybe I had better not—"

"Ah, do stay!" exclaimed Taverner, hurrying toward him, while the eyes popped in van Rijn's piratical visage and my pulse ran wild.

Taverner took the newcomer by the elbow and steered him toward us. "By all means, do," he urged. "True, we've had a scene, but harmless, yes, I'd say benign. And here's a gentleman I know you've been wanting to meet." He reached our table and made a grand flourish. "Messer Leonardo da Vinci . . . Herr Doktor Albert Einstein. . . ." I suppose he included me.

Of course, the Italian had not heard of the Jew, but he sensed what was afoot and bowed deeply. Einstein, more diffident, nevertheless responded with similar grace and sat down amidst polite noises all around. "Do you mind if I smoke?" he asked. We didn't, so he kindled a pipe while the barmaid brought new drinks. Neither of my tablemates did more than sip, however, and I wasn't about to spoil this for myself by getting drunk the way they were doing over at the bar.

Besides, I must be interpreter. Einstein's Italian was limited, and of a date centuries later than Leonardo's, who had neither German nor English. I interpreted. Do you see why I will never risk my standing at the Old Phoenix?

They needed a while to warm up. Einstein was eager to learn what this or that cryptic notation of Leonardo's referred to. But Leonardo must have Einstein's biography related to him.

When he realized what that signified, his blue eyes became blowtorches, and I had trouble following every word that torrented from him. We thus got some pauses. Furthermore, occasionally even those chain lightning minds must halt and search before going on.

Hence, unavoidably, I noticed Héloise and Abélard anew.

They sat kissing, whispering, trembling. This was the sole night they could have, she alive, he his entire self—the odds against their ever chancing to meet here were unmeasurably huge—and what was allowed them, by the law of their hostel and the law of their holy orders? Tick, said a grandfather clock by the wall, tick, tick; here too, a night is twelve hours long.

Taverner scuttled around in the unobtrusive way he can don when he wants to. They started trading songs at the bar. The taproom is big enough that that doesn't annoy anyone who hasn't a very good ear; and Einstein and Leonardo, who did, were too engaged with each other.

What does the smile mean upon Mona Lisa and your several Madonnas?

Will you give to me again that melody of Bach's?

How did you fare under Sforza, how under Borgia, how under King Francis?

How did you fare in Switzerland, how against Hitler, how with Roosevelt?

What physical considerations led you to think men might build wings?

What evidence proves that the earth goes around the sun, that light has a finite speed, that the stars are also suns?

What makes you doubt the finiteness of the universe?

Well, sir, why have you not analyzed your concept of space-time as follows?

Taverner and the barmaid spoke low behind their hands. Finally she went to Héloise and Abélard. "Go on upstairs," she said through tears of her own. "You've only this while, and it's wearing away."

He looked up like a blind man. "We took vows," came from his lips.

Héloise closed them with hers. "Thou didst break thine before," she told him, "and we praised the goodness of God."

"Go, go," said the barmaid. Almost by herself, she raised them to their feet. I saw them leave, I heard them on the stairs.

And then Leonardo: "Doctor Alberto, you waste your efforts." He grimaced; the hands knotted around his goblet. "I cannot follow your mathematics, your logic. I have not the knowledge—"

But Einstein leaned forward, and his voice too was less than steady. "You have the brain. And, yes, a fresh view, an insight not blinkered by four centuries of progress point by point . . . down a single road, when we know in this room there are many, many. . . ."

"You cannot explain to me in a few hours—"

"No, but you can get a general idea of what I mean, and I think you, out of everybody who ever lived, can see where . . . where I am astray—and from me, you can carry back home—"

Leonardo flamed.

"No."

That was Taverner. He had come up on the empty side of our table; and he no longer seemed stumpy or jolly.

"No, gentlemen," he said in language after language. His tone was not stern, it was regretful, but it never wavered. "I fear I must ask you to change the subject. You would learn more than should be. Both of you."

We stared at him, and the silence around us turned off the singing. Leonardo's countenance froze. Finally Einstein smiled lopsidedly, scraped back his chair, stood, knocked the dottle from his pipe. Its odor was bittersweet. "My apologies, Herr Gastwirt," he said in his soft fashion. "You are right. I forgot." He bowed. "This evening has been an honor and a delight. Thank you."

Turning, his stooped form departed.

When the door had shut on him, Leonardo sat unmoving for another while. Taverner threw me a rueful grin and went back to his visiting mysteries. The men at the bar, who had sensed a problem and quieted down, now cheered up and grew rowdier yet. When Mrs. Hauksbee walked in, they cheered.

Leonardo cast his goblet on the floor. Glass flew outward, wine fountained red. "Héloise and Abélard!" he roared. "*They* will have had their night!"

The Tale of Hauk

The Icelandic Eddas and sagas include some of the finest literature in the world. I do not pretend that this story equals those told about Egil, Njál, Grettir, and others, but it is among my tributes to them.

A man called Geirolf dwelt on the Great Fjord in Raumsdal. His father was Bui Hardhand, who owned a farm inland near the Dofra Fell. One year Bui went in viking to Finnmark and brought back a woman he dubbed Gydha. She became the mother of Geirolf. But because Bui already had children by his wife, there would be small inheritance for this by-blow.

Folk said uncanny things about Gydha. She was fair to see, but spoke little, did no more work than she must, dwelt by herself in a shack out of sight of the garth, and often went for long stridings alone on the upland heaths, heedless of cold, rain, and rovers. Bui did not visit her often. Her son Geirolf did. He too was a moody sort, not much given to playing with others, quick and harsh of temper. Big and strong, he went abroad with his father already when he was twelve, and in the next few years won the name of a mighty though ruthless fighter.

Then Gydha died. They buried her near her shack, and it was whispered that she spooked around it of nights. Soon after, walking home with some men by moonlight from a feast at a neighbor's, Bui clutched his breast and fell dead. They wondered if Gydha had called him, maybe to accompany her home to Finnmark, for there was no more sight of her.

Geirolf bargained with his kin and got the price of a ship for himself. Thereafter he gathered a crew, mostly younger sons and a wild lot, and fared west. For a long while he harried Scotland, Ireland, and the coasts south of the Channel, and won much booty. With some of this he bought his farm on the Great Fjord. Meanwhile he courted Thyra, a daughter of the yeoman Sigtryg Einarsson, and got her.

They had one son early on, Hauk, a bright and lively lad. But thereafter five years went by until they had a daughter who lived, Unn, and two years later a boy they called Einar. Geirolf was in viking every summer, and sometimes wintered over in the Westlands. Yet he was a kindly father, whose children were always glad to see him come roaring home. Very tall and broad in the shoulders, he had long red-brown hair and a full beard around a broad blunt-nosed face whose eyes were ice-blue and slanted. He liked fine clothes and heavy gold rings, which he also lavished on Thyra.

Then the time came when Geirolf said he felt poorly and would not fare elsewhere that season. Hauk was fourteen years old and had been wild to go. "I'll keep my promise to you as well as may be," Geirolf said, and sent men asking around. The best he could do was get his son a bench on a ship belonging to Ottar the Wide-Faring from Haalogaland in the north, who was trading along the coast and meant to do likewise overseas.

Hauk and Ottar took well to each other. In England, the man got the boy prime-signed so he could deal with Christians. Though neither was baptized, what he heard while they wintered there made Hauk thoughtful. Next spring they fared south to trade among the Moors, and did not come home until late fall.

Ottar was Geirolf's guest for a while, though he scowled to himself when his host broke into fits of deep coughing. He offered to take Hauk along on his voyages from now on and start the youth toward a good livelihood.

"You a chapman—the son of a viking?" Geirolf sneered. He had grown surly of late.

Hauk flushed. "You've heard what we did to those vikings who set on *us*," he answered.

"Give our son his head," was Thyra's smiling rede, "or he'll take the bit between his teeth."

The upshot was that Geirolf grumbled agreement, and Hauk fared off. He did not come back for five years.

Long were the journeys he took with Ottar. By ship and horse, they made their way to Uppsala in Svithjodh, thence into the wilderness of the Keel after pelts; amber they got on the windy strands of Jutland, salt herring along the Sound; seeking beeswax, honey, and tallow, they pushed beyond Holmgard to the fair at Kiev; walrus ivory lured them past North Cape, through bergs and floes to the land of the fur-clad Biarmians; and they bore many goods west. They did not hide that the wish to see what was new to them drove them as hard as any hope of gain.

In those days King Harald Fairhair went widely about in Norway, bringing all the land under himself. Lesser kings and chieftains must either plight faith to him or meet his wrath; it crushed whomever would stand fast. When he entered Raumsdal, he sent men from garth to garth as was his wont, to say he wanted oaths and warriors.

"My older son is abroad," Geirolf told these, "and my younger still a stripling. As for myself—" He coughed, and blood flecked his beard. The king's men did not press the matter.

But now Geirolf's moods grew ever worse. He snarled at everybody, cuffed his children and housefolk, once drew a dagger and stabbed to death a thrall who chanced to spill some soup on him. When Thyra reproached him for this, he said only, "Let them know I am not altogether hollowed out. I can still wield blade." And he looked at her so threateningly from beneath his shaggy brows that she, no coward, withdrew in silence.

A year later, Hauk Geirolfsson returned to visit his parents.

That was on a chill fall noontide. Whitecaps chopped beneath a whistling wind and cast spindrift salty onto lips. Clifftops on either side of the fjord were lost in mist. Above blew cloud wrack like smoke. Hauk's ship, a wide-beamed knorr, rolled, pitched, and creaked as it beat its way under sail. The owner stood in the bows, wrapped in a flame-red cloak, an uncommonly big young man, yellow hair tossing around a face akin to his father's, weatherbeaten though still scant of beard. When he saw the arm of the fjord that he wanted to enter, he pointed with a spear at whose head he had bound a silk pennon. When he saw Disafoss pouring in a white stream down the blue-gray stone wall to larboard, and beyond the waterfall at the end of that arm lay his old home, he shouted for happiness.

Geirolf had rich holdings. The hall bulked over all else, heavy-timbered, brightly painted, dragon heads arching from rafters and gables. Elsewhere around the yard were cookhouse, smokehouse, bathhouse, storehouses, workshop, stables, barns, women's bower. Several cabins for hirelings and their families were strewn beyond. Fishing boats lay on the strand near a shed which held the master's dragonship. Behind the steading, land sloped sharply upward through a narrow dale, where fields were walled with stones grubbed out of them and now stubbled after harvest. A bronze-leaved oakenshaw stood untouched not far from the buildings; and a mile inland, where hills humped themselves toward the mountains, rose a darkling wall of pinewood.

Spearheads and helmets glimmered ashore. But men saw it was a single craft bound their way, white shield on the mast. As the hull slipped alongside the little wharf, they lowered their weapons. Hauk sprang from bow to dock in a single leap and whooped.

Geirolf trod forth. "Is that you, my son?" he called. His voice was hoarse from coughing; he had grown gaunt and sunken-eyed; the ax that he bore shivered in his hand.

"Yes, father, yes, home again," Hauk stammered. He could not hide his shock.

Maybe this drove Geirolf to anger. Nobody knew; he had become impossible to get along with. "I could well-nigh have hoped otherwise," he rasped. "An unfriend would give me something better than straw-death."

The rest of the men, housecarls and thralls alike, flocked about Hauk to bid him welcome. Among them was a burly, grizzled yeoman whom he knew from aforetime, Leif Egilsson, a neighbor come to dicker for a horse. When he was small, Hauk had often wended his way over a woodland trail to Leif's garth to play with the children there.

He called his crew to him. They were not just Norse, but had among them Danes, Swedes, and English, gathered together over the years as he found them trustworthy. "You brought a mickle for me to feed," Geirolf said. Luckily, the wind bore his words from all but Hauk. "Where's your master Ottar?"

The young man stiffened. "He's my friend, never my master," he answered. "This is my own ship, bought with my own earnings. Ottar abides in England this year. The West Saxons have a new king, one Alfred, whom he wants to get to know."

"Time was when it was enough to know how to get sword past a Westman's shield," Geirolf grumbled.

Seeing peace down by the water, women and children hastened from the hall to meet the newcomers. At their head went Thyra. She was tall and deep-bosomed; her gown blew around a form still straight and freely striding. But as she neared, Hauk saw that the gold of her braids was dimmed and sorrow had furrowed her face. Nonetheless she kindled when she knew him. "Oh, thrice welcome, Hauk!" she said low. "How long can you bide with us?"

After his father's greeting, it had been in his mind to say he must soon be off. But when he spied who walked behind his mother, he said, "We thought we might be guests here the winter through, if that's not too much of a burden."

"Never—" began Thyra. Then she saw where his gaze had gone, and suddenly she smiled.

Alfhild Leifsdottir had joined her widowed father on this visit. She was two years younger than Hauk, but they had been glad of each other as playmates. Today she stood a maiden grown, lissome in a blue wadmal gown, heavily crowned with red locks above great green eyes, straight nose, and gently curved mouth. Though he had known many a woman, none struck him as being so fair.

He grinned at her and let his cloak flap open to show his finery of broidered, fur-lined tunic, linen shirt and breeks, chased leather boots, gold on arms and neck and sword-hilt. She paid them less heed than she did him when they spoke.

Thus Hauk and his men moved to Geirolf's hall. He brought plentiful gifts, there was ample food and drink, and their tales of strange lands—their songs, dances, games, jests, manners—made them good housefellows in these lengthening nights.

Already on the next morning, he walked out with Alfhild. Rain had cleared the air, heaven and fjord sparkled, wavelets chuckled beneath a cool breeze from the woods. Nobody else was on the strand where they went.

"So you grow mighty as a chapman, Hauk," Alfhild teased. "Have you never gone in viking . . . only once, only to please your father?"

"No," he answered gravely. "I fail to see what manliness lies in falling on those too weak to defend themselves. We traders must be stronger and more war-skilled than any who may seek to plunder us." A thick branch of driftwood, bleached and hardened, lay nearby. Hauk picked it up and snapped it between his hands. Two other men would have had trouble doing that. It gladdened him to see Alfhild glow at the sight. "Nobody has tried us twice," he said.

They passed the shed where Geirolf's dragon lay on rollers. Hauk opened the door for a peek at the remembered slim shape. A sharp whiff from the gloom within brought his nose wrinkling.

"Whew!" he snorted. "Dry rot."

"Poor *Fireworm* has long lain idle," Alfhild sighed. "In later years, your father's illness has gnawed him till he doesn't even see to the care of his ship. He knows he will never take it a-roving again."

"I feared that," Hauk murmured.

"We grieve for him on our own garth too," she said. "In former days, he was a staunch friend to us. Now we bear with his ways, yes, insults that would make my father draw blade on anybody else."

"That is dear of you," Hauk said, staring straight before him. "I'm very thankful."

"You have not much cause for that, have you?" she asked. "I mean, you've been away so long . . . Of course, you have your mother. She's borne the brunt, stood like a shield before your siblings—" She touched her lips. "I talk too much."

"You talk as a friend," he blurted. "May we always be friends."

They wandered on, along a path from shore to fields. It went by the shaw. Through boles and boughs and falling leaves, they saw Thor's image and altar among the trees. "I'll make offering here for my father's health," Hauk said, "though truth to tell, I've more faith in my own strength than in any gods."

"You have seen lands where strange gods rule," she nodded.

"Yes, and there too, they do not steer things well," he said. "It was in a Christian realm that a huge wolf came raiding flocks, on which no iron would bite. When it took a baby from a hamlet near our camp, I thought I'd be less than a man did I not put an end to it."

"What happened?" she asked breathlessly, and caught his arm.

"I wrestled it barehanded—no foe of mine was ever more fell—and at last broke its neck." He pulled back a sleeve to show scars of terrible bites. "Dead, it changed into a man they had outlawed that year for his evil deeds. We burned the lich to make sure it would not walk again, and thereafter the folk had peace. And . . . we had friends, in a country otherwise wary of us."

She looked on him in the wonder he had hoped for.

Erelong she must return with her father. But the way between the garths was just a few miles, and Hauk often rode or skied through the woods. At home, he and his men helped do what work there was, and gave merriment where it had long been little known.

Thyra owned this to her son, on a snowy day when they were by themselves. They were in the women's bower, whither they had gone to see a tapestry she was weaving. She wanted to know how it showed against those of the Westlands; he had brought one such, which hung above the benches in the hall. Here, in the wide quiet room, was dusk, for the day outside had become a tumbling whiteness. Breath steamed from lips as the two of them spoke. It smelled sweet; both had drunk mead until they could talk freely.

"You did better than you knew when you came back," Thyra said. "You blew like spring into this winter of ours. Einar and Unn were withering; they blossom again in your nearness."

"Strangely has our father changed," Hauk answered sadly. "I remember once when I was small, how he took me by the hand on a frost-clear night, led me forth under the stars, and named for me the pictures in them, Thor's Wain, Freyja's Spindle—how wonderful he made them, how his deep slow laughterful voice filled the dark.''

''A wasting illness draws the soul inward,'' his mother said. ''He . . . has no more manhood . . . and it tears him like fangs that he will die helpless in bed. He must strike out at someone, and here we are.''

She was silent a while before she added: ''He will not live out the year. Then you must take over.''

''I must be gone when weather allows,'' Hauk warned. ''I promised Ottar.''

''Return as soon as may be,'' Thyra said. ''We have need of a strong man, the more so now when yonder King Harald would reave their freehold rights from yeomen.''

''It would be well to have a hearth of my own.'' Hauk stared past her, toward the unseen woods. Her worn face creased in a smile.

Suddenly they heard yells from the yard below. Hauk ran out onto the gallery and looked down. Geirolf was shambling after an aged carl named Atli. He had a whip in his hand and was lashing it across the white locks and wrinkled cheeks of the man, who could not run fast either and who sobbed.

''What is this?'' broke from Hauk. He swung himself over the rail, hung, and let go. The drop would at least have jarred the wind out of most. He, though, bounced from where he landed, ran behind his father, caught hold of the whip and wrenched it from Geirolf's grasp. ''What are you doing?''

Geirolf howled and struck his son with a double fist. Blood trickled from Hauk's mouth. He stood fast. Atli sank to his knees and fought not to weep.

''Are you also a heelbiter of mine?'' Geirolf bawled.

''I'd save you from your madness, father,'' Hauk said in pain. ''Atli followed you to battle ere I was born—he dandled me on his knee—and he's a free man. What has he done, that you'd bring down on us the anger of his kinfolk?"

"Harm not the skipper, young man," Atli begged. "I fled because I'd sooner die than lift hand against my skipper."

"Hell swallow you both!" Geirolf would have cursed further, but the coughing came on him. Blood drops flew through the snowflakes, down onto the white earth, where they mingled with the drip from the heads of Hauk and Atli. Doubled over, Geirolf let them half lead, half carry him to his shut-bed. There he closed the panel and lay alone in darkness.

"What happened between you and him?" Hauk asked.

"I was fixing to shoe a horse," Atli said into a ring of gaping onlookers. "He came in and wanted to know why I'd not asked his leave. I told him 'twas plain Kolfaxi needed new shoes. Then he hollered, "I'll show you I'm no log in the woodpile!" and snatched yon whip off the wall and took after me." The old man squared his shoulders. "We'll speak no more of this, you hear?" he ordered the household.

Nor did Geirolf, when next day he let them bring him some broth.

For more reasons than this, Hauk came to spend much of his time at Leif's garth. He would return in such a glow that even the reproachful looks of his young sister and brother, even the sullen or the weary greeting of his father, could not dampen it.

At last, when lengthening days and quickening blood bespoke seafarings soon to come, that happened which surprised nobody. Hauk told them in the hall that he wanted to marry Alfhild Leifsdottir, and prayed Geirolf press the suit for him. "What must be, will be," said his father, a better grace than awaited. Union of the families was clearly good for both.

Leif Egilsson agreed, and Alfhild had nothing but aye to say. The betrothal feast crowded the whole neighborhood together in cheer. Thyra hid the trouble within her, and Geirolf himself was calm if not blithe.

Right after, Hauk and his men were busking themselves to fare. Regardless of his doubts about gods, he led in offering for a safe voyage to Thor, Aegir, and St. Michael. But Alfhild found herself a quiet place alone, to cut runes on an ash tree in the name of Freyja.

When all was ready, she was there with the folk of Geirolf's stead to see the sailors off. That morning was keen, wind roared in trees and skirled between cliffs, waves ran green and white beneath small flying clouds. Unn could not but hug her brother who was going, while Einar gave him a handclasp that shook. Thyra said, "Come home hale and early, my son." Alfhild mostly stored away the sight of Hauk. Atli and others of the household mumbled this and that.

Geirolf shuffled forward. The cane on which he leaned rattled among the stones of the beach. He was hunched in a hairy cloak against the sharp air. His locks fell tangled almost to the coal-smoldering eyes. "Father, farewell," Hauk said, taking his free hand.

"You mean 'fare far,' don't you?" Geirolf grated. " 'Fare far and never come back.' You'd like that, wouldn't you? But we will meet again. Oh, yes, we will meet again."

Hauk dropped the hand. Geirolf turned and sought the house. The rest behaved as if they had not heard, speaking loudly, amidst yelps of laughter, to overcome those words of foreboding. Soon Hauk called his orders to begone.

Men scrambled aboard the laden ship. Its sail slatted

aloft and filled, the mooring lines were cast loose, the hull stood out to sea. Alfhild waved until it was gone from sight behind the bend where Disafoss fell.

The summer passed—plowing, sowing, lambing, calving, farrowing, hoeing, reaping, flailing, butchering—rain, hail, sun, stars, loves, quarrels, births, deaths—and the season wore toward fall. Alfhild was seldom at Geirolf's garth, nor was Leif; for Hauk's father grew steadily worse. After midsummer he could no longer leave his bed. But often he whispered, between lung-tearing coughs, to those who tended him, "I would kill you if I could."

On a dark day late in the season, when rain roared about the hall and folk and hounds huddled close to fires that hardly lit the gloom around, Geirolf awoke from a heavy sleep. Thyra marked it and came to him. Cold and dankness gnawed their way through her clothes. The fever was in him like a brand. He plucked restlessly at his blanket, where he half sat in his short shut-bed. Though flesh had wasted from the great bones, his fingers still had strength to tear the wool. The mattress rustled under him. "Straw-death, straw-death," he muttered.

Thyra laid a palm on his brow. "Be at ease," she said.

It dragged from him: "You'll not be rid . . . of me . . . so fast . . . by straw-death." An icy sweat broke forth and the last struggle began.

Long it was, Geirolf's gasps and the sputtering flames the only noises within that room, while rain and wind ramped outside and night drew in. Thyra stood by the bedside to wipe the sweat off her man, blood and spittle from his beard. A while after sunset, he rolled his eyes back and died.

Thyra called for water and lamps. She cleansed him,

clad him in his best, and laid him out. A drawn sword was on his breast.

In the morning, thralls and carls alike went forth under her orders. A hillock stood in the fields about half a mile inland from the house. They dug a grave chamber in the top of this, lining it well with timber. ''Won't you bury him in his ship?'' asked Atli.

''It is rotten, unworthy of him,'' Thyra said. Yet she made them haul it to the barrow, around which she had stones to outline a hull. Meanwhile folk readied a grave-ale, and messengers bade neighbors come.

When all were there, men of Geirolf's carried him on a litter to his resting place and put him in, together with weapons and a jar of Southland coins. After beams had roofed the chamber, his friends from aforetime took shovels and covered it well. They replaced the turfs of sere grass, leaving the hillock as it had been save that it was now bigger. Einar Thorolfsson kindled his father's ship. It burned till dusk, when the horns of the new moon stood over the fjord. Meanwhile folk had gone back down to the garth to feast and drink. Riding home next day, well gifted by Thyra, they told each other that this had been an honorable burial.

The moon waxed. On the first night that it rose full, Geirolf came again.

A thrall named Kark had been late in the woods, seeking a strayed sheep. Coming home, he passed near the howe. The moon was barely above the pines; long shivery beams of light ran on the water, lost themselves in shadows ashore, glinted wanly anew where a bedewed stone wall snaked along a stubblefield. Stars were few. A great stillness lay on the land, not even an owl hooted, until all at once dogs down in the garth began howling. It was not the way they howled at the moon; across the mile between, it sounded ragged and terrified. Kark felt the chill close in around him, and hastened toward home.

Something heavy trod the earth. He looked around and saw the bulk of a huge man coming across the field from the barrow. "Who's that?" he called uneasily. No voice replied, but the weight of those footfalls shivered through the ground into his bones. Kark swallowed, gripped his staff, and stood where he was. But then the shape came so near that moonlight picked out the head of Geirolf. Kark screamed, dropped his weapon, and ran.

Geirolf followed slowly, clumsily behind.

Down in the garth, light glimmered red as doors opened. Folk saw Kark running, gasping for breath. Atli and Einar led the way out, each with a torch in one hand, a sword in the other. Little could they see beyond the wild flame-gleam. Kark reached them, fell, writhed on the hard-beaten clay of the yard, and wailed.

"What is it, you lackwit?" Atli snapped, and kicked him. Then Einar pointed his blade.

"A stranger—" Atli began.

Geirolf rocked into sight. The mould of the grave clung to him. His eyes stared unblinking, unmoving, blank in the moonlight, out of a gray face whereon the skin crawled. The teeth in his tangled beard were dry. No breath smoked from his nostrils. He held out his arms, crook-fingered.

"Father!" Einar cried. The torch hissed from his grip, flickered weakly at his feet, and went out. The men at his back jammed the doorway of the hall as they sought its shelter.

"The skipper's come again," Atli quavered. He sheathed his sword, though that was hard when his hand shook, and made himself step forward. "Skipper, d'you know your old shipmate Atli?"

The dead man grabbed him, lifted him, and dashed him to earth. Einar heard bones break. Atli jerked once and lay still. Geirolf trod him and Kark underfoot. There was a sound of cracking and rending. Blood spurted forth.

Blindly, Einar swung blade. The edge smote but would not bite. A wave of grave-chill passed over him. He whirled and bounded back inside.

Thyra had seen. "Bar the door," she bade. The windows were already shuttered against frost. "Men, stand fast. Women, stoke up the fires."

They heard the lich groping about the yard. Walls creaked where Geirolf blundered into them. Thyra called through the door. "Why do you wish us ill, your own household?" But only those noises gave answer. The hounds cringed and whined.

"Lay iron at the doors and under every window," Thyra commanded. "If it will not cut him, it may keep him out."

All that night, then, folk huddled in the hall. Geirolf climbed onto the roof and rode the ridge-pole, drumming his heels on the shakes till the whole building boomed. A little before sunrise, it stopped. Peering out by the first dull dawnlight, Thyra saw no mark of her husband but his deep-sunken footprints and the wrecked bodies he had left.

"He grew so horrible before he died," Unn wept. "Now he can't rest, can he?"

"We'll make him an offering," Thyra said through her weariness. "It may be we did not give him enough when we buried him."

Few would follow her to the howe. Those who dared, brought along the best horse on the farm. Einar, as the son of the house when Hauk was gone, himself cut its throat after a sturdy man had given the hammer-blow. Carls and wenches butchered the carcass, which Thyra and Unn cooked over a fire in whose wood was blent the charred rest of the dragonship. Nobody cared to eat much of the flesh or broth. Thyra poured what was left over the bones, upon the grave.

Two ravens circled in sight, waiting for folk to go so they could take the food. "Is that a good sign?" Thyra sighed. "Will Odin fetch Geirolf home?"

That night everybody who had not fled to neighboring steads gathered in the hall. Soon after the moon rose, they heard the footfalls come nearer and nearer. They heard Geirolf break into the storehouse and worry the laid-out bodies of Atli and Kark. They heard him kill cows in the barn. Again he rode the roof.

In the morning Leif Egilsson arrived, having gotten the news. He found Thyra too tired and shaken to do anything further. "The ghost did not take your offering," he said, "but maybe the gods will."

In the oakenshaw, he led the giving of more beasts. There was talk of a thrall for Odin, but he said that would not help if this did not. Instead, he saw to the proper burial of the slain, and of those kine which nobody would dare eat. That night he abode on the farm.

And Geirolf came back. Throughout the darkness, he tormented the home which had been his.

"I will bide here one more day," Leif said next sunrise. "We all need rest—though ill is it that we must sleep during the daylight when we've so much readying for winter to do."

By that time, some other neighborhood men were also on hand. They spoke loudly of how they would hew the lich asunder.

"You know not what you boast of," said aged Grim

the Wise. "Einar smote, and he strikes well for a lad, but the iron would not bite. It never will. Ghost-strength is in Geirolf, and all the wrath he could not set free during his life."

That night folk waited breathless for moonrise. But when the gnawed shield climbed over the pines, nothing stirred. The dogs, too, no longer seemed cowed. About midnight, Grim murmured into the shadows, "Yes, I thought so. Geirolf walks only when the moon is full."

"Then tomorrow we'll dig him up and burn him!" Leif said.

"No," Grim told them. "That would spell the worst of luck for everybody here. Don't you see, the anger and unpeace which will not let him rest, those would be forever unslaked? They could not but bring doom on the burners."

"What then can we do?" Thyra asked dully.

"Leave this stead," Grim counselled, "at least when the moon is full."

"Hard will that be," Einar sighed. "Would that my brother Hauk were here."

"He should have returned erenow," Thyra said. "May we in our woe never know that he has come to grief himself."

In truth, Hauk had not. His wares proved welcome in Flanders, where he had bartered for cloth that he took across to England. There Ottar greeted him, and he met the young King Alfred. At that time there was no war going on with the Danes, who were settling into the Danelaw and thus in need of household goods. Hauk and Ottar did a thriving business among them. This led them to think they might do as well in Iceland, whither Norse folk were moving who liked not King Harald Fair-hair. They made a voyage to see. Foul winds hampered them on the way home. Hence fall was well along when Hauk's ship returned.

The day was still and cold. Low overcast turned sky and water the hue of iron. A few gulls cruised and mewed, while under them sounded creak and splash of oars, swearing of men, as the knorr was rowed. At the end of the fjord-branch, garth and leaves were tiny splashes of color, lost against rearing cliffs, brown fields, murky wildwood. Straining ahead from afar, Hauk saw that a bare handful of men came down to the shore, moving listlessly more than watchfully. When his craft was unmistakable, though, a few women—no youngsters—sped from the hall as if they could not wait. Their cries came to him more thin than the gulls'.

Hauk lay alongside the dock. Springing forth, he called merrily, "Where is everybody? How fares Alfhild?" His words lost themselves in silence. Fear touched him. "What's wrong?"

Thyra trod forth. Years might have gone by during his summer abroad, so changed was she. "You are barely in time," she said in an unsteady tone. Taking his hands, she told him how things stood.

Hauk stared long into emptiness. At last, "Oh, no," he whispered. "What's to be done?"

"We hoped you might know that, my son," Thyra answered. "The moon will be full tomorrow night."

His voice stumbled. "I am no wizard. If the gods themselves would not lay this ghost, what can I do?"

Einar spoke, in the brashness of youth: "We thought you might deal with him as you did with the werewolf."

"But that was—No, I cannot!" Hauk croaked. "Never ask me."

"Then I fear we must leave," Thyra said. "For aye.

You see how many have already fled, thrall and free alike, though nobody else has a place for them. We've not enough left to farm these acres. And who would buy them of us? Poor must we go, helpless as the poor ever are.''

''Iceland—'' Hauk wet his lips. ''Well, you shall not want while I live.'' Yet he had counted on this homestead, whether to dwell on or sell.

''Tomorrow we move over to Leif's garth, for the next three days and nights,'' Thyra said.

Unn shuddered. ''I know not if I can come back,'' she said. ''This whole past month here, I could hardly ever sleep.'' Dulled skin and sunken eyes bore her out.

''What else would you do?'' Hauk asked.

''Whatever I can,'' she stammered, and broke into tears. He knew: wedding herself too young to whoever would have her dowryless, poor though the match would be—or making her way to some town to turn whore, his little sister.

''Let me think on this,'' Hauk begged. ''Maybe I can hit on something.''

His crew were also daunted when they heard. At eventide they sat in the hall and gave only a few curt words about what they had done in foreign parts. Everyone lay down early on bed, bench, or floor, but none slept well.

Before sunset, Hauk had walked forth alone. First he sought the grave of Atli. ''I'm sorry, dear old friend,'' he said. Afterward, he went to Geirolf's howe. It loomed yellow-gray with withered grass wherein grinned the skull of the slaughtered horse. At its foot were strewn the charred bits of the ship, inside stones which outlined a greater but unreal hull. Around reached stubblefields and walls, hemmed in by woods on one side and water on the other, rock lifting sheer beyond. The chill and the quiet had deepened.

Hauk climbed to the top of the barrow and stood there a while, head bent downward. "Oh, father," he said, "I learned doubt in Christian lands. What's right for me to do?" There was no answer. He made a slow way back to the dwelling.

All were up betimes next day. It went slowly over the woodland path to Leif's, for animals must be herded along. The swine gave more trouble than most. Hauk chuckled once, not very merrily, and remarked that at least this took folk's minds off their sorrows. He raised no mirth.

But he had Alfhild ahead of him. At the end of the way, he sprinted shouting into the yard. Leif owned less land than Geirolf, his buildings were smaller and fewer, most of his guests must house outdoors in sleeping bags. Hauk paid no heed. "Alfhild!" he called. "I'm here!"

She left the dough she was kneading and sped to him. They hugged each other hard and long, in sight of the whole world. None thought that shame, as things were. At last she said, striving not to weep, "How we've longed for you! Now the nightmare can end."

He stepped back. "What mean you?" he muttered slowly, knowing full well.

"Why—" She was bewildered. "Won't you give him his second death?"

Hauk gazed past her for some heartbeats before he said: "Come aside with me."

Hand in hand, they wandered off. A meadow lay hidden from the garth by a stand of aspen. Elsewhere around, pines speared into a sky that today was bright.

Clouds drifted on a nipping breeze. Far off, a stag bugled.

Hauk spread feet apart, hooked thumbs in belt, and made himself meet her eyes. "You think over-highly of my strength," he said.

"Who has more?" she asked. "We kept ourselves going by saying you would come home and make things good again."

"What if the drow is too much for me?" His words sounded raw through the hush. Leaves dropped yellow from their boughs.

She flushed. "Then your name will live."

"Yes—" Softly he spoke the words of the High One:

> *"Kine die, kinfolk die,*
> *and so at last oneself.*
> *This I know that never dies:*
> *how dead men's deeds are deemed."*

"You will do it!" she cried gladly.

His head shook before it drooped. "No. I will not. I dare not."

She stood as if he had clubbed her.

"Won't you understand?" he began.

The wound he had dealt her hopes went too deep. "So you show yourself a nithing!"

"Hear me," he said, shaken. "Were the lich anybody else's—"

Overwrought beyond reason, she slapped him and choked, "The gods bear witness, I give them my holiest oath, never will I wed you unless you do this thing. See, by my blood I swear." She whipped out her dagger and gashed her wrist. Red rills coursed out and fell in drops on the fallen leaves.

He was aghast. "You know not what you say. You're too young, you've been too sheltered. *Listen.*"

She would have fled from him, but he gripped her shoulders and made her stand. "Listen," went between his teeth. "Geirolf is still my father—my father who begot me, reared me, named the stars for me, weaponed me to make my way in the world. How can I fight him? Did I slay him, what horror would come upon me and mine?"

"O-o-oh," broke from Alfhild. She sank to the ground and wept as if to tear loose her ribs.

He knelt, held her, gave what soothing he could. "Now I know," she mourned. "Too late."

"Never," he murmured. "We'll fare abroad if we must, take new land, make new lives together."

"No," she gasped. "Did I not swear? What doom awaits an oathbreaker?"

Then he was long still. Heedlessly though she had spoken, her blood lay in the earth, which would remember.

He too was young. He straightened. "I will fight," he said.

Now she clung to him and pleaded that he must not. But an iron calm had come over him. "Maybe I will not be cursed," he said. "Or maybe the curse will be no more than I can bear."

"It will be mine too, I who brought it on you," she plighted herself.

Hand in hand again, they went back to the garth. Leif spied the haggard look on them and half guessed what had happened. "Will you fare to meet the drow, Hauk?" he asked. "Wait till I can have Grim the Wise brought here. His knowledge may help you."

"No," said Hauk. "Waiting would weaken me. I go this night."

Wide eyes stared at him—all but Thyra's; she was too torn.

Toward evening he busked himself. He took no helm, shield, or byrnie, for the dead man bore no weapons. Some said they would come along, armored themselves well, and offered to be at his side. He told them to follow him, but no farther than to watch what happened. Their iron would be of no help, and he thought they would only get in each other's way, and his, when he met the over-human might of the drow. He kissed Alfhild, his mother, and his sister, and clasped hands with his brother, bidding them stay behind if they loved him.

Long did the few miles of path seem, and gloomy under the pines. The sun was on the world's rim when men came out in the open. They looked past fields and barrow down to the empty garth, the fjordside cliffs, the water where the sun lay as half an ember behind a trail of blood. Clouds hurried on a wailing wind through a greenish sky. Cold struck deep. A wolf howled.

"Wait here," Hauk said.

"The gods be with you," Leif breathed.

"I've naught tonight but my own strength," Hauk said. "Belike none of us ever had more."

His tall form, clad in leather and wadmal, showed black athwart the sunset as he walked from the edge of the woods, out across plowland toward the crouching howe. The wind fluttered his locks, a last brightness until the sun went below. Then for a while the evenstar alone had light.

Hauk reached the mound. He drew sword and leaned on it, waiting. Dusk deepened. Star after star came forth, small and strange. Clouds blowing across them picked up a glow from the still unseen moon.

It rose at last above the treetops. Its ashen sheen stretched gashes of shadow across the earth. The wind loudened.

The grave groaned. Turves, stones, timbers swung aside. Geirolf shambled out beneath the sky. Hauk felt the ground shudder under his weight. There came a carrion stench, though the only sign of rotting was on the dead man's clothes. His eyes peered dim, his teeth gnashed dry in a face at once well remembered and hideously changed. When he saw the living one who waited, he veered and lumbered thitherward.

"Father," Hauk called. "It's I, your eldest son."

The drow drew nearer.

"Halt, I beg you," Hauk said unsteadily. "What can I do to bring you peace?"

A cloud passed over the moon. It seemed to be hurtling through heaven. Geirolf reached for his son with fingers that were ready to clutch and tear. "Hold," Hauk shrilled. "No step farther."

He could not see if the gaping mouth grinned. In another stride, the great shape came well-nigh upon him. He lifted his sword and brought it singing down. The edge struck truly, but slid aside. Geirolf's skin heaved, as if to push the blade away. In one more step, he laid grave-cold hands around Hauk's neck.

Before that grip could close, Hauk dropped his useless weapon, brought his wrists up between Geirolf's, and mightily snapped them apart. Nails left furrows, but he was free. He sprang back, into a wrestler's stance.

Geirolf moved in, reaching. Hauk hunched under those arms and himself grabbed waist and thigh. He threw his shoulder against a belly like rock. Any live man would have gone over, but the lich was too heavy.

Geirolf smote Hauk on the side. The blows drove

him to his knees and thundered on his back. A foot lifted to crush him. He rolled off and found his own feet again. Geirolf lurched after him. The hastening moon linked their shadows. The wolf howled anew, but in fear. Watching men gripped spearshafts till their knuckles stood bloodless.

Hauk braced his legs and snatched for the first hold, around both of Geirolf's wrists. The drow strained to break loose and could not; but neither could Hauk bring him down. Sweat ran moon-bright over the son's cheeks and darkened his shirt. The reek of it was at least a living smell in his nostrils. Breath tore at his gullet. Suddenly Geirolf wrenched so hard that his right arm tore from between his foe's fingers. He brought that hand against Hauk's throat. Hauk let go and slammed himself backward before he was throttled.

Geirolf stalked after him. The drow did not move fast. Hauk sped behind and pounded on the broad back. He seized an arm of Geirolf's and twisted it around. But the dead cannot feel pain. Geirolf stood fast. His other hand groped about, got Hauk by the hair, and yanked. Live men can hurt. Hauk stumbled away. Blood ran from his scalp into his eyes and mouth, hot and salt.

Geirolf turned and followed. He would not tire. Hauk had no long while before strength ebbed. Almost, he fled. Then the moon broke through to shine full on his father. "You . . . shall not . . . go on . . . like that," Hauk mumbled while he snapped after air.

The drow reached him. They closed, grappled, swayed, stamped to and fro, in wind and flickery moonlight. Then Hauk hooked an ankle behind Geirolf's and pushed. With a huge thud, the drow crashed to earth. He dragged Hauk along.

Hauk's bones felt how terrible was the grip upon him. He let go on his own hold. Instead, he arched his back and pushed himself away. His clothes ripped. But he burst free and reeled to his feet.

Geirolf turned over and began to crawl up. His back was once more to Hauk. The young man sprang. He got a knee hard in between the shoulderblades, while both his arms closed on the frosty head before him.

He hauled. With the last and greatest might that was in him, he hauled. Blackness went in tatters before his eyes.

There came a loud snapping sound. Geirolf ceased pawing behind him. He sprawled limp. His neck was broken, his jawbone wrenched from the skull. Hauk climbed slowly off him, shuddering. Geirolf stirred, rolled, half rose. He lifted a hand toward Hauk. It traced a line through the air and a line growing from beneath that. Then he slumped and lay still.

Hauk crumpled too.

"Follow me who dare!" Leif roared, and went forth across the field. One by one, as they saw nothing move ahead of them, the men came after. At last they stood hushed around Geirolf—who was only a harmless dead man now, though the moon shone bright in his eyes—and on Hauk, who had begun to stir.

"Bear him carefully down to the hall," Leif said. "Start a fire and tend it well. Most of you, take from the woodpile and come back here. I'll stand guard meanwhile . . . though I think there is no need."

And so they burned Geirolf there in the field. He walked no more.

In the morning, they brought Hauk back to Leif's garth. He moved as if in dreams. The others were too awestruck to speak much. Even when Alfhild ran to meet him, he could only say, "Hold clear of me. I may be under a doom."

"Did the drow lay a weird on you?" she asked, spear-stricken.

"I know not," he answered. "I think I fell into the dark before he was wholly dead."

"What?" Leif well-nigh shouted. "You did not see the sign he drew?"

"Why, no," Hauk said. "How did it go?"

"Thus. Even afar and by moonlight, I knew." Leif drew it.

"That is no ill-wishing!" Grim cried. "That's naught but the Hammer."

Life rushed back into Hauk. "Do you mean what I hope?"

"He blessed you," Grim said. "You freed him from what he had most dreaded and hated—his straw-death. The madness in him is gone, and he has wended hence to the world beyond."

Then Hauk was glad again. He led them all in heaping earth over the ashes of his father, and in setting things right on the farm. That winter, at the feast of Thor, he and Alfhild were wedded. Afterward he became well thought of by King Harald, and rose to great wealth. From him and Alfhild stem many men whose names are still remembered. Here ends the tale of Hauk the Ghost Slayer.

Fairy Gold

Romance need not divorce itself from reality. It can speak with its own voice, but as clearly and to the point as any naturalism, about our world and our living selves. Thus Tolkien touched on matters of good and evil, sin and redemption, and the human spirit. Cabell unmercifully satirized his contemporary America. And here, on a less exalted plane, is a small object lesson in elementary economics.

Women, weather, and wizardy are alike in this, that their beneficences are apt to be as astonishing as their betrayals.

—The Aphorisms of Rhoene

It is an old tale, often told: a young man loved a young woman, and she him, but they quarreled, whereupon he went off in search of desperate adventure while she wept in solitude. However, this time it was not quite so. Arvel stormed down Hammerhead Street toward the Drum and Trumpet, where he intended to get drunk. Lona, after a few angry tears, uttered many curses and then returned to her pottery, where she punished the clay with her fists and pedaled the wheel until it shrieked.

The hour being scarcely past noon, Arvel found none of his cronies in the tavern, only a half-dozen sailors. Trade had grown listless throughout Caronne, after much of the kingdom's treasure bled away abroad during the Dynasts' War. Ships that came to Seilles often lay docked for weeks before their masters had sold all cargo. The markets at Croy were a little better, but the Tauran League now held a monopoly of them.

These men were off a vessel that had arrived on the morning's tide. They sat together, drinking like walruses rescued from a desert, rumbling mirth and brags, pawing at the wench whenever she came to refill a goblet. Arvel recognized the language of Norren, though he did not speak it. A couple of them were not of that land, but dark-hued, while the manes and beards of the rest were sun-bleached nearly white and their skins turned to red leather. Evidently they had been in the tropics.

Worldfarers! His longing took Arvel by the throat. He flung himself down at a table in a corner, hard enough to bruise his bottom. A sunbeam struck through a window leaded together out of stained glass scraps, to shatter in rainbows on the scarred wood. Smoke and kitchen smells lapped around him.

The wench came through the gloom, her clogs loud on the floor. "Joy to you," she greeted. Surprise caught her. "Why, Arvel, what a thundercloud in your face. Did a ghost dog bite you today?"

"A pack of them, and the Huntsman himself to egg them on," he snarled. "Wine—the cheapest, because I'll want a plenty."

She fetched, took his coin, and settled on the bench opposite. Pity dwelt in her voice and countenance. "It's about your girl, isn't it?" she asked low.

He gave her a startled blue glance. "How can you tell?"

"Why, everyone knows you're mad with your wish to go oversea, and never a hope. But that's had you adrift by day, not at drink before evening. Something new must have gone awry to bring you in here so early, and what could it be save what touches your betrothal?"

Arvel swallowed a draught. Sourness burned its way down his gullet. "You're shrewd, Ynis," he mumbled. "Yes, we're done with each other, Lona Grancy and I."

The wench looked long at him. "I never thought her a fool," she said.

Despite his misery, Arvel preened a trifle. He was, after all, quite young, and various women had assured him he was handsome—tall, wide-shouldered, lithe, with straight features, slightly freckle-dusted, framed by fiery hair that curled past his earrings. As a scion of a noble family, albeit of the lowest rank, he was entitled to bear a sword and generally did, along with his knife; both were of the finest steel and their handles silver-chased. Otherwise, though, he perforce went shabby these days. The saffron of his shirt was faded and its lace frayed, his hose were darned, the leather of his jerkin and shoes showed wear, the cloak he had folded beside him was of a cut no longer modish.

"Well," he said, after a more reasonable gulp of wine than his first, "she wanted to make a potter of me. A potter! Told me I must scuttle my dream, settle down, learn a—" he snorted— "an honest trade—"

"And cease being a parasite," Ynis finished sharply.

Arvel jerked where he sat, flushed, and rapped in answer. "I've never taken more than is my right."

"Aye, your allowance. Which is meager, for the bastard son of a house that the war ruined. What use your courtliness any more, Arvel Tarabine, or your horsemanship, swordsmanship, woodsmanship?"

"I guide—"

"Indeed. You garner an argent here and there, taking out parties of fat merchants and rich foreigners who like to pretend they're born to the chase. If they stand you drink afterward, you'll brag of what you did in the war, and sing 'em a song or two. And always you babble about Sir Falcovan and that expedition he's getting up. Is this how you'll spend the rest of your years, till you're too old and sodden for it and slump into beggary? No, your Lona is not a fool. You are, who wouldn't listen to her."

He stiffened. "You get above yourself."

Ynis eased and smiled. "I get motherly, I do." She was plump, not uncomely but beginning to fade, a widow who had three children to nurture and, maybe, a dream or two of her own. "You're a good fellow, mauger your folly, and besides, I like your girl. Go back, make amends—"

"Hej, pige!" bawled a Norrener from across the taproom, so loudly that a mouse fled along a rafter. *"Mer vin!"*

Ynis sighed, rose, and went to serve him. She had been about to quench the rage that her words had refuelled in Arvel. Now it flamed up afresh. He could not endure to sit still. He tossed off his drink, surged from the bench, and went out the door, banging it shut behind him.

* * *

To Lona came Jans Orliand, chronicler at the Scholarium of Seilles and friend of her late father. This was not as strange as it might seem, for Jans was of humble birth himself and had married a cousin of the potter. Afterward he prospered modestly through his talents, without turning aloof from old acquaintances, until the hard times struck him too.

Lona had just put a fresh charge of charcoal under her kiln and pumped it akindle with the bellows. She was returning to her wheel when his gaunt form shadowed the entrance. She kept the shed open while she worked, even in winter, lest heat and fumes overcome her; and this was an amiable summer day. Nevertheless she had a healthy smell about her, of the sweat that dampened her smock. A smudge went across her snub nose. A kerchief covered most of her gold-brown hair.

''Joy to you,'' Jans hailed. He paused, to squint nearsightedly at her small, sturdy frame and into her green-brown eyes, until he said: ''Methinks you've need of the reality, not the mere ritual.''

''Is it that plain to see?'' she wondered. ''Well—whoops!'' In an expansive gesture, he had almost thrown a sleeve of his robe around one of the completed vessels that lined her shelves. She stopped him before he sent it acrash to the floor. ''Here, sit down, do.'' She offered him a stool. ''How may I please you, good sir?''

''Oh, let us not be formal,'' he urged, while he folded his height downward. She perched on the workbench and swung her feet in unladylike wise; but then, she was an artisan, in what was considered a man's occupation. ''I require cups, dishes, pots of attractive style; and you, no doubt, will be glad of the sale.''

Lona nodded, with less eagerness than she would

ordinarily have felt. Feeling his gaze searching her yet, she forced herself to tease: "What, have you broken that much? And why have you not sent your maidservant or your son?"

"I felt I had better choose the articles myself," Jans explained. "See you, I have decided on renting out the new house, but its bareness has seemed to repel what few prospective tenants have appeared."

"The new house?"

"Have you forgotten? Ah, well, it was years ago. My wife and I bought it, thinking we would move thither as soon as we could sell the old one. But the war came, and her death, and these lean days. I can no longer afford the staff so large a place would demand, only my single housekeeper. The taxes on it are a vampire drain, and no one who wants it can afford to buy it. I've posted my offer on every market board and had it cried aloud through every street—without result. So at last my hopes are reduced to becoming a landlord."

"Oh, yes, I do recall. Let's pick you out something pretty, then."

Still Lona could not muster any sparkle. Jans stroked his bald pate. "What hurts you, my dear?" he asked in a most gentle tone.

She snapped after air. "You . . . may as well hear . . . now. Soon it will be common knowledge. Arvel and I . . . have parted."

"What? But this is terrible. How? Why?"

"He—he *will* not be sensible. He cannot confess . . . to himself . . . that Sir Falcovan Roncitar's fleet is going to sail beyond the sunset without him—" Lona fought her wish to weep, or to smash something. She stared at her fingers, where they wrestled in her lap. "When that happens . . . I dread what may become of him. We could, could survive together . . . in this trade

. . . and today I told him we must . . . b-because the father of my children shall not be a drunken idler—And he—O-o-oh!'' She turned her wail into an oath and ended bleakly: ''I wish him luck. He'll need it.''

In his awkward fashion, Jans went to her and patted her shoulder. ''Poor lass, you've never fared on a smooth road, have you?'' he murmured. ''A child when you lost your mother; and your father perforce made you his helper; and when he too wended hence, there was no better inheritance for you than this.''

Lona lifted her head. ''It's not a bad little shop. It keeps me alive. It could keep a family.''

Jans winced. She saw, and welcomed the chance to escape from herself. ''What pains you?'' she demanded. ''It's your turn for telling.''

He stood aside from her. His back sagged, while a sad little smile tugged his lips upward. ''Oh, an irony,'' he replied. ''The single form of humor the gods know, I believe.''

''I don't understand.''

''Quite simple, 'tis. Hark.'' He confronted her. ''When for a time it appeared that Arvel might indeed sail off to the New Lands, and you with him as his bride, were you not also ablaze? Be honest; we speak in confidence.''

''Well—'' She swallowed. ''Not in his way. I would have been sorry to forsake this my home for a wilderness. Nonetheless, I was ready to go for his sake, even if I must sell out at a great loss. And in truth, I would have welcomed such a chance to better ourselves and bequeath a good life to our children.'' She spread her empty hands. ''Of course, I knew from the first it was likeliest a will-o'-the-wisp. He would have had to borrow the sum required, and where, without security? His father's estate entailed. Nobody who might desire this shop and cottage is able to pay a reasonable price, wherefore they are just as unmortgageable. After he tried, and failed, I besought him to settle down here and at least earn a steady living; but there it was I who failed.''

Jans raised a finger to hush her. ''No matter that,'' he said. ''My first point has been made. Id est, imprimis, you would have left these premises if you could.

''Secundus, the dowries for my daughters exhausted my savings, and nature has not outfitted my son for my own sort of career. You know Denn Orliand for a good lad, and good with his hands, who at present toils as a day laborer, for miserable wages, whenever he can find work. I could buy him a shop of some kind, as it might be this very one, were my small capital not trapped by that incubus of a second house.''

''We're all trapped,'' Lona whispered.

''Tertius,'' the dry voice marched on, ''I looked forward to your wedding, for I am fond of you and Arvel is by no means a bad fellow. I had a book for a gift, a geography which migrants to the New Lands should find helpful or at least amusing, as the case may be, and which is in any event a sumptuous volume—''

''Jans.'' She took his nearer hand in both of hers.

''Quartus,'' he ended, ''you might have had occasion to send me a wedding gift from oversea in your turn.''

''What?'' she exclaimed.

He glanced away and cleared his throat. ''Um-m . . . a lady in reduced circumstances, forced to work in a tavern—but a fine person. As a matter of fact, I met her when Arvel once took me to the, m-m, Drum and Trumpet.''

''Ynis!'' Lona trilled. ''Why, I've met her myself a time or two, but I never suspected—''

"Well, but of course I cannot think of assuming any fresh obligation before I have provided for the last child that my Iraine gave me, namely, Denn. The, m-hm, the lady in question agrees."

"Does Denn?" Scorn tinged her voice.

"Oh, he has no idea of all this," Jans answered hastily. "Pray do keep silence about it. And bear in mind, too, that . . . Ynis . . . would be most unwise to give up her present position, distasteful though it often is to her, and marry an aging widower, unless her stepson is able to provide for her and her children if necessary. Denn is loyal, he would do so, but he must have a foundation for his own life before he can, must he not? We are being sensible, even as you are."

Lona swallowed again. "Yes." She jumped down from the bench. "Come," she said, around an uncertain smile, "let's choose your things."

Natan Sandana the jeweler was visiting Vardrai of Syr the courtesan. The occasion was not the usual one. The small gray man had always contented himself with his wife, rather than spend money on the favors of other women, especially when they were as expensive as Vardrai's. His desire was for a different sort of joining.

"I tell you, we cannot lose," he urged, while he paced excitedly back and forth. The rug drank down every footfall. "My guild maintains a farflung web of communication—which stays healthy, sick though business has otherwise become. I had word of that Norrener ship soon after she had sailed from Owaio. Scarcely was she moored at the Longline this morning but I was aboard, to speak with her captain and look into his strongbox. The news was true. Besides his cargo of spices and rare woods, he has, for himself, such a store of pearls as I never saw aforetime. White, rosy, black, all huge, all perfect, oh, I have today let Beauty's embodied being trickle through these fingers!''

''How did he get them?'' asked Vardrai from the couch whereon she had curled her magnificent body. She continued to stroke a comb through the mahogany sheen of her tresses.

Natan shrugged. ''He did not say. But it's known that while they were down among yon islands, the Norreners lent their aid—ship, cannon, pikes—in a war between two kinglets, for hire. I conjecture that the good Haako picked up some booty about which he did not inform his royal employer.''

''And he'd fain sell the lot?''

''What else? He can get a substantial price at home. However, he understands it will be but a fraction of the true value. If we, here, outbid it, we shall still have a fantastic bargain.''

Vardrai set the comb down and touched the necklace that her throat graced. ''Pearls are fine to wear,'' she observed, ''but who can eat them? If you can scarcely move what stock you have in your shop, Master Sandana, how can you realize a profit on such a hoard?''

''Some can be sold quickly,'' he maintained. ''Not everyone suffers in this abominable climate of trade. Zulio Pandric, for example, waxes fat, and nowadays is my best customer.''

She grimaced the least bit. ''And mine, or one of them,'' she murmured, half to herself. ''I wish I could charge some less than others. A lusty young man would make up for a bloated old moneylender. But he and his kind seem to have all the gold, and I dare not risk word leaking out that Vardrai of Syr can be had cheaply.''

"For the most part, the pearls will have to be held for several years, perhaps as much as a decade, until conditions improve," Natan admitted. "But conditions will. They must. If nothing else, once Sir Falcovan Roncitar has established his colony overseas, the wealth of the New Lands will begin flowing back to Caronne, and we know with certainty how lavish the gods were when they fashioned that part of the world. Gems will not only command their present rightful price, they will have appreciated enormously. Think, my lady. How would you like a profit of two or three hundred per centum?"

The woman sighed. Her glance strayed to an open window which, from this upper floor, overlooked King's Newmarket. The breeze that blew in was soft and quiet, for little of the olden bustle stirred on the square; dwindled were the very odors of foodstalls and horse droppings. Cultivated musicality slipped from her voice as she said, in the provincial accent of her childhood, "The trick is to stay alive till then. How much do you need?"

"I bargained him down to four hundred aureates—"

Vardrai whistled.

"—of which I can provide half, if I pledge sufficient property to Master Pandric," Natan said. "But we must be swift. Unlike so many merchant skippers, Haako expects to sell his cargo at a brisk rate, to wholesalers as well as the rich and the noble. Then he'll be off."

The jeweler halted before Vardrai's couch. "My lady," he pleaded, "I came to you because your trade is still faring well, and it is general knowledge that you are not extravagant, but put money aside. What say you to a partnership, share and share alike?"

Slowly, she shook her lovely head. "I say wonderful—but impossible," she told him with regret. "I have not the likes of such cash, nor could I leave it with you to ripen for ten years or so if I did."

"But," he protested. "But."

"I know." She gestured at those velvet hangings, ivory-inlaid furnishings, crystal chandeliers, fragrant incense burners which decorated the room. She ran a palm down the thin silk which draped her in luster. "I command high prices, because the alternative is to be poor, miserable, and abused down in Docktown or along the canals. But this means my gentlemen are not many. It also means that they expect this sort of environs, and much else that is costly; and it must be often changed, lest they weary of sameness. No, it's true that large monies pass through my hands, but what remains is scant, hard though I pinch. Besides, as I said, I cannot wait ten years."

"Why not?"

Vardrai turned her left cheek toward the window and pointed to the corner of that deep-violet eye. A sunbeam, slanting over a roof opposite, brought forth the tiny crow's-feet as shadows. "I am less young than you may think," she said quietly. "Time gnaws. I have seen what becomes of old whores."

Despite his disappointment, Natan felt a tinge of compassion. "What will you do?"

She smiled. "Why, I hope within that decade to have collected the wherewithal to buy a house and start an establishment wherein several girls work, paying commissions to me. That will give me my security and . . . and freedom."

Her gaze went outward again, fell on a red-haired youth who was crossing the marketplace with furious long strides, and followed him. A madam could have whatever lovers she chose, requiring no more of them than that they please her.

A gong sounded. "Come in," Vardrai called. A maidservant opened the door and announced: "My lady, there's a patron. Somebody new."

"Indeed?" Interest quickened the courtesan's tone. "Who?"

"He's a Norrener, my lady, but seems quite decent. Says he's the captain of a ship."

Natan chuckled, a trifle bitterly. "Ah, ha!" he remarked. "I expect you'll find Haako Grayfellsson rather a change from Zulio Pandric."

"Let me hope so," Vardrai replied. "Well, go back, Jayinn, and entertain him while I make ready. I fear you must leave now, Master Sandana; and I *am* sorry I couldn't help you.

Over the cobblestones, between high, half-timbered walls, through arcades, beneath overhangs, across the plazas and a bridge spanning the Imperial Canal, Arvel Tarabine stalked. Almost, he ran. Passersby whom he jostled would begin to curse, espy the fury on his brow and the white knuckles on his fists, and keep silent. A couple of wagoners halted their mules to let him by, as if otherwise he would have cut a way for himself. Dogs barked at him, but from a safe distance.

Truth to tell, he fled his rage and grief, lest they cause him indeed to harm someone; but they rode along with him, inside his breast. They kicked his heart, squeezed his lungs, clambered about on his rib cage, and mouthed at him. Perhaps, he thought, he could exorcise them by wearing his body down to exhaustion—but how much liefer would he have gotten into a fight!

Out the Eastport he went, and soon left Tholis Way for a trail northward. Seilles had long since outgrown its old defensive walls, but not far in that direction, because there the land climbed steeply, in cliff and crag and ravine. Not even shepherds cared to make use of it, nor did noblemen risk breaking their horses' legs in the chase. Peasants sometimes went afoot after deer, or set snares for birds and rabbits—yet seldom, for wolves prowled these reaches and, it was whispered, beings more uncanny than that.

The trail was merely a track winding up hillsides and along ridges, often overgrown by whins. Strong though he was, after two hours of it Arvel must stop to catch his breath. He looked about him.

Stillness and warmth pressed down out of a sky where no clouds were, only a hawk whose wings shone burnished. The air had a scorched smell. Gorse and scrub trees grew around strewn boulders, save where the heights plunged sheer. Afar and below was a forest canopy, richly green, and beyond it the Ilwen estuary gleamed like a drawn blade. He could just discern the city, walls, towers, ruddy-tiled roofs, temple spire, Scholarium dome, Hall of Worthies and palace of the Lord Mayor, warehouses and a couple of ships at the Longline, all tiny at this distance and not quite real. It was as if Lona were a dear dream from which he had been shaken awake.

His glance traveled westward. The sun cast a blaze off the rim of the world yonder—the bay, and behind it the ocean. Despair lifted overwhelmingly in him. That dream was also lost. Everything was lost.

How he had implored Sir Falcovan! "I proved myself a good fighting man in the war, one who can lead other men, did I not? Your colony may well need defenders. It will certainly need explorers, surveyors, hunters, and you know I can handle such matters too. As for a regular business, well, I'd be ill at ease on a plantation, but the trade in timber, furs, gold, ores—Take me, my lord!"

The great adventurer twirled his mustachios. "Most gladly, son," he answered, "if you can outfit yourself and engage whatever underlings you require, as well as help pay our mutual costs. Two hundred and fifty aureates is the price of a share in the enterprise. The Company cannot take less, not in justice to those who've already bought in. And you'll need another hundred or so for your own expenses."

That much money would keep a family in comfort for some years, or buy a large house or a small shop here at home. "My lord, I—I'll have to borrow."

"Against prospective earnings?" Sir Falcovan raised his brows. "Well, you can try. But don't dawdle. The ships have begun loading at Croy. We must sail before autumn."

"My . . . my wife, the wife I'll have, she's strong and willing the same as I," Arvel begged. "We've talked about it. We'll go indentured if we can't find the money." Lona had resisted that idea violently before she gave in, and he misliked it himself, but passage to the New Lands, to a reborn hope for the future, would be worth seven years of bondage.

The knight shook his head. "No, we've no dearth of such help—nigh more than we can find use for, to be frank. It's capital we still need: that, and qualities of leadership." His weathered visage softened. "I understand your feelings, lad. I was your age once. May the gods smile on you."

They had not done so.

Abruptly Arvel could no longer stand in place. He spun about on his heel and resumed his flight.

The weariness that he sought, he won after a few more hours. He staggered up Cromlech Hill and flopped to the ground, his back against the warm side of a megalith. A forgotten tribe had raised this circle on the brow of this tor, unknown millennia ago, and practised their rites, whatever those were, at the altar in the middle. Now the pillars stood alone, gray, worn, lichenous, in grass that the waning summer had turned to hay, and held their stony memories to themselves. People shunned them. Arvel cared nothing. He thought that he'd welcome a bogle or a werewolf, anything he could rightfully kill.

The heat, the redolence, a drowsy buzzing of insects, all entered him. He slept.

Chill awakened him. He sat up with a gasp and saw that the sun was down. Deep blue in the west, where the evenstar glowed lamplike, heaven darkened to purple overhead. It lightened again in the east, ahead of a full moon that would shortly rise, but murk already laired among the megaliths.

"Good fortune, mortal." The voice, male, sang rather than spoke.

Arvel gasped. The form that loomed before him was tall, and huge slanty eyes caught what luminance there was and gave it back as the eyes of a cat do. Otherwise it was indistinct, more than this dimness could reasonably have caused. He thought he saw a cloak, its flaring collar suggestive of bat wings, and silvery hair around a narrow face; but he could not be sure.

He scrambled to his feet. "Joy to you, sir," he said in haste while he stepped backward, hand on sword. His heart, that would have exulted to meet an avowed enemy, rattled, and his gullet tightened.

Yet the stranger made no threatening move, but remained as quiet in the dusk as the cromlech. "Have no fear of *me*, Arvel Tarabine,'' he enjoined. ''Right welcome you are.''

The man wet his lips. ''You have the advantage of me, sir,'' he croaked. ''I do not think I have had the pleasure of meeting you erenow.''

''No; for who remembers those who came to their cradles by night and drew runes in the air above them?'' A fluid shrug. ''Names are for mortals and for gods, not for the Fair Folk. But call me Irrendal if you wish.''

Arvel stiffened. His pulse roared in his ears. ''No! Can't be!''

Laughter purled. ''Ah, you think Irrendal and his elves are mere figures in nursery tales? Well, you have forgotten this too; but know afresh, from me, that the culture of children is older than history and the lore which its tales preserve goes very deep.''

Arvel gathered nerve. ''Forgive me, sir, but I have simply your word for that.''

''Granted. Nor will I offer you immediate evidence, because it must needs be of a nature harmful to you.'' The other paused. ''However,'' he proposed slowly, ''if you will follow me, you shall perceive evidence enough, aye, and receive it, too.''

''Why—what, what—?—'' stammered Arvel. He felt giddy. The evenstar danced in his vision, above the stranger's head.

Graveness responded: ''You are perhaps he for whom the elvenfolk have yearned, working what poor small magics are ours in these iron centuries, in hopes that the time-flow would guide him hither. You can perhaps release us from misery. Take heed: the enterprise is perilous. You could be killed, and the kites and foxes pick your bones.'' A second quicksilver laugh. ''Ah, what difference between them and the worms?

We believe you can prevail, else I would not have appeared to you. And if you do, we will grant you your heart's desire.''

There being no clear and present menace to him, a measure of calm descended upon Arvel. Beneath it, excitement thrummed. ''What would you of me?'' he asked with care.

''Twelve years and a twelvemonth ago,'' related he who used the name Irrendal, ''an ogre came into these parts. We think hunger drove him from the North, after men had cleared and plowed his forest. For him, our country is well-nigh as barren; unicorn, lindworm, jack-o'-dance, all such game has become rare. Thus he turned on us, not only our orchards and livestock but our very selves. Male and female elf has he seized and devoured. Worse, he has taken of our all too few and precious children. His strength is monstrous: gates has he torn from their hinges, walls has he battered down, and entered ravening. Warriors who sought him out never came back, save when he has thrown a gnawed skull into a camp of ours while his guffaws rolled like thunder in the dark. Spells have we cast, but they touched him no deeper than would a springtime rain. To the gods have we appealed, but they answered not and we wonder if those philosophers may be right who declare that the gods are withdrawing from a world where, ever more, men exalt Reason. Sure it is that the Fair Folk must abide, or perish, in whatever countrysides they have been the tutelaries; we cannot flee. Hushed are our mirth and music. O mortal, save us!''

A tingle went along Arvel's backbone. The hair stirred on his head. ''Why do you suppose I can do aught, when you are helpless?'' he forced forth.

''For the same reason that the ogre has not troubled your race,'' Irrendal told him. ''You have powers denied those of the Halfworld—power to be abroad by daylight and to wield cold iron. Uha, so named by the Northerners, knows better than to provoke a human hunt after him. We elves have already tried to get aid from men, but too much iron is in their homes, we cannot go near; and in these wilds we found none but stray peasants, who fled in terror at first sight of one like me. You do not. Moreover, you are a fighting man, and bear steel."

His voice rang: "Follow me to Uha's lair. Slay him. You shall have glory among us, and the richest of rewards."

"Unless he slays me," Arvel demurred.

"Aye, that could happen." Scorn flickered. "If you are afraid, I will not detain you further. Go back to your safe little life."

The rage, that had smoldered low in the man, flared anew, high and white-hot. An ogre? Had he, Arvel, not wished for something to attack? "Have done!" he shouted. "Let's away!"

"Oh, wonder of wonders," Irrendal exulted. And the moon rose.

Its radiance dimmed the stars that were blinking forth, turned grass and gorse hoar, frosted the starkness of stones. It did not make the elf any more clear in the man's sight. "Follow me, follow me," Irrendal called and slipped off, shadow-silent.

Arvel came after. He saw well enough by the icy light to trot without stumbling; but the hillscape seemed unreal, a mirage through which he passed. Only his footfalls and smoke-white breath made any sound. The chill grew ever deeper. Now and then he thought he glimpsed strangenesses flitting by, but they were never there when he looked closer.

Once Irrendal showed him a spring, where he

quenched his thirst, and once a silvery tree whereon glowed golden fruit; he ate thereof, and an intoxicating sweetness removed all hunger from him. Otherwise he followed his half-seen guide while the moon climbed higher and the constellations trekked westward. The time seemed endless and the time seemed like naught until he came to the cave of the ogre.

It yawned jagged-edged in a cliff, like a mouth full of rotten teeth. Despite the cold, a graveyard stench billowed from it, to make Arvel gag. The bones, tatters of clothing, bronze trappings that lay scattered around declared that Irrendal had spoken truth.

Or had he? Sudden doubt assailed Arvel. Fragmentary recollections of the nursery tales floated up into his mind. Did they not say the elves were a tricksy lot, light-willed and double-tongued, whose choicest jape was to outwit a mortal? Was it not the case that nothing of theirs could have enduring value to a man? Irrendal had promised Arvel his heart's desire, but what might that actually prove to be?

Doubt became dread. Arvel was on the point of bolting. Then Irrendal winded a horn he had brought forth from somewhere, and it was too late. Cruelly beautiful, the notes were a challenge and a mockery; and they had no echoes, even as the bugler had no shadow.

Hu-hu, hu-hu, attend your doom!

The ogre appeared in the cave mouth. Monstrous he was, broad and thick as a horse, taller than a man despite a stoop that brought his knuckles near the ground. Eyes like a swine's glittered beneath a shelf of brow, above noseless nostrils and a jaw where fangs sprouted. The moon grizzled his coarse pelt. Earth quivered to each shambling step he took. Hatred rumbled from his throat as he saw the elf, and he gathered himself to charge.

"Draw blade, man, or die!" Irrendal cried.

Arvel's weapon snaked forth. Moonlight poured along it. Fear fled before battle joy. His left hand took his knife, and thus armed, he advanced.

The ogre grew aware of him, bawled dismay, and sought to scuttle off. Faster on his feet, Arvel barred escape, forced his enemy back against the cliff, and sprang in for the kill.

Uha was as brave as any cornered beast. An arm swept in an arc that would have smeared Arvel's brains over the talons had it made connection. The human barely skipped aside. He had accomplished only a shallow slash of sword. But where the steel had been, ogre-flesh charred and smoked.

Uha lumbered after him. Arvel bounded in and out. His sword whistled. When a hand clutched close, he seared it with his knife. Uha bellowed, clattered his teeth, flailed and kicked. Irrendal stood apart, impassive.

The fight lasted long. Afterward Arvel recalled but little of it. Finally Uha won back into his den. The man pursued—altogether recklessly, for in there he was blind. Yet that was where the nightmare combat ended.

Arvel reeled out, fell prone upon the blessed sane earth, and let darkness whirl over him.

He regained strength after some while, sat painfully up, and beheld Irrendal. "You have conquered, you have freed us," the elf sang. "Hero, go home."

"Will . . . we meet . . . again?" Arvel mumbled with mummy-parched tongue.

"Indeed we shall, a single time," Irrendal vowed, "for have I not promised you reward? Await me tomorrow dusk beneath the Dragon Tower. Meanwhile—" he paused— "leave your steel that slew the ogre, for henceforth it is unlucky."

The thought passed through Arvel's exhaustion that thus far his pay was the loss of two good, costly blades. However, he dared not disobey.

"Farewell, warrior," Irrendal bade him, "until next twilight," and was gone.

Slowly, Arvel observed that the moon had passed its height. Before the western ridges hid it from him, he had best be in familiar territory; nor did he wish to linger *here* another minute.

He crawled to his feet and limped away.

Entering Seilles at dawn, he sought the sleazy lodging house where he had a room, fell into bed, and slept until late afternoon. Having cleansed off grime and dried sweat with a sponge and a basin of cold water, and having donned fresh albeit threadbare garments, he proceeded to the Drum and Trumpet, benched himself, and called for bread, meat, and ale.

Ynis regarded him closely. "You seem awearied," she remarked. "What's happened?"

"You'd not believe it if I told you," he answered, "nor would I."

In truth, he was unsure whether he remembered more than a wild dream on Cromlech Hill. Nothing spoke for its reality save aches, bruises, and the absence of his edged metal. The loss of Lona was more comprehensible, and hurt worse.

Eating and drinking, he wondered if his wits had left him. That was a thought to shudder at, madness. But life as a hale man would be dreary at best. What could he do?

Not creep back to Lona, whine for forgiveness, and seek to become a potter. She would despise him for that, after the hard words he had uttered yesterday, as much as he would himself. Besides, he'd never make a worthwhile partner in the shop. His hands lacked the deftness of hers and his tongue the unction of a seller—not that she ever truckled to anybody.

If he stayed on in Seilles, he had no prospect other than a continuation of his present miserable, cadging existence. Opportunities elsewhere—for instance, going to sea—where niggardly. But at least he would be making his own way in the world.

As he had wished to do, and been sure he could do magnificently, in the New Lands. Well-a-day, how many mortals ever win to their heart's desire?

Arvel sat bolt upright. Ale splashed from the goblet in his grasp.

"What is it that's wrong, dearie?" Ynis asked.

"Nothing . . . or everything. . . . I know not," he muttered.

The sun had gone behind the houses across the street. Soon it would go behind the horizon. Irrendal had said to meet him at the Dragon Tower.

What was there to lose? Simply time, if last night's business had been delirium after all, and time was a burden on Arvel.

Granted, legend maintained that the elves were a shifty folk, and their powers among men weak and evanescent. He must not let any hopes fly upward. But did it do harm if his blood surged and he forgot his pains?

Swallowing the last of his meal, Arvel hastened out. "Farewell," Ynis called. He did not hear. Sighing, she moved toward a tableful of rowdies who whooped for service.

Hemmed in by walls, the streets were already dark, but people moved about. Linkmen were lighting the great lamps on their iron standards, while windows and shopfronts came aglow. Since the advent of modern illumination in Caronne, city dwellers kept late hours. Even those who had no work to do or money to spend enjoyed strolling and staring in the coolth of day's end. Arvel could understand why creatures of night and magic now avoided the homes of men.

Sunset chimes pealed from the temple as he passed Hardan's Port. It no longer existed save as a name; cannon had crumbled it and its whole section of wall during the Baronial War, and nobody felt a restoration was worth undertaking. Instead, the then Lord Mayor had turned the area into a public park. Trees that he planted on the borders had since grown tall enough to screen off view of surrounding mansions. Only the highest spires of the city pierced heaven above their shadowiness. Gravel scrunched under Arvel's feet, along labyrinthine flowerbeds. Their perfumes were faint at this eventide hour. A nightingale chanted through the bell-tones and fireflies wavered in air. No lovers had arrived, which struck him as odd.

At the center of a greensward reared that remnant of the old fortifications known as the Dragon Tower. Ivy entwined it, and the fierce heads carven under the battlements were weathered into shapelessness. Here an elf might well venture. Arvel's pulse fluttered. He took stance at the doorway. The chimes fell silent. The gloaming deepened. Stars trembled into view.

"Greeting, friend." Whence had the vague tall shape come? Arvel felt after the sword he no longer wore.

Laughter winged around him. "Be at ease," Irrendal sang. "You've naught to fear but folly."

Arvel felt himself redden.

"Against that, no sorcery prevails, nor the gods themselves," Irrendal continued. With the weight of the ogre off it, his slightly wicked merriment danced free. "Nor can the Halfworld ever be more in men's lives than transient, a sparkle, a breeze, a snowflake, a handful of autumn leaves blowing past. Still . . . much may be done with very little, if cunning suffices.

"I pledged to you your heart's desire, Arvel Tarabine. You must choose what that is. I can but hope you choose aright. I think, though, this should cover the price. Hold out your hand."

Dazedly, the man did. A gesture flickered. A weight dropped. Almost, in his surprise, he let the thing fall, before he closed fingers upon it.

"A coin of some value as men reckon value," Irrendal declared. "Spend it wisely—but swiftly this same night, lest your newly won luck go aglimmer."

Was there a least hint of wistfulness in the melody? "Fare you well, always well, over the sea and beyond," Irrendal bade him. "Remember me. Tell your children and ask them to tell theirs, that elvenkind not be forgotten. Farewell, farewell."

And he was gone.

Long did Arvel stand alone, upbearing the heaviness in his hand, while his thoughts surged to and fro. At last he departed.

A street lamp glared where the city began. He stopped to look at what he held. Yellow brilliance sheened. He caught his breath, and again stood mute and moveless for a space. Then, suddenly, he ran.

Zulio Pandric the banker sat late at his desk, going through an account book which was not for anyone else's eyes, least of all those of the king's tax assessors. Lantern globes shone right, left, and above, to brighten the work, massive furniture, walnut wainscot, his gross corpulence and ivory-rimmed spectacles. From time to time he reached into a porcelain bowl for a sweetmeat. Incense made the air equally sticky.

To him entered the butler, who said with diffidence, "Sir, a young man demands immediate audience. I told him to apply tomorrow during your regular hours, but he was most insistent. Shall I have the watchman expel him?"

"Um," grunted Zulio. "Did he give you his name?"

"Yes, sir, of course I obtained that. Arvel Tarabine. He does not seem prosperous, sir, nor is his manner dignified."

"Arvel Tarabine. Hm." Zulio rubbed a jowl while he searched through his excellent memory. "Ah, yes. A byblow of Torric, Landholder Merlinhurst. Father impoverished, barely able to maintain the estate. Son, I hear, a wastrel. . . . Admit him." Zulio had long pondered how he might lay such families under obligation. Here, conceivably, was a weak spot in the independence of one of them.

Eagerness made the fellow who entered as vivid as his flame-red hair. "I've a marvel to show you, Master Pandric, a whopping marvel!" he declaimed.

"Indeed? Be seated, pray." The moneylender waved at a chair. "What is this matter that cannot wait until morning?"

"Behold," said Arvel. He did not sit but, instead, leaned over the desk. From beneath his cloak he took a thing that thudded when he slapped it down.

Zulio barely suppressed an exclamation of his own. It was a gold coin that gleamed before him—but such a coin, as broad as his palm and as thick as his thumb. In a cautious movement, he laid hold on it and hefted. The weight was easily five pounds avoirdupois, belike more; and the metal was pure, he felt its softness give beneath his thumbnail.

A sense of the eerie crept along his nerves. "How did you come by this, young sir?" he asked low.

"Honestly." Arvel jittered from foot to foot.

"What do you wish of me?"

"Why, that you change it into ordinary pieces of money. It's far too large for my use."

"Let us see, let us see." Zulio puffed out of his chair and across the room to a sideboard. Thereon stood scales of several sizes, a graduated glass vessel half full of water, an arithmetical reckoner, and certain reference works. He needed no more than a pair of minutes to verify the genuineness of the gold and establish its exact value at those present rates of exchange which scarcity had created—four hundred aureates.

He brought the coin closer to a lantern and squinted. The lettering upon it was of no alphabet he knew, and he had seen many. The obverse bore a portrait of someone crowned who was not quite human, the reverse a gryphon.

Abruptly he knew what he held. Chill shivered through his blubber. He turned about, stared at Arvel, and said, each word falling like lead down a shot tower: "This is fairy gold."

"Well—" The youth reached a decision. "Yes, it is. I did a service for the elves, and it is my reward. There's naught unlawful about that, is there? I'd simply liefer the tale not be noised abroad. Too many people have an unreasoning dread of the Fair Folk."

"As well one might, considering their notorious deviousness. Don't you know—" Zulio checked himself. "May I ask why this haste to be rid of it?"

"I told you. I cannot spend it as it is. You can find a buyer, or have it melted into bullion, and none will suspect you of robbery as they could perchance suspect me. Chiefly, though, I want to travel. This will buy me a share in Sir Falcovan Roncitar's enterprise, and whatever else I'll need to win my fortune in the New Lands.''

''Could you not at least wait until morning?''

''No. I was counselled—well, I know nothing about these matters, only that he warned me I'd lose my luck if I didn't act at once—and I do want to leave. Come morning I'll buy a horse and a new sword and be off to Croy, out of this wretched town forever!''

Zulio decided Arvel was honest. He really had no idea of the curious property of fairy gold. His impatience might be due to something as trivial as a love affair gone awry.

Yes, probe that. ''No farewells, no sweetheart?'' Zulio asked slyly.

Arvel whitened, flushed, and whitened. ''She never wants to see me again—What's that to you, you fat toad? Break my coin and take your commission, or I'll find me another banker.''

''I fear—'' Zulio began, and stopped.

''What?'' Arvel demanded.

Zulio had changed his mind. He did not need to explain the situation. He would be extravagantly foolish to do so.

''I fear,'' he said, ignoring the insult, ''that I shall have to charge you more than the usual brokerage fee. As you yourself realize, a coin so valuable, and alien to boot, is not easily exchanged. It will take time. It will require paperwork, to stave off the royal revenue collectors. Meanwhile the money I give you is earning no interest for me, and I must purchase additional precautions against theft—''

Arvel proved to be even less versed in finance and bargaining that Zulio had hoped. The banker got the elven piece for three hundred and fifty aureates, paid over in gold and silver of ordinary denominations while the watchman witnessed the proceedings.

''Help the gentleman carry these bags back to his lodgings, Darron,'' Zulio ordered courteously. ''As for you, Master Tarabine, let me wish you every success and happiness in your New Lands. Should you find you have banking needs, the house of Pandric is at your service.''

''Thank you,'' Arvel snapped. ''Goodnight. Goodbye.'' Somehow, the immense adventure before him had not brought joy into his eyes. He lifted his part of the money easily enough, but walked out as if he were under a heavy burden.

Scarcely were the two men gone when Zulio stuffed the coin into a satchel and waddled forth to Crystal Street by himself. He could realize a large profit this night, but only this night. If he waited until dawn, he loss would be vast.

He did not think that Natan Sandana the jeweler, whose family and associates had been city-bred for generations, had heard anything about fairy gold. Quite probably Sandana did not believe the Halfworld was more than a nursery tale. Zulio came of backwoods peasant stock, and had dabbled in magic—without result, save that he acquired much arcane lore. Panting, sweating, he elbowed onward through crowds, amidst their babble and the plangencies of beggar musicians, underneath walls and galleries and lamp-flare, until he reached the home he wanted.

Natan was at his fireside, reading aloud from an old book—the verses of wayward Cappen Varra, which this prudent, wizened modern man loved—to his wife and younger children. He did not like or trust Zulio Pandric, and received his guest with an ill grace. Nevertheless, manners demanded that he take the banker into a private room as requested, and have the maid-servant bring mulled wine.

Candles in antique silver holders threw mild light over bookshelves and paintings. The leather of his chair creaked beneath Natan as he leaned back, bridged his fingertips, and inquired the visitor's wishes.

"This is an irregular hour, yes," Zulio admitted. "I'd not ordinarily trouble you now. But the circumstances tonight are special. You are a man of discretion, Master Sandana; you will understand if I spare you long and tedious explanations. Suffice it that I have urgent need of gemstones, and do not wish to risk it becoming a subject of gossip."

Natan grinned. Zulio knew, annoyed, that he was thinking of the courtesan Vardrai. Well, what did his sniggers count for? He'd assuredly forget them in the morning. "I have therefore taken a rare coin, a virtual ingot, from my vaults and brought it hither," Zulio said. "Observe. Let us talk."

Discussion occupied an hour. Natan Sandana was not so rude to a prominent man of affairs that he tested the gold himself . . . then. He did ask for, and get, a certification of value. In return, Zulio accepted a receipt for payment in full. "Have a care," he warned, as he put four hundred aureates' worth of the finest diamonds into his satchel—or better, because the jeweler had been still more anxious to deal than the slack market warranted. "Some evilly gifted thieves have been at work of late, I heard. Rumor goes that they employ actual witchcraft. That is why my attestation explicitly disavows responsibility for any effects of sorcery, as well as mundane malfeasance. You could open your strongbox and find nothing but a pile of rubbish, left as a jeer at you."

"I thank you, but I doubt it will happen, and not just because I equate the supernatural with superstition," the other man replied. A feverish intensity had come upon him. Zulio wondered why.

No matter. He had his profit, a clear fifty aureates above what he had paid out to Arvel Tarabine, in the form of gems negotiable piecemeal. Puffing, chuckling, jiggling, Zulio Pandric hastened back to his ledger and his sweetmeats.

"I must go out, dear," Natan Sandana told his wife. "Don't wait up for me."

"What has happened?" she asked.

"An unbelievable stroke of luck, I hope," he said, and kissed her fondly. "I'll tell you later, if all goes well."

As he stepped forth, the coin in his pouch dragged at his belt. He felt as if every passing glance lingered on the bulge, and pulled his cloak around it. Should he have waited for morning, when he could engage a guard? But that would have been to make conspicuous a transaction best kept secret. Tax collectors were as rapacious as any unofficial robber.

Besides, who would think that a drably clad little gray man carried a fortune on his person? Especially nowadays, when that fortune had been languishing for years in stock he could not sell.

Natan took Serpentine Street, the best-lit and safest way through Docktown, to the Longline. There he must pass a number of empty berths before he reached *Sea Mule.*

Fore and aft, the castles of the Norrener carrack loomed darkling. Between them, her guns glimmered dully by the light of wharf lamps and lanterns of the watch on board; her three masts stood gaunt athwart a lately risen moon. Its glade trembled on the river, which murmured with currents and tide. Rigging creaked as hemp contracted in the night's damp chill.

"Oh-hoa!" Natan called. "Lower the gangplank. I've business with your captain."

The pikemen obliged, which relieved him. Haako Grayfellsson might have been ashore carousing. Instead, the big man slumped in his cabin, amidst the malodor of bear-tallow candles, and swigged from a bottle of rum.

"Well met, Master Sandana," he said in accented Caronnean and a tone which all but added, "I suppose."

"I'm happy to find you here," Natan said.

Haako stroked his red, barbaric beard. "You wouldn't have, if I'd not blown over-much money on a vixen I'd heard praised—Enough. What would you of me?"

Natan laid palms on the table and leaned across it. "No need to pussyfoot," he said. "About our conversation the day before yesterday. I am prepared to buy your pearls at the price we mentioned."

An oath blasted from Haako's lips, but it was a sound of utter delight. Briefly, Natan recalled Vardrai. Poor woman; in a way it was a shame how she had missed her chance at this investment. Well, so much the more for those whom he held dear.

"Why, welcome again," the courtesan purred. She undulated into a position where light shone through her shift and outlined every curve against a nighted window.

This time her pleasure and seductiveness were sincere. The Norrener seaman was a little uncouth, true, but he possessed a vigor which he used with some skill. She had been sorry when he told her that he could not afford a second visit.

He stood awkwardly in the scented room, twisting between his fingers a fur pouch that contained something round. Through the windowpane drifted a vibrancy of violin and flute. Vardrai made it worth those beggar musicians' while to keep station below this wall.

"I . . . have a . . . proposition for you," he mumbled. Strange how he blushed, like a virginal boy, this man who had dared hurricanes and spears.

"Oh, I *like* propositions." Vardrai drew close to him and ruffled his whiskers.

He seized her and kissed her. She seldom wanted a kiss on the mouth, but found that this time it was different. "What a woman you are," he groaned.

"Thank you, kind sir," she laughed, and fluttered her lashes at him. "Shall we try if that be true?"

"A moment, I beg you." Haako stepped back and took her by the shoulders. His callouses scratched her slightly, arousingly, as he shivered. Otherwise he was gentle. His eyes sought hers. "Vardrai, I—I've come into a chunk of money. Left to myself, I'll drink and dice it away, and soon have nothing for you . . . and my ship will be calling two or three times yearly in Seilles hereafter, it will." The words tumbled from him. "Here's my proposition. What say I give you the sum, right this now, in pure gold—and you let me see you free of charge, always after, whenever I'm in port? Is that a fair offer, I ask you? Oh, Vardrai, Vardrai—"

Wariness congealed her. "What sum do you speak of?" she asked.

"I've the coin right here, and a paper from banker Pandric to give the worth," he blurted, while he fumbled in his pouch. "Four hundred aureates, 'tis."

Her world swooped around her. She stumbled

against him. He upheld her. "Four hundred aureates!" she whispered.

The moon sank west. Streets were deserted, save for the Lord Mayor's patrols, or peasants carting their produce to market, or less identifiable persons. The sounds of their passage rang hollow beneath the stars. Hither and yon, though, windows were coming to life with lamplight.

One belonged to the kitchen of Jans Orliand. Having slept poorly ever since he lost his wife, the chronicler was often up this early. He sat with a dish of porridge he had cooked for himself and read a book as he ate.

A knock on the door lifted his attention. Surprised, slightly apprehensive, he went to unlatch it. If that was a robber, he could shout and rouse his son Denn—but it was a woman who slipped through, and when she removed her hooded cloak, she was seen to be glorious.

"Vardrai of Syr!" Jans exclaimed. They had never met, but she was too famous for him not to recognize when they chanced to pass each other in the open. "Why, why, what brings you? Sit down, do, let me brew some herbal tea—"

"I have heard it cried that you've a house for sale, a large one with many rooms," she said.

He looked closer at her. Cosmetics did not altogether hide the darknesses below her eyes, or the pallor of cheeks and lips. She must have lain sleepless hour after hour, thinking about this, until she could wait no longer.

"Well, well, yes, I do," he replied. "Not that I expected—"

The wish exploded from her: "Could you show it to

me? Immediately? If it suits, I can buy it on the instant.''

Lona Grancy had also slept ill. The moon had not yet gone behind western roofs, and the east showed just the faintest silver, when she trudged from cottage to shed, lighted its lamps, and commenced work. ''May as well,'' she said. ''Not that customers will crowd our place, eh?''—this to her cat, which returned a wise green gaze before addressing itself to the saucer of milk she set forth.

The maiden pummeled clay, threw it upon the turntable, sat down, and spun the wheel with more ferocity than needful. It shrilled and groaned. She shivered in the cold which crept out from between her arrayed wares. The hour before dawn is the loneliest of all.

A man came in off the street. ''Master Orliand!'' she hailed him. ''What on earth?'' The spinning died away.

''I thought . . . I hoped I might find you awake,'' the scholar said. Breath smoked ragged with each word. ''I am pushing matters, true, but—well, every moment's delay is a moment additional before I can seek out a, a certain lady and—Could we talk, my dear?''

''Of course, old friend.'' Lona rose. ''Let me put this stuff aside and clean my hands, then I'll fetch us a bite of food and—But what do you want?''

''Your property,'' said Jans. ''I can give you an excellent price.''

Again by herself, for her visitor had staggered off to his bed, Lona stood in her home and looked down at the coin. It covered her hand; its weight felt like the weight of the world; strange glimmers and glistens rippled across the profile upon it. Silence pressed inward. Wicks guttered low.

So, she thought, now she had sold everything. Jans would not force her to leave unduly fast, but leave she must. Why had she done it—and in such haste, too?

Well, four hundred aureates was no mean sum of cash. No longer was she bound to the shop which had bound her father to itself. She could fare elsewhere, to opportunities in Croy, for example; or, of course, this was a dowry which could buy her a desirable match. Yes, a good, steady younger son of a nobleman or merchant, who would make cautious investments and—

"And hell take him!" she screamed, grabbed the coin to her, and fled.

Arvel tried for a long while to sleep. Finally he lost patience, dressed in the dark, and fumbled his way downstairs. Lamps still burned along the street, but their glow was pale underneath a sinking moon and lightening sky, pale as the last stars. Dew shimmered on cobbles. Shadows made mysterious the carvings upon timbers, the arcades and alleys around him.

He would go to the farmers' market, he decided, break his fast, and search for a horse. When that was done, the shops would be open wherein he could obtain the rest of his equipage. By noon he could be on the road to Croy and his destiny. The prospect was oddly desolate.

However, no doubt he would meet another girl somewhere, and—

A small, sturdy figure rounded a corner, stopped for an instant, and sped toward him. "Oh, Arvel!" Echoes gave back Lona's cry, over and over. Light went liquid across the disc she carried. "See what I have for you! Our passage to the New Lands!"

"But—but how in creation did you get hold of that?" he called. Bewilderment rocked him. "And I thought you—you and I—"

"I've sold out!" she jubilated as she ran. "We can go!"

She caromed against him, and he wasted no further time upon thought.

When they came up for air, he mumbled, "I already have the price of our migration, dear darling. But that you should offer me this, out of your love, why, that's worth more than, than all the rest of the world, and heaven thrown in."

She crowed for joy and nestled close. Again he gathered her to him. In her left hand, behind his shoulder, she gripped the fairy gold. The sun came over a rooftop, and smote. Suddenly she held nothing. A few dead leaves blew away upon the dawn breeze, with a sound like dry laughter.

The Valor of Cappen Varra

Romance has its humor, including the blessed ability to make game of itself. This little yarn affectionately turns the work of Robert E. Howard and his followers on its head. Rather than a barbarian wandering into civilized lands, I thought, why not a civilized man who winds up among barbarians? Historically, that's a much likelier situation. But let's keep the rough-hewn narrative style—

This wasn't my only source. I also drew on a lively folk ballad from the Danish Middle Ages. They could laugh back then, too.

The wind came from the north with sleet on its back. Raw shuddering gusts whipped the sea till the ship lurched and men felt driven spindrift stinging their faces. Beyond the rail there was winter night, a moving blackness where the waves rushed and clamored; straining into the great dark, men sensed only the bitter salt of sea-scud, the nettle of sleet and the lash of wind.

Cappen lost his footing as the ship heaved beneath

him, his hands were yanked from the icy rail and he went stumbling to the deck. The bilge water was new coldness on his drenched clothes. He struggled back to his feet, leaning on a rower's bench and wishing miserably that his quaking stomach had more to lose. But he had already chucked his share of stockfish and hardtack, to the laughter of Svearek's men, when the gale started.

Numb fingers groped anxiously for the harp on his back. It still seemed intact in its leather case. He didn't care about the sodden wadmal breeks and tunic that hung around his skin. The sooner they rotted off him, the better. The thought of the silks and linens of Croy was a sigh in him.

Why had he come to Norren?

A gigantic form, vague in the whistling dark, loomed beside him and gave him a steadying hand. He could barely hear the blond giant's bull tones: "Ha, easy there, lad. Methinks the sea horse road is overly rough for yer feet."

"Ulp," said Cappen. His slim body huddled on the bench, too miserable to care. The sleet pattered against his shoulders and the spray congealed in his red hair.

Torbek of Norren squinted into the night. It made his leathery face a mesh of wrinkles. "A bitter feast of Yolner we hold," he said. " 'Twas a madness of the king's, that he would guest with his brother across the water. Now the other ships are blown from us and the fire is drenched out and we lie alone in the Wolf's Throat."

Wind piped shrill in the rigging. Cappen could just see the longboat's single mast reeling against the sky. The ice on the shrouds made it a pale pyramid. Ice everywhere, thick on the rails and benches, sheathing the dragon head and the carved stern-post, the ship rolling and staggering under the great march of waves, men bailing and bailing in the half-frozen bilge to keep her afloat, and too much wind for sail or oars. Yes—a cold feast!

"But then, Svearek has been strange since the troll took his daughter, three years ago," went on Torbek. He shivered in a way the winter had not caused. "Never does he smile, and his once open hand grasps tight about the silver and his men have poor reward and no thanks. Yes, strange—" His small frost-blue eyes shifted to Cappen Varra, and the unspoken thought ran on beneath them: Strange, even that he likes you, the wandering bard from the south. Strange, that he will have you in his hall when you cannot sing as his men would like.

Cappen did not care to defend himself. He had drifted up toward the northern barbarians with the idea that they would well reward a minstrel who could offer them something more than their own crude chants. It had been a mistake; they didn't care for roundels or sestinas, they yawned at the thought of roses white and red under the moon of Caronne, a moon less fair than my lady's eyes. Nor did a man of Croy have the size and strength to compel their respect; Cappen's light blade flickered swiftly enough so that no one cared to fight him, but he lacked the power of sheer bulk. Svearek alone had enjoyed hearing him sing, but he was niggardly and his brawling thorp was an endless boredom to a man used to the courts of southern princes.

If he had but had the manhood to leave—But he had delayed, because of a hope that Svearek's coffers would open wider; and now he was dragged along over the Wolf's Throat to a mid-winter feast which would have to be celebrated on the sea.

"Had we but fire—" Torbek thrust his hands inside his cloak, trying to warm them a little. The ship rolled till she was almost on her beam ends; Torbek braced himself with practiced feet, but Cappen went into the bilge again.

He sprawled there for a while, his bruised body refusing movement. A weary sailor with a bucket glared at him through dripping hair. His shout was dim under the hoot and skirl of wind: "If ye like it so well down here, then help us bail!"

" 'Tis not yet my turn," groaned Cappen, and got slowly up.

The wave which had nearly swamped them had put out the ship's fire and drenched the wood beyond hope of lighting a new one. It was cold fish and sea-sodden hardtack till they saw land again—if they ever did.

As Cappen raised himself on the leeward side, he thought he saw something gleam, far out across the wrathful night. A wavering red spark—He brushed a stiffened hand across his eyes, wondering if the madness of wind and water had struck through into his own skull. A gust of sleet hid it again. But—

He fumbled his way aft between the benches. Huddled figures cursed him wearily as he stepped on them. The ship shook herself, rolled along the edge of a boiling black trough, and slid down into it; for an instant, the white teeth of combers grinned above her rail, and Cappen waited for an end to all things. Then she mounted them again, somehow, and wallowed toward another valley.

King Svearek had the steering oar and was trying to hold the longboat into the wind. He had stood there since sundown, huge and untiring, legs braced and the bucking wood cradled in his arms. More than human he seemed, there under the icicle loom of the stern-post, his gray hair and beard rigid with ice. Beneath the horned helmet, the strong moody face turned right and left, peering into the darkness. Cappen felt smaller than usual when he approached the steersman.

He leaned close to the king, shouting against the blast of winter: "My lord, did I not see firelight?"

"Aye. I spied it an hour ago," grunted the king. "Been trying to steer us a little closer to it."

Cappen nodded, too sick and weary to feel reproved. "What is it?"

"Some island—there are many in this stretch of water—now shut up!"

Cappen crouched under the rail and waited.

The lonely red gleam seemed nearer when he looked again. Svearek's tones were lifting in a roar that hammered through the gale from end to end of the ship: "Hither! Come hither to me, all men not working!"

Slowly, they groped to him, great shadowy forms in wool and leather, bulking over Cappen like storm-gods. Svearek nodded toward the flickering glow. "One of the islands, somebody must be living there. I cannot bring the ship closer for fear of surf, but one of ye should be able to take the boat thither and fetch us fire and dry wood. Who will go?"

They peered overside, and the uneasy movement that ran among them came from more than the roll and pitch of the deck underfoot.

Beorna the Bold spoke at last, it was hardly to be heard in the noisy dark: "I never knew of men living hereabouts. It must be a lair of trolls."

"Aye, so . . . aye, they'd but eat the man we sent . . . out oars, let's away from here though it cost our lives . . ." The frightened mumble was low under the jeering wind.

Svearek's face drew into a snarl. "Are ye men or

puling babes? Hack yer way through them, if they be trolls, but bring me fire!''

''Even a she-troll is stronger than fifty men, my king,'' cried Torbek. ''Well ye know that, when the monster woman broke through our guards three years ago and bore off Hildigund.''

''Enough!'' It was a scream in Svearek's throat. ''I'll have yer craven heads for this, all of ye, if ye gang not to the isle!''

They looked at each other, the big men of Norren, and their shoulders hunched bearlike. It was Beorna who spoke it for them: ''No, that ye will not. We are free housecarls, who will fight for a leader—but not for a madman.''

Cappen drew back against the rail, trying to make himself small.

''All gods turn their faces from ye!'' It was more than weariness and despair which glared in Svearek's eyes, there was something of death in them. ''I'll go myself, then!''

''No, my king. That we will not find ourselves in.''

''I am the king.''

''And we are yer housecarls, sworn to defend ye—even from yerself. Ye shall not go.''

The ship rolled again, so violently that they were all thrown to starboard. Cappen landed on Torbek, who reached up to shove him aside and then closed one huge fist on his tunic.

''Here's our man!''

''Hi!'' yelled Cappen.

Torbek hauled him roughly back to his feet. ''Ye cannot row or bail yer fair share,'' he growled, ''nor do ye know the rigging or any skill of a sailor—'tis time ye made yerself useful!''

''Aye, aye—let little Cappen go—mayhap he can sing

the trolls to sleep—'' The laughter was hard and barking, edged with fear, and they all hemmed him in.

''My lord!'' bleated the minstrel. ''I am your guest—''

Svearek laughed unpleasantly, half crazily. ''Sing them a song,'' he howled. ''Make a fine roun—whatever ye call it—to the troll-wife's beauty. And bring us some fire, little man, bring us a flame less hot than the love in yer breast for yer lady!''

Teeth grinned through matted beards. Someone hauled on the rope from which the ship's small boat trailed, dragging it close. ''Go, ye scut!'' A horny hand sent Cappen stumbling to the rail.

He cried out once again. An ax lifted above his head. Someone handed him his own slim sword, and for a wild moment he thought of fighting. Useless—too many of them. He buckled on the sword and spat at the men. The wind tossed it back in his face, and they raved with laughter.

Over the side! The boat rose to meet him, he landed in a heap on drenched planks and looked up into the shadowy faces of the northmen. There was a sob in his throat as he found the seat and took out the oars.

An awkward pull sent him spinning from the ship, and then the night had swallowed it and he was alone. Numbly, he bent to the task. Unless he wanted to drown, there was no place to go but the island.

He was too weary and ill to be much afraid, and such fear as he had was all of the sea. It could rise over him, gulp him down, the gray horses would gallop over him and the long weeds would wrap him when he rolled dead against some skerry. The soft vales of Caronne and the roses in Croy's gardens seemed like a dream. There was only the roar and boom of the northern sea, hiss of sleet and spindrift, crazed scream of wind, he was alone as man had ever been and he would go down to the sharks alone.

The boat wallowed, but rode the waves better than the longship. He grew dully aware that the storm was pushing him toward the island. It was becoming visible, a deeper blackness harsh against the night.

He could not row much in the restless water; he shipped the oars and waited for the gale to capsize him and fill his mouth with the sea. And when it gurgled in his throat, what would his last thought be? Should he dwell on the lovely image of Ydris in Seilles, she of the long bright hair and the singing voice? But then there had been the tomboy laughter of dark Falkny, he could not neglect her. And there were memories of Elvanna in her castle by the lake, and Sirann of the Hundred Rings, and beauteous Vardry, and hawk-proud Lona, and—No,he could not do justice to any of them in the little time that remained. What a pity it was!

No, wait, that unforgettable night in Nienne, the beauty which had whispered in his ear and drawn him close, the hair which had fallen like a silken tent about his cheeks . . . ah, that had been the summit of his life, he would go down into darkness with her name on his lips . . . But hell! What *had* her name been, now?

Cappen Varra, minstrel of Croy, clung to the bench and sighed.

The great hollow voice of surf lifted about him, waves sheeted across the gunwale and the boat danced in madness. Cappen groaned, huddling into the circle of his own arms and shaking with cold. Swiftly, now, the end of all sunlight and laughter, the dark and lonely road which all men must tread. *O Ilwarra of Syr, Aedra in Tholis, could I but kiss you once more—*

Stones grated under the keel. It was a shock like a

sword going through him. Cappen looked unbelievingly up. The boat had drifted to land—he was alive!

It kindled the sun in his breast. Weariness fell from him, and he leaped overside, not feeling the chill of the shallows. With a grunt, he heaved the boat up on the narrow strand and knotted the painter to a fang-like jut of reef.

Then he looked about him. The island was small, utterly bare, a savage loom of rock rising out of the sea that growled at its feet and streamed off its shoulders. He had come into a little cliff-walled bay, somewhat sheltered from the wind. He was here!

For a moment he stood, running through all he had learned about the trolls which infested these northlands. Hideous and soulless dwellers underground, they knew not old age; a sword could hew them asunder, but before it reached their deep-seated life, their inhuman strength had plucked a man apart. Then they ate him—

Small wonder the northmen feared them. Cappen threw back his head and laughed. He had once done a service for a mighty wizard in the south, and his reward hung about his neck, a small silver amulet. The wizard had told him that no supernatural being could harm anyone who carried a piece of silver.

The Northmen said that a troll was powerless against a man who was not afraid; but, of course, only to see one was to feel the heart turn to ice. They did not know the value of silver, it seemed—odd that they shouldn't, but they did not. Because Cappen Varra did, he had no reason to be afraid; therefore he was doubly safe, and it was but a matter of talking the troll into giving him some fire. If indeed there was a troll here, and not some harmless fisherman.

He whistled gaily, wrung part of the water from his

cloak and ruddy hair, and started along the beach. In the sleety gloom, he could just see a hewn-out path winding up one of the cliffs and he set his feet on it.

At the top of the path, the wind ripped his whistling from his lips. He hunched his back against it and walked faster, swearing as he stumbled on hidden rocks. The ice-sheathed ground was slippery underfoot, and the cold bit like a knife.

Rounding a crag, he saw redness glow in the face of a steep bluff. A cave mouth, a fire within—he hastened his steps, hungering for warmth, until he stood in the entrance.

''Who comes?''

It was a hoarse bass cry that rang and boomed between walls of rock; ice and horror were in it, and for a moment Cappen's heart stumbled. Then he remembered the amulet and strode boldly inside.

''Good evening, mother,'' he said cheerily.

The cave widened out into a stony hugeness that gaped with tunnels leading further underground. The rough, soot-blackened walls were hung with plundered silks and cloth-of-gold, gone ragged through age and damp; the floor was strewn with stinking rushes, and gnawed bones were heaped in disorder. Cappen saw the skulls of men among them. In the center of the room, a great fire leaped and blazed, throwing billows of heat against him; some of its smoke went up a hole in the roof, the rest stung his eyes to watering and he sneezed.

The troll-wife crouched on the floor, snarling at him. She was quite the most hideous thing Cappen had ever seen: nearly as tall as he, she was twice as broad and thick, and the knotted arms hung down past bowed knees till their clawed fingers brushed the ground. Her head was beast-like, almost split in half by the tusked mouth, the eyes wells of darkness, the nose an ell long; her hairless skin was green and cold, moving on her bones. A tattered shift covered some of her monstrousness, but she was still a nightmare.

"Ho-ho, ho-ho!" Her laughter roared out, hungry and hollow as the surf around the island. Slowly, she shuffled closer. "So my dinner comes walking in to greet me, ho, ho, ho! Welcome, sweet flesh, welcome, good marrow-filled bones, come in and be warmed."

"Why, thank you, good mother." Cappen shucked his cloak and grinned at her through the smoke. He felt his clothes steaming already. "I love you too."

Over her shoulder, he suddenly saw the girl. She was huddled in a corner, wrapped in fear, but the eyes that watched him were as blue as the skies over Caronne. The ragged dress did not hide the gentle curves of her body, nor did the tear-streaked grime spoil the lilt of her face. "Why, 'tis springtime in here," cried Cappen, "and Primavera herself is strewing flowers of love."

"What are you talking about, crazy man?" rumbled the troll-wife. She turned to the girl. "Heap the fire, Hildigund, and set up the roasting spit. Tonight I feast!"

"Truly I see heaven in female form before me," said Cappen.

The troll scratched her misshapen head.

"You must surely be from far away, moonstruck man," she said.

"Aye, from golden Croy am I wandered, drawn over dolorous seas and empty wild lands by the fame of loveliness waiting here; and now that I have seen you, my life is full." Cappen was looking at the girl as he spoke, but he hoped the troll might take it as aimed her way.

"It will be fuller," grinned the monster. "Stuffed with hot coals while yet you live." She glanced back at the girl. "What, are you not working yet, you lazy tub of lard? Set up the spit, I said!"

The girl shuddered back against a heap of wood. "No," she whispered. "I cannot—not . . . not for a man."

"Can and will, my girl," said the troll, picking up a bone to throw at her. The girl shrieked a little.

"No, no, sweet mother. I would not be so ungallant as to have beauty toil for me." Cappen plucked at the troll's filthy dress. "It is not meet—in two senses. I only came to beg a little fire; yet will I bear away a greater fire within my heart."

"Fire in your guts, you mean! No man ever left me save as picked bones."

Cappen thought he heard a worried note in the animal growl. "Shall we have music for the feast?" he asked mildly. He unslung the case of his harp and took it out.

The troll-wife waved her fists in the air and danced with rage. "Are you mad? I tell you, you are going to be eaten!"

The minstrel plucked a string on his harp. "This wet air has played the devil with her tone," he murmured sadly.

The troll-wife roared wordlessly and lunged at him. Hildigund covered her eyes. Cappen tuned his harp. A foot from his throat, the claws stopped.

"Pray do not excite yourself, mother," said the bard. "I carry silver, you know."

"What is that to me? If you think you have a charm which will turn me, know that there is none. I've no fear of your metal!"

Cappen threw back his head and sang:

"A lovely lady full oft lies.
The light that lies within her eyes
and lies and lies, is no surprise.
All her unkindness can devise
to trouble hearts that seek the prize
which is herself, are angel lies—"

"*Aaaarrgh!*" It was like thunder drowning him out. The troll-wife turned and went on all fours and poked up the fire with her nose.

Cappen stepped softly around her and touched the girl. She looked up with a little whimper.

"You are Svearek's only daughter, are you not?" he whispered.

"Aye—" She bowed her head, a strengthless despair weighing it down. "The troll stole me away three winters agone. It has tickled her to have a princess for slave—but soon I shall roast on her spit, even as ye, brave man—"

"Ridiculous. So fair a lady is meant for another kind of, um, never mind! Has she treated you very ill?"

"She beats me now and again—and I have been so lonely, naught here at all save the troll-wife and I—" The small work-roughened hands clutched desperately at his waist, and she buried her face against his breast. "Can ye save us?" she gasped. "I fear 'tis for naught ye ventured yer life, bravest of men. I fear we'll soon both sputter on the coals."

Cappen said nothing. If she wanted to think he had come especially to rescue her, he would not be so ungallant to tell her otherwise.

The troll-wife's mouth gashed in a grin as she walked through the fire to him. "There is a price," she said. "If you cannot tell me three things about myself which are true beyond disproving, not courage nor amulet nor the gods themselves may avail to keep that head on your shoulders.''

Cappen clapped a hand to his sword. ''Why, gladly,'' he said; this was a rule of magic he had learned long ago, that three truths were the needful armor to make any guardian charm work. ''Imprimis, yours is the ugliest nose I ever saw poking up a fire. Secundus, I was never in a house I cared less to guest at. Tertius, even among trolls you are little liked, being one of the worst.''

Hildigund moaned with terror as the monster swelled in rage. But there was no movement. Only the leaping flames and the eddying smoke stirred.

Cappen's voice rang out, coldly: ''Now the king lies on the sea, frozen and wet, and I am come to fetch a brand for his fire. And I had best also see his daughter home.''

The troll shook her head, suddenly chuckling. ''No. The brand you may have, just to get you out of this cave, foulness; but the woman is in my thrall until a man sleeps with her—here—for a night. And if he does, I may have him to break my fast in the morning!''

Cappen yawned mightily. ''Thank you, mother. Your offer of a bed is most welcome to these tired bones, and I accept gratefully.''

''You will die tomorrow!'' she raved. The ground shook under the huge weight of her as she stamped. ''Because of the three truths, I must let you go tonight; but tomorrow I may do what I will!''

''Forget not my little friend, mother,'' said Cappen, and touched the cord of the amulet.

''I tell you, silver has no use against me—''

Cappen sprawled on the floor and rippled fingers across his harp. *''A lovely lady full oft lies—''*

The troll-wife turned from him in a rage. Hildigund

ladled up some broth, saying nothing, and Cappen ate it with pleasure, though it could have used more seasoning.

After that he indited a sonnet to the princess, who regarded him wide-eyed. The troll came back from a tunnel after he finished, and said curtly: "This way." Cappen took the girl's hand and followed her into a pitchy, reeking dark.

She plucked an arras side to show a room which surprised him by being hung with tapestries, lit with candles, and furnished with a fine broad featherbed. "Sleep here tonight, if you dare," she growled. "And tomorrow I shall eat you—and you, worthless lazy she-trash, will have the hide flayed off your back!" She barked a laugh and left them.

Hildigund fell weeping on the mattress. Cappen let her cry herself out while he undressed and got between the blankets. Drawing his sword, he laid it carefully in the middle of the bed.

The girl looked at him through jumbled fair locks. "How can ye dare?" she whispered. "One breath of fear, one moment's doubt, and the troll is free to rend ye."

"Exactly." Cappen yawned. "Doubtless she hopes that will come to my lying wakeful in the night. Wherefore 'tis but a question of going gently to sleep. O Svearek, Torbek, and Beorna, could you but see how I am resting now!"

"But . . . the three truths ye gave her . . . how knew ye . . . ?"

"Oh, those. Well, see you, sweet lady, Primus and Secundus were my own thoughts, and who is to disprove them? Tertius was also clear, since you said there had been no company here in three years—yet are there many trolls in these lands, ergo even they cannot stomach our gentle hostess.'' Cappen watched her through heavy-lidded eyes.

She flushed deeply, blew out the candles, and he heard her slip off her garment and get in with him. There was a long silence.

Then: ''Are ye not—''

''Yes, fair one?'' he muttered through his drowsiness.

''Are ye not . . . well, I am here and ye are here and—''

''Fear not,'' he said. ''I laid my sword between us. Sleep in peace.''

''I . . . would be glad—ye have come to deliver—''

''No, fair lady. No man of gentle breeding could so abuse his power. Goodnight.'' He leaned over, brushing his lips gently across hers, and lay down again.

''Ye are . . . I never thought man could be so noble,'' she whispered.

Cappen mumbled something. As his soul spun into sleep, he chuckled. Those unresting days and nights on the sea had not left him fit for that kind of exercise. But, of course, if she wanted to think he was being magnanimous, it could be useful later—

He woke with a start and looked into the sputtering glare of a torch. Its light wove across the crags and gullies of the troll-wife's face and shimmered wetly off the great tusks in her mouth.

''Good morning, mother,'' said Cappen politely.

Hildigund thrust back a scream.

''Come and be eaten,'' said the troll-wife.

''No, thank you,'' said Cappen, regretfully but firmly. '' 'Twould be ill for my health. No, I will but trouble you for a firebrand and then the princess and I will be off.''

"If you think that stupid bit of silver will protect you, think again," she snapped. "Your three sentences were all that saved you last night. Now I hunger."

"Silver," said Cappen didactically, "is a certain shield against all black imagics. So the wizard told me, and he was such a nice white-bearded old man I am sure even his attendant devils never lied. Now please depart, mother, for modesty forbids me to dress before your eyes."

The hideous face thrust close to his. He smiled dreamily and tweaked her nose—hard.

She howled and flung the torch at him. Cappen caught it and stuffed it into her mouth. She choked and ran from the room.

"A new sport—trollbaiting," said the bard gaily into the sudden darkness. "Come, shall we not venture out?"

The girl trembled too much to move. He comforted her, absentmindedly, and dressed in the dark, swearing at the clumsy leggings. When he left, Hildigund put on her clothes and hurried after him.

The troll-wife squatted by the fire and glared at them as they went by. Cappen hefted his sword and looked at her. "I do not love you," he said mildly, and hewed out.

She backed away, shrieking as she slashed at her. In the end, she crouched at the mouth of a tunnel, raging futilely. Cappen pricked her with his blade.

"It is not worth my time to follow you down underground," he said, "but if ever you trouble men again, I will hear of it and come and feed you to my dogs. A piece at a time—a very small piece—do you understand?"

She snarled at him.

"An *extremely* small piece," said Cappen amiably. "Have you heard me?"

Something broke in her. "Yes," she whimpered. He let her go, and she scuttled from him like a rat.

He remembered the firewood and took an armful; on the way, he thoughtfully picked up a few jeweled rings which he didn't think she would be needing and stuck them in his pouch. Then he led the girl outside.

The wind had laid itself, a clear frosty morning glittered on the sea and the longship was a distant sliver against white-capped blueness. The minstrel groaned. "What a distance to row! Oh, well—"

They were at sea before Hildigund spoke. Awe was in the eyes that watched him. "No man could be so brave," she murmured. "Are ye a god?"

"Not quite," said Cappen. "No, most beautiful one, modesty grips my tongue. 'Twas but that I had the silver and was therefore proof against her sorcery."

"But the silver was no help!" she cried.

Cappen's oar caught a crab. "What?" he yelled.

"No—no—why, she told ye so her own self—"

"I thought she lied. I *know* the silver guards against—"

"But she used no magic! Trolls have but their own strength!"

Cappen sagged in his seat. For a moment he thought he was going to faint. Then only his lack of fear had armored him; and if he had known the truth, that would not have lasted a minute.

He laughed shakily. Another score for his doubts about the overall value of truth!

The longship's oars bit water and approached him. Indignant voices asking why he had been so long on his errand faded when his passenger was seen. And

Svearek the king wept as he took his daughter back into his arms.

The hard brown face was still blurred with tears when he looked at the minstrel, but the return of his old self was there too. "What ye have done, Cappen Varra of Croy, is what no other man in the world could have done."

"Aye—aye—" The rough northern voices held adoration as the warriors crowded around the slim red-haired figure.

"Ye shall have her whom ye saved to wife," said Svearek, "and when I die ye shall rule all Norren."

Cappen swayed and clutched the rail.

Three nights later he slipped away from their shore camp and turned his face southward.

The Gate of the Flying Knives

When Robert Asprin was planning the first of his popular *Thieves' World* anthologies, he asked me for a contribution. It sounded like fun. Furthermore, it offered a chance to bring back Cappen Varra. I rather like that scoundrel.

Again penniless, houseless, and ladyless, Cappen Varra made a brave sight just the same as he wove his way amidst the bazaar throng. After all, until today he had for some weeks been in, if not quite of, the household of Molin Torchholder, as much as he could contrive. Besides the dear presence of ancilla Danlis, he had received generous reward from the priest-engineer whenever he sang a song or composed a poem. That situation had changed with suddenness and terror, but he still wore a bright green tunic, scarlet cloak, canary hose, soft half-boots trimmed in silver, and plumed beret. Though naturally heartsick at what had happened, full of dread for his darling, he saw no reason to sell the garb yet. He could raise enough money in various ways to live on while he searched for her. If need be, as often before, he could pawn the harp that a goldsmith was presently redecorating.

If his quest had not succeeded by the time he was reduced to rags, then he would have to suppose Danlis and the Lady Rosanda were forever lost. But he had never been one to grieve over future sorrows.

Beneath a westering sun, the bazaar surged and clamored. Merchants, artisans, porters, servants, slaves, wives, nomads, courtesans, entertainers, beggars, thieves, gamblers, magicians, acolytes, soldiers, and who knew what else mingled, chattered, chaffered, quarreled, plotted, sang, played games, drank, ate, and who knew what else. Horsemen, cameldrivers, wagoners pushed through, raising waves of curses. Music tinkled and tweedled from wineshops. Vendors proclaimed the wonders of their wares from booths, neighbors shouted at each other, and devotees chanted from flat rooftops. Smells thickened the air, of flesh, sweat, roast meat and nuts, aromatic drinks, leather, wool, dung, smoke, oils, cheap perfume.

Ordinarily, Cappen Varra enjoyed this shabby-colorful spectacle. Now he single-mindedly hunted through it. He kept full awareness, of course, as everybody must in Sanctuary. When light fingers brushed him, he knew. But whereas aforetime he would have chuckled and told the pickpurse, "I'm sorry, friend; I was hoping I might lift somewhat off you," at this hour he clapped his sword in such forbidding wise that the fellow recoiled against a fat woman and made her drop a brass tray full of flowers. She screamed and started beating him over the head with it.

Cappen didn't stay to watch.

On the eastern edge of the marketplace he found what he wanted. Once more Illyra was in the bad graces of her colleagues and had moved her trade to a stall available elsewhere. Black curtains framed it, against a mud-brick wall. Reek from a nearby tannery well-nigh drowned the incense she burned in a curious holder, and would surely overwhelm any of her herbs. She herself also lacked awesomeness, such as most seeresses, mages, conjurers, scryers, and the like affected. She was too young; she would have looked almost wistful in her flowing, gaudy S'danzo garments, had she not been so beautiful.

Cappen gave her a bow in the manner of Caronne. "Good day, Illyra the lovely," he said.

She smiled from the cushion whereon she sat. "Good day to you, Cappen Varra." They had had a number of talks, usually in jest, and he had sung for her entertainment. He had hankered to do more than that, but she seemed to keep all men at a certain distance, and a hulk of a blacksmith who evidently adored her saw to it that they respected her wish.

"Nobody in these parts has met you for a fair while," she remarked. "What fortune was great enough to make you forget old friends?"

"My fortune was mingled, inasmuch as it left me without time to come down here and behold you, my sweet," he answered out of habit.

Lightness departed from Illyra. In the olive countenance, under the chestnut mane, large eyes focused hard on her visitor. "You find time when you need help in disaster," she said.

He had not patronized her before, or indeed any fortune-teller or thaumaturge in Sanctuary. In Caronne, where he grew up, most folk had no use for magic. In his later wanderings he had encountered sufficient strangeness to temper his native skepticism. As shaken as he already was, he felt a chill go along his spine. "Do you read my fate without even casting a spell?"

She smiled afresh, but bleakly. "Oh, no. It's simple reason. Word did filter back to the Maze that you were residing in the Jewelers' Quarter and a frequent guest at the mansion of Molin Torchholder. When you appear on the heels of a new word—that last night his wife was reaved from him—plain to see is that you've been affected yourself."

He nodded. "Yes, and sore afflicted. I have lost—" He hesitated, unsure whether it would be quite wise to say "—my love—" to this girl whose charms he had rather extravagantly praised.

"—your position and income," Illyra snapped. "The high priest cannot be in any mood for minstrelsy. I'd guess his wife favored you most, anyhow. I need not guess you spent your earnings as fast as they fell to you, or faster, were behind in your rent, and were accordingly kicked out of your choice apartment as soon as rumor reached the landlord. You've returned to the Maze because you've no place else to go, and to me in hopes you can wheedle me into giving you a clue—for if you're instrumental in recovering the lady, you'll likewise recover your fortune, and more."

"No, no, no," he protested. "You wrong me."

"The high priest will appeal only to his Rankan gods," Illyra said, her tone changing from exasperated to the thoughtful. She stroked her chin. "He, kinsman of the Emperor, here to direct the building of a temple which will overtop that if Ils, can hardly beg aid from the old gods of Sanctuary, let alone from our wizards, witches, and seers. But you, who belong to no part of the Empire, who drifted hither from a kingdom far in the West . . . you may seek anywhere. The idea is your own; else he would furtively have slipped you some gold, and you have engaged a diviner with more reputation than is mine.''

Cappen spread his hands. ''You reason eerily well, dear lass,'' he conceded. ''Only about the motives are you mistaken. Oh, yes, I'd be glad to stand high in Molin's esteem, be richly rewarded, and so forth. Yet I feel for him; beneath that sternness of his, he's not a bad sort, and he bleeds. Still more do I feel for his lady, who was indeed kind to me and who's been snatched away to an unknown place. But before all else—'' He grew quite earnest. ''The Lady Rosanda was not seized by herself. Her ancilla has also vanished, Danlis. And—Danlis is she whom I love, Illyra, she whom I meant to wed.''

The maiden's looked probed him further. She saw a young man of medium height, slender but tough and agile. (That was due to the life he had had to lead; by nature he was indolent, except in bed.) His features were thin and regular on a long skull, clean-shaven, eyes bright blue, black hair banged and falling to the shoulders. His voice gave the language a melodious accent, as if to bespeak white cities, green fields and woods, quicksilver lakes, blue sea, of the homeland he left in search of his fortune.

''Well, you have charm, Cappen Varra,'' she murmured, ''and how you do know it.'' Alert: ''But coin you lack. How do you propose to pay me?''

''I fear you must work on speculation, as I do myself,'' he said. ''If our joint efforts lead to a rescue, why, then we'll share whatever material reward may come. Your part might buy you a home on the Path of Money.'' She frowned. ''True,'' he went on, ''I'll get more than my share of the immediate bounty that Molin bestows. I will have my beloved back. I'll also regain the priest's favor, which is moderately lucrative.

Yet consider. You need but practice your art. Thereafter any effort and risk will be mine."

"What makes you suppose a humble fortune-teller can learn more than the Prince Governant's investigator guardsmen?" she demanded.

"The matter does not seem to lie within their jurisdiction," he replied.

She leaned forward, tense beneath the layers of clothing. Cappen bent toward her. It was as if the babble of the marketplace receded, leaving these two alone with their wariness.

"I was not there," he said low, "but I arrived early this morning after the thing had happened. What's gone through the city has been rumor, leakage that cannot be caulked, household servants blabbing to friends outside and they blabbing onward. Molin's locked away most of the facts till he can discover what they mean, if ever he can. I, however, I came on the scene while chaos still prevailed. Nobody kept me from talking to folk, before the lord himself saw me and told me to begone. Thus I know about as much as anyone, little though that be."

"And—?" she prompted.

"And it doesn't seem to have been a worldly sort of capture, for a worldly end like ransom. See you, the mansion's well guarded, and neither Molin nor his wife have ever gone from it without escort. His mission here is less than popular, you recall. Those troopers are from Ranke and not subornable. The house stands in a garden, inside a high wall whose top is patrolled. Three leopards run loose on the grounds after dark.

"Molin had business with his kinsman the Prince, and spent the night at the palace. His wife, the Lady Rosanda, stayed home, retired, later came out and complained she could not sleep. She therefore had

Danlis wakened. Danlis is no chambermaid; there are plenty of those. She's amanuensis, adviser, confidante, collector of information, ofttimes guide or interpreter—oh, she earns her pay, does my Danlis. Despite she and I having a dawntide engagement, which is why I arrived then, she must now out of bed at Rosanda's whim, to hold milady's hand or take dictation of milady's letters or read to milady from a soothing book—but I'm a spendthrift of words. Suffice to say that they two sought an upper chamber which is furnished as both solarium and office. A single staircase leads thither, and it is the single room at the top. There is a balcony, yes; and, the night being warm, the door to it stood open, as well as the windows. But I inspected the facade beneath. That's sheer marble, undecorated save for varying colors, devoid of ivy or of anything that any climber might cling to, save he were a fly.

"Nevertheless . . . just before the east grew pale, shrieks were heard. The watch pelted to the stair and up it. They must break down the inner door, which was bolted. I suppose that was merely against chance interruptions, for nobody had felt threatened. The solarium was in disarray; vases and things were broken; shreds torn off a robe and slight traces of blood lay about. Aye, Danlis, at least, would have resisted. But she and her mistress were gone.

"A couple of sentries on the garden wall reported hearing a loud sound as of wings. The night was cloudy-dark and they saw nothing for certain. Perhaps they imagined the noise. Suggestive is that the leopards were found cowering in a corner and welcomed their keeper when he would take them back to their cages.

"And this is the whole of anyone's knowledge, Illyra," Cappen ended. "Help me, I pray you, help me get back my love!"

She was long quiet. Finally she said, in a near whisper, "It could be a worse matter than I'd care to peer into, let alone enter."

"Or it could not," Cappen urged.

She gave him a quasi-defiant stare. "My mother's people reckon it unlucky to do any service for a Shavakh—a person not of their tribe—without recompense. Pledges don't count."

Cappen scowled. "Well, I could go to a pawnshop and—But no, time may be worth more than rubies." From the depths of unhappiness, his grin broke forth. "Poems also are valuable, right? You S'danzo have your ballads and love ditties. Let me indite a poem, Illyra, that shall be yours alone."

Her expression quickened. "Truly?"

"Truly. Let me think . . . Aye, we'll begin thus." And, venturing to take her hands in his, Cappen murmured:

> *"My lady comes to me like break of day.*
> *I dream in darkness if it chance she tarries,*
> *Until the banner of her brightness harries*
> *The hosts of Shadowland from off the way—"*

She jerked free and cried, "No! You scoundrel, that has to be something you did for Danlis—or for some earlier woman you wanted in your bed—"

"But it isn't finished," he argued. "I'll complete it for you, Illyra."

Anger left her. She shook her head, clicked her tongue, and sighed. "No matter. You're incurably yourself. And I . . . am only half S'danzo. I'll attempt your spell."

"By every love goddess I ever heard of," he promised unsteadily, "you shall indeed have your own poem after this is over."

"Be still," she ordered. "Fend off anybody who comes near."

He faced about and drew his sword. The slim, straight blade was hardly needed, for no other enterprise had site within several yards of hers, and as wide a stretch of paving lay between him and the fringes of the crowd. Still, to grasp the hilt gave him a sense of finally making progress. He had felt helpless for the first hours, hopeless, as if his dear had actually died instead of—of what? Behind him he heard cards riffled, dice cast, words softly wailed.

All at once Illyra strangled a shriek. He whirled about and saw how the blood had left her olive countenance, turning it grey. She hugged herself and shuddered.

"What's wrong?" he blurted in fresh terror.

She did not look at him. "Go away," she said in a thin voice. "Forget you ever knew that woman."

"But—but what—"

"Go away, I told you! Leave me alone!"

Then somehow she relented enough to let forth: "I don't know. I dare not know. I'm just a little half-breed girl who has a few cantrips and a tricksy second sight, and—and I saw that this business goes outside of space and time, and a power beyond any magic is there—Enas Yorl could tell more, but he himself—" Her courage broke. "Go away!" she screamed. "Before I shout for Dubro and his hammer!"

"I beg your pardon," Cappen Varra said, and made haste to obey.

He retreated into the twisting streets of the Maze. They were narrow; most of the mean buildings around him were high; gloom already filled the quarter. It was as if he had stumbled into the same night when Danlis had gone . . . Danlis, creature of sun and horizons. . . . If she lived, did she remember their last time together as he remembered it, a dream dreamed centuries ago?

Having the day free, she had wanted to explore the countryside north of town. Cappen had objected on three counts. The first he did not mention; that it would require a good deal of effort, and he would get dusty and sweaty and saddlesore. She despised men who were not at least as vigorous as she was, unless they compensated by being venerable and learned.

The second he hinted at. Sleazy though most of Sanctuary was, he knew places within it where a man and a woman could enjoy themselves, comfortably, privately—his apartment, for instance. She smiled her negation. Her family belonged to the old aristocracy of Ranke, not the newly rich, and she had been raised in its austere tradition. Albeit her father had fallen on evil times and she had been forced to take service, she kept her pride, and proudly would she yield her maidenhead to her bridegroom. Thus far she had answered Cappen's ardent declarations with the admission that she liked him and enjoyed his company and wished he would change the subject. (Buxom Lady Rosanda seemed as if she might be more approachable, but there he was careful to maintain a cheerful correctness.) He did believe she was getting beyond simple enjoyment, for her patrician reserve seemed less each time they saw each other. Yet she could not altogether have forgotten that he was merely the bastard of a minor nobleman in a remote country, himself disinherited and a footloose minstrel.

His third objection he dared say forth. While the hinterland was comparatively safe, Molin Torchholder would be furious did he learn that a woman of his household had gone escorted by a single armed man, and he no professional fighter. Molin would probably have been justified, too. Danlis smiled again and said, "I could ask a guardsman off duty to come along. But you have interesting friends, Cappen. Perhaps a warrior is among them?"

As a matter of fact, he knew any number, but doubted she would care to meet them—with a single exception. Luckily, Jamie the Red had no prior commitment, and agreed to join the party. Cappen told the kitchen staff to pack a picnic hamper for four.

Jamie's girls stayed behind; this was not their sort of outing, and the sun might harm their complexions. Cappen thought it a bit ungracious of the Northerner never to share them. That put him, Cappen, to considerable expense in the Street of Red Lanterns, since he could scarcely keep a paramour of his own while wooing Danlis. Otherwise he was fond of Jamie. They had met after Rosanda, chancing to hear the minstrel sing, had invited him to perform at the mansion, and then invited him back, and presently Cappen was living in the Jeweler's Quarter. Jamie had an apartment nearby.

Three horses and a pack mule clopped out of Sanctuary in the new-born morning, to a jingle of harness bells. That merriment found no echo in Cappen's head; he had been drinking past midnight, and in no case enjoyed rising before noon. Passive, he listened to Jamie:

"—Aye, milady, they're mountaineers where I hail from, poor folk but free folk. Some might call us barbarians, but that might be unwise in our hearing. For we've tales, songs, laws, ways, gods as old as any in the world, and as good. We lack much of your

Southern lore, but how much of ours do you ken? Not that I boast, please understand. I've seen wonders in my wanderings. But I do say we've a few wonders of our own at home."

"I'd like to hear of them," Danlis responded. "We know almost nothing about your country in the Empire—hardly more than mentions in the chronicles of Venafer and Mattathan, or the *Natural History* of Kahayavesh. How do you happen to come here?"

"Oh-ah, I'm a younger son of our king, and I thought I'd see a bit of the world before settling down. Not that I packed any wealth along to speak of. But what with one thing and another, hiring out hither and yon for this or that, I get by." Jamie paused. "You, uh, you've far more to tell, milady. You're from the crown city of the Empire, and you've got book learning, and at the same time you come out to see for yourself what land and rocks and plants and animals are like."

Cappen decided he had better get into the conversation. Not that Jamie would undercut a friend, nor Danlis be unduly attracted by a wild highlander. Nevertheless—

Jamie wasn't bad-looking in his fashion. He was huge, topping Cappen by a head and disproportionately wide in the shoulders. His loose-jointed appearance was deceptive, as the bard had learned when they sported in a public gymnasium; those were heavy bones and oak-hard muscles. A spectacular red mane drew attention from boyish face, mild blue eyes, and slightly diffident manner. Today he was plainly clad, in tunic and cross-gaitered breeks; but the knife at his belt and the ax at his saddlebow stood out.

As for Danlis, well, what could a poet do but struggle for words which might embody a ghost of her glory? She was tall and slender, her features almost cold in their straight-lined perfection and alabaster hue—till you observed the big grey eyes, golden hair piled on high, curve of lips whence came that husky voice. (How often had he lain awake yearning for her lips! He would console himself by remembering the strong, delicately blue-veined hand that she did let him kiss.) Despite waxing warmth and dust puffed up from the horses' hoofs, her cowled riding habit remained immaculate and no least dew of sweat was on her skin.

By the time Cappen got his wits out of the blankets wherein they had still been snoring, talk had turned to gods. Danlis was curious about those of Jamie's country, as she was about most things. (She did shun a few subjects as being unwholesome.) Jamie in his turn was eager to have her explain what was going on in Sanctuary. "I've heard but the one side of the matter, and Cappen's indifferent to it," he said. "Folk grumble about your master—Molin, is that his name—?"

"He is not my master," Danlis made clear. "I am a free woman who assists his wife. He himself is a high priest in Ranke, also an engineer."

"Why is the Emperor angering Sanctuary? Most places I've been, colonial governments know better. They leave the local gods be."

Danlis grew pensive. "Where shall I start? Doubtless you know that Sanctuary was originally a city of the kingdom of Ilsig. Hence it has built temples to the gods of Ilsig—notably Ils, Lord of Lords, and his queen Shipri the All-Mother, but likewise others—Anen of the Harvests, Thufir the tutelary of pilgrims—"

"But none to Shalpa, patron of thieves," Cappen put in, "though these days he has the most devotees of any."

Danlis ignored his jape. "Ranke was quite a different

country, under quite different gods,'' she continued. ''Chief of these are Savankala the Thunderer, his consort Sabellia, Lady of Stars, their son Vashanka the Tenslayer, and his sister and consort Azyuna—gods of storm and war. According to Venafer, it was they who made Ranke supreme at last. Mattathan is more prosaic and opines that the martial spirit they inculcated was responsible for the Rankan Empire finally taking Ilsig into itself.''

''Yes, milady, yes, I've heard this,'' Jamie said, while Cappen reflected that if his beloved had a fault, it was her tendency to lecture.

''Sanctuary has changed from of yore,'' she proceeded. ''It has become polyglot, turbulent, corrupt, a canker on the body politic. Among its most vicious elements are the proliferating alien cults, not to speak of necromancers, witches, charlatans, and similar predators on the people. The time is overpast to restore law here. Nothing less than the Imperium can do that. A necessary preliminary is the establishment of the Imperial deities, the gods of Ranke, for everyone to see: symbol, rallying point, and actual presence.''

''But they *have* their temples,'' Jamie argued.

''Small, dingy, to accommodate Rankans, few of whom stay in the city for long,'' Danlis retorted. ''What reverence does that inspire, for the pantheon and the state? No, the Emperor has decided that Savankala and Sabellia must have the greatest fane, the most richly endowed, in this entire province. Molin Torchholder will build and consecrate it. Then can the degenerates and warlocks be scourged out of Sanctuary. Afterward the Prince Government can handle common felons.''

Cappen didn't expect matters would be that simple. He got no chance to say so, for Jamie asked at once, ''Is this wise, milady? True, many a soul hereabouts worships foreign gods, or none. But many still adore the old gods of Ilsig. They look on your, uh, Savankala as an intruder. I intend no offense, but they do. They're outraged that he's to have a bigger and grander house than Ils of the Thousand Eyes. Some fear what Ils may do about it."

"I know," Danlis said. "I regret any distress caused, and I'm sure Lord Molin does too. Still, we must overcome the agents of darkness, before the disease that they are spreads throughout the Empire."

"Oh, no," Cappen managed to insert, "I've lived here awhile, mostly down in the Maze. I've had to do with a good many so-called magicians, of either sex or in between. They aren't that bad. Most I'd call pitiful. They just use their little deceptions to scrabble out what living they can, in this crumbly town where life has trapped them."

Danlis gave him a sharp glance. "You've told me people think ill of sorcery in Caronne," she said.

"They do," he admitted. "But that's because we incline to be rationalists, who consider nearly all magic a bag of tricks. Which is true. Why, I've learned a few sleights myself."

"You have?" Jamie rumbled in surprise.

"For amusement," Cappen said hastily, before Danlis could disapprove. "Some are quite elegant, virtual exercises in three-dimensional geometry." Seeing interest kindle in her, he added, "I studied mathematics in boyhood; my father, before he died, wanted me to have a gentleman's education. The main part has rusted away in me, but I remember useful or picturesque details."

"Well, give us a show, come luncheon time," Jamie proposed.

Cappen did, when they halted. That was on a hillside above the White Foal River. It wound gleaming through farmlands whose intense green denied that desert lurked on the rim of sight. The noonday sun baked strong odors out of the earth: humus, resin, juice of wild plants. A solitary plane tree graciously gave shade. Bees hummed.

After the meal, and after Danlis had scrambled off to get a closer look at a kind of lizard new to her, Cappen demonstrated his skill. She was especially taken—enchanted—by his geometric artifices. Like any Rankan lady, she carried a sewing kit in her gear; and being herself, she had writing materials along. Thus he could apply scissors and thread to paper. He showed how a single ring may be cut to produce two that are interlocked, and how a strip may be twisted to have but one surface and one edge, and whatever else he knew. Jamie watched with pleasure, if with less enthusiasm.

Observing how delight made her glow, Cappen was inspired to carry on the latest poem he was composing for her. It had been slower work than usual. He had the conceit, the motif, a comparison of her to the dawn, but hitherto only the first few lines had emerged, and no proper structure. In this moment—

—the banner of her brightness harries
The hosts of Shadowland from off the way
That she now wills to tread—for what can stay
The triumph of that radiance she carries?

Yes, it was clearly going to be a rondel. Therefore the next two lines were:

My lady comes to me like break of day.
I dream in darkness if it chance she tarries.

He had gotten that far when abruptly she said: "Cappen, this is such a fine excursion, such splendid scenery. I'd like to watch sunrise over the river tomorrow. Will you escort me?"

Sunrise? But she was telling Jamie, "We need not trouble you about that. I had in mind a walk out of town to the bridge. If we choose the proper route, it's well guarded everywhere, perfectly safe."

And scant traffic moved at that hour; besides, the monumental statues along the bridge stood in front of bays which they screened from passersby—"Oh, yes, indeed, Danlis, I'd love to," Cappen said. For such an opportunity, he could get up before cockcrow.

—When he reached the mansion, she had not been there.

Exhausted after his encounter with Illyra, Cappen hied him to the Vulgar Unicorn and related his woes to One-Thumb. The big man had come on shift at the inn early, for a fellow boniface had not yet recovered from the effects of a dispute with a patron. (Shortly thereafter, the patron was found floating face down under a pier. Nobody questioned One-Thumb about this; his regulars knew that he preferred the establishment safe, if not always orderly.) He offered taciturn sympathy and the loan of a bed upstairs. Cappen scarcely noticed the insects that shared it.

Waking about sunset, he found water and a washcloth, and felt much refreshed—hungry and thirsty, too. He made his way to the taproom below. Dusk was blue in windows and open door, black under the rafters. Candles smeared weak light along counter and main board and on lesser tables at the walls. The air had grown cool, which allayed the stenches of the Maze. Thus Cappen was acutely aware of the smells of beer—old in the rushes underfoot, fresh where a trio of men had settled down to guzzle—and of spitted meat, wafting from the kitchen.

One-Thumb approached, a shadowy hulk save for highlights on his bald pate. "Sit," he grunted. "Eat. Drink." He carried a great tankard and a plate bearing a slab of roast beef on bread. These he put on a corner table, and himself on a chair.

Cappen sat also and attacked the meal. "You're very kind," he said between bites and draughts.

"You'll pay when you get coin, or if you don't, then in songs and magic stunts. They're good for trade." One-Thumb fell silent and peered at his guest.

When Cappen was done, the innkeeper said, "While you slept, I sent out a couple of fellows to ask around. Maybe somebody saw something that might be helpful. Don't worry—I didn't mention you, and it's natural I'd be interested to know what really happened."

The minstrel stared. "You've gone to a deal of trouble on my account."

"I told you, I want to know for my own sake. If deviltry's afoot, where could it strike next?" One-Thumb rubbed a finger across the toothless part of his gums. "Of course, if you should luck out—I don't expect it, but in case you do—remember who gave you a boost." A figure appeared in the door and he went to render service.

After a bit of muttered talk, he led the newcomer to Cappen's place. When the minstrel recognized the lean youth, his pulse leaped. One-Thumb would not have brought him and Hanse together without cause; bard and thief found each other insufferable. They nodded coldly but did not speak until the tapster returned with a round of ale.

When the three were seated, One-Thumb said, "Well, spit it out, boy. You claim you've got news."

"For him?" Hanse flared, gesturing at Cappen.

"Never mind who. Just talk."

Hanse scowled. "I don't talk for a single lousy mugful."

"You do if you want to keep on coming in here."

Hanse bit his lip. The Vulgar Unicorn was a rendezvous virtually indispensable to one in his trade.

Cappen thought best to sweeten the pill: "I'm known to Molin Torchholder. If I can serve him in this matter, he won't be stingy. Nor will I. Shall we say—hm—ten gold royals to you?"

The sum was not princely, but on that account plausible. "Awright, awright," Hanse replied. "I'd been casing a job I might do in the Jewelers' Quarter. A squad of the watch came by toward morning and I figured I'd better go home, not by the way I came, either. So I went along the Avenue of Temples, as I might be wanting to stop in and pay my respects to some god or other. It was a dark night, overcast, the reason I'd been out where I was. But you know how several of the temples keep lights going. There was enough to see by, even upward a ways. Nobody else was in sight. Suddenly I heard a kind of whistling, flapping noise aloft. I looked and—"

He broke off.

"And what?" Cappen blurted. One-Thumb sat impassive.

Hanse swallowed. "I don't swear to this," he said. "It was still dim, you realize. I've wondered since if I didn't see wrong."

"What was it?" Cappen gripped the table edge till his fingernails whitened.

Hanse wet his throat and said in a rush: "What it

seemed like was a huge black thing, almost like a snake, but bat-winged. It came streaking from, oh, more or less the direction of Molin's, I guess now that I think back. And it was aimed more or less toward the temple of Ils. There was something that dangled below, as it might be a human body or two. I didn't stay to watch, I ducked into the nearest alley and waited. When I came out, it was gone."

He knocked back his ale and rose. "That's all," he snapped. "I don't want to remember the sight any longer, and if anybody ever asks, I was never here tonight."

"Your story's worth a couple more drinks," One-Thumb invited.

"Another evening," Hanse demurred. "Right now I need a whore. Don't forget those ten royals, singer." He left, stiff-legged.

"Well," said the innkeeper after a silence, "what do you make of this latest?"

Cappen suppressed a shiver. His palms were cold. "I don't know, save that what we confront is not of our kind."

"You told me once you've got a charm against magic."

Cappen fingered the little silver amulet, in the form of a coiled snake, he wore around his neck. "I'm not sure. A wizard I'd done a favor for gave me this, years ago. He claimed it'd protect me against spells and supernatural beings of less than godly rank. But to make it work, I have to utter three truths about the spellcaster or the creature. I've done that in two or three scrapes, and come out of them intact, but I can't prove the talisman was responsible."

More customers entered, and One-Thumb must go to serve them. Cappen nursed his ale. He yearned to get drunk and belike the landlord would stand him what was needful, but he didn't dare. He had already learned more than he thought the opposition would approve of—whoever or whatever the opposition was. They might have means of discovering this.

His candle flickered. He glanced up and saw a beardless fat man in an ornate formal robe, scarcely normal dress for a visit to the Vulgar Unicorn. "Greeting," the person said. His voice was like a child's.

Cappen squinted through the gloom. "I don't believe I know you," he replied.

"No, but you will come to believe it, oh, yes, you will." The fat man sat down. One-Thumb came over and took an order for red wine— "a decent wine, mine host, a Zhanuvend or Baladach." Coin gleamed forth.

Cappen's heart thumped. "Enas Yorl?" he breathed.

The other nodded. "In the flesh, the all too mutable flesh. I do hope my curse strikes again soon. Almost any shape would be better than this. I hate being overweight. I'm a eunuch, too. The times I've been a woman were better than this."

"I'm sorry, sir," Cappen took care to say. Though he could not rid himself of the spell laid on him, Enas Yorl was a powerful thaumaturge, no mere prestidigitator.

"At least I've not been arbitrarily displaced. You can't imagine how annoying it is, suddenly to find oneself elsewhere, perhaps miles away. I was able to come here in proper wise, in my litter. Faugh, how can anyone voluntarily set shoes to these open sewers they call streets in the Maze?" The wine arrived. "Best we speak fast and to the point, young man, that we may finish and I get home before the next contretemps."

Enas Yorl sipped and made a face. "I've been swindled," he whined. "This is barely drinkable, if that."

''Maybe your present palate is at fault, sir,'' Cappen suggested. He did not add that the tongue definitely had a bad case of logorrhea. It was an almost physical torture to sit stalled, but he had better humor the mage.

''Yes, quite probably. Nothing has tasted good since—Well. To business. On hearing that One-Thumb was inquiring about last night's incident, I sent forth certain investigators of my own. You will understand that I've been trying to find out as much as I can.'' Enas Yorl drew a sign in the air. ''Purely precautionary. I have no desire whatsoever to cross the Powers concerned in this.''

A wintry tingle went through Cappen. ''You know who they are, what it's about?'' His tone wavered.

Enas Yorl wagged a finger. ''Not so hasty, boy, not so hasty. My latest information was of a seemingly unsuccessful interview you had with Illyra the seeress. I also learned you were now in this hostel and close to its landlord. Obviously you are involved. I must know why, how, how much—everything.''

''Then you'll help—sir?''

A headshake made chin and jowls wobble. ''Absolutely not. I told you I want no part of this. But in exchange for whatever data you possess, I am willing to explicate as far as I am able, and to advise you. Be warned: my advice will doubtless be that you drop the matter and perhaps leave town.''

And doubtless he would be right, Cappen thought. It simply happened to be counsel that was impossible for a lover to follow . . . unless—O kindly gods of Caronne, no, no!—unless Danlis was dead.

The whole story spilled out of him, quickened and deepened by keen questions. At the end, he sat breathless while Enas Yorl nodded.

''Yes, that appears to confirm what I suspected,'' the

mage said most softly. He stared past the minstrel, into shadows that loomed and flickered. Buzz of talk, clink of drinking ware, occasional gust of laughter among customers seemed remoter than the moon.

"What was it?" broke from Cappen.

"A sikkintair, a Flying Knife. It can have been nothing else."

"A—what?"

Enas focused on his companion. "The monster that took the women," he explained. "Sikkintairs are an attribute of Ils. A pair of sculptures on the grand stairway of his temple represent them."

"Oh, yes, I've seen those, but never thought—"

"No, you're not a votary of any gods they have here. Myself, when I got word of the abduction, I sent my familiars scuttling about and cast spells of inquiry. I received indications. . . . I can't describe them to you, who lack arcane lore. I established that the very fabric of space had been troubled. Vibrations had not quite damped out as yet, and were centered on the temple of Ils. You may, if you wish a crude analogy, visualize a water surface and the waves, fading to ripples and finally to naught, when a diver has passed through."

Enas Yorl drank more in a gulp than was his wont. "Civilization was old in Ilsig when Ranke was still a barbarian village," he said, as though to himself; his gaze had drifted away again, toward darkness. "Its myths depicted the home of the gods as being outside the world—not above, not below, but outside. Philosophers of a later, more rationalistic era elaborated this into a theory of parallel universes. My own researches—you will understand that my condition has made me especially interested in the theory of dimensions, the subtler aspects of geometry—my own researches have demonstrated the possibility of transference between these different spaces.

"As another analogy, consider a pack of cards. One is inhabited by a king, one by a knight, one by a deuce, et cetera. Ordinarily none of the figures can leave the plane on which it exists. If, however, a very thin piece of absorbent material soaked in a unique kind of solvent were laid between two cards, the dyes that form them could pass through: retaining their configuration, I trust. Actually, of course, this is a less than ideal comparison, for the transference is accomplished through a particular contortion of the continuum—"

Cappen could endure no more pedantry. He crashed his tankard down on the table and shouted, "By all the hells of all the cults, will you get to the point?"

Men stared from adjacent seats, decided no fight was about to erupt, and went back to their interests. These included negotiations with streetwalkers who, lanterns in hand, had come in looking for trade.

Enas Yorl smiled. "I forgive your outburst, under the circumstances," he said. "I too am occasionally young.

"Very well. Given the foregoing data, including yours, the infrastructure of events seems reasonably evident. You are aware of the conflict over a proposed new temple, which is to outdo that of Ils and Shipri. I do not maintain that the god has taken a direct hand. I certainly hope he feels that would be beneath his dignity; a theomachy would not be good for us, to understate the case a trifle. But he may have inspired a few of his more fanatical priests to action. He may have revealed to them, in dreams or visions, the means whereby they could cross to the next world and there make the sikkintairs do their bidding. I hypothesize that the Lady Rosanda—and, to be sure, her coadjutrix, your inamorata—are incarcerated in that world. The temple is too full of priests, deacons, acolytes, and lay people for hiding the wife of a magnate. However, the gate need not be recognizable as such."

Cappen controlled himself with an inward shudder and made his trained voice casual: "What might it look like, sir?"

"Oh, probably a scroll, taken from a coffer where it had long lain forgotten, and now unrolled—yes, I should think in the sanctum, to draw power from the sacred objects and to be seen by as few persons as possible who are not in the conspiracy—" Enas Yorl came out of his abstraction. "Beware! I deduce your thought. Choke it before it kills you."

Cappen ran sandy tongue over leathery lips. "What . . . should we . . . expect to happen, sir?"

"That is an interesting question," Enas Yorl said. "I can but conjecture. Yet I am well acquainted with the temple hierarchy and—I don't think the Archpriest is privy to the matter. He's too aged and weak. On the other hand, this is quite in the style of Hazroah, the High Flamen. Moreover, of late he has in effect taken over the governance of the temple from his nominal superior. He's bold, ruthless—should have been a soldier—Well, putting myself in his skin, I'll predict that he'll let Molin stew a while, then cautiously open negotiations—a hint at first, and always a claim that this is the will of Ils.

"None but the Emperor can cancel an undertaking for the Imperial deities. Persuading him will take much time and pressure. Molin is a Rankan aristocrat of the old school; he will be torn between his duty to his gods, his state, and his wife. But I suspect that eventually he can be worn down to the point where he agrees that it is, in truth, bad policy to exalt Savankala and Sabellia in a city whose tutelaries they have never been. He in his turn can influence the Emperor as desired."

"How long would this take, do you think?" Cappen whispered. "Till the women are released?"

Enas York shrugged. "Years, possibly. Hazroah may try to hasten the process by demonstrating that the Lady Rosanda is subject to punishment. Yes, I should imagine that the remains of an ancilla who had been tortured to death, delivered on Molin's doorstep, would be a rather strong argument."

His look grew intense on the appalled countenance across from him. "I know," he said. "You're breeding fever-dreams of a heroic rescue. It cannot be done. Even supposing that somehow you won through the gate and brought her back, the gate would remain. I doubt Ils would personally seek revenge; besides being petty, that could provoke open strife with Savankala and his retinue, who're formidable characters themselves. But Ils would not stay the hand of the Flamen Hazroah, who is a most vengeful sort. If you escaped his assassins, a sikkintair would come after you, and nowhere in the world could you and she hide. Your talisman would be of no avail. The sikkintair is not supernatural, unless you give that designation to the force which enables so huge a mass to fly; and it is from no magician, but from the god.

"So forget the girl. The town is full of them." He fished in his purse and spilled a handful of coins on the table. "Go to a good whorehouse, enjoy yourself, and raise one for poor old Enas Yorl."

He got up and waddled off. Cappen sat staring at the coins. They made a generous sum, he realized vaguely: silver lunars, to the number of thirty.

One-Thumb came over. "What'd he say?" the taverner asked.

"I should abandon hope," Cappen muttered. His eyes stung; his vision blurred. Angrily, he wiped them.

"I've a notion I might not be smart to hear more." One-Thumb laid his mutilated hand on Cappen's shoulder. "Care to get drunk? On the house. I'll have to take your money or the rest will want free booze too, but I'll return it tomorrow."

"No, I—I thank you, but—but you're busy, and I need someone I can talk to. Just lend me a lantern, if you will."

"That might attract a robber, fellow, what with those fine clothes of yours."

Cappen gripped swordhilt. "He'd be very welcome, the short while he lasted," he said in bitterness.

He climbed to his feet. His fingers remembered to gather the coins.

Jamie let him in. The Northerner had hastily thrown a robe over his massive frame; he carried the stone lamp that was a night light. "Sh," he said. "The lassies are asleep." He nodded toward a closed door at the far end of this main room. Bringing the lamp higher, he got a clear view of Cappen's face. His own registered shock. "Hey-o, lad, what ails you? I've seen men poleaxed who looked happier."

Cappen stumbled across the threshold and collapsed in an armchair. Jamie barred the outer door, touched a stick of punk to the lamp flame and lit candles, filled wine goblets. Drawing a seat opposite, he sat down, laid red-furred right shank across left knee, and said gently, "Tell me."

When it had spilled from Cappen, he was a long span quiet. On the walls shimmered his weapons, among pretty pictures that his housemates had selected. At last he asked low, "Have you quit?"

"I don't know, I don't know," Cappen groaned.

"I think you can go on a ways, whether or not things are as the witchmaster supposes. We hold where I come from that no man can flee his weird, so he may as well meet it in a way that'll leave a good story. Besides, this may not be our deathday; and I doubt yon dragons are unkillable, but it could be fun finding out; and chiefly, I was much taken with your girl. Not many like her, my friend. They also say in my homeland, " 'Waste not, want not.' "

Cappen lifted his glance, astounded. "You mean I should try to free her?" he exclaimed.

"No, I mean *we* should." Jamie chuckled. "Life's gotten a wee bit dull for me of late—aside from Butterfly and Light-of-Pearl, of course. Besides, I could use a share of reward money."

"I . . . I want to," Cappen stammered. "How I want to! But the odds against us—"

"She's your girl, and it's your decision. I'll not blame you if you hold back. Belike, then, in your country, they don't believe a man's first troth is to his woman and kids. Anyway, for you that was no more than a hope."

A surge went through the minstrel. He sprang up and paced, back and forth, back and forth. "But what could we do?"

"Well, we could scout the temple and see what's what," Jamie proposed. "I've been there once in a while, reckoning 'twould do no hurt to give those gods their honor. Maybe we'll find that indeed naught can be done in aid. Or maybe we won't, and go ahead and do it."

Danlis—

Fire blossomed in Cappen Varra. He was young. He

drew his sword and swung it whistling on high. "Yes! We will!"

A small grammarian part of him noted the confusion of tenses and moods in the conversation.

The sole traffic on the Avenue of Temples was a night breeze, cold and sibilant. Stars, as icy to behold, looked down on its broad emptiness, on darkened buildings and weather-worn idols and rustling gardens. Here and there flames cast restless light, from porticoes or gables or ledges, out of glass lanterns or iron pots or pierced stone jars. At the foot of the grand staircase leading to the fane of Ils and Shipri, fire formed halos on the enormous figures, male and female in robes of antiquity, that flanked it.

Beyond, the god-house itself loomed, porticoed front, great bronze doors, granite walls rising sheer above to a gilt dome from which light also gleamed; the highest point in Sanctuary.

Cappen started up. "Halt," said Jamie, and plucked at his cloak. "We can't walk straight in. They keep guards in the vestibule, you know."

"I want a close view of those sikkintairs," the bard explained.

"Um, well, maybe not a bad idea, but let's be quick. If a squad of the watch comes by, we're in trouble." They could not claim they simply wished to perform their devotions, for a civilian was not allowed to bear more arms in this district than a knife. Cappen and Jamie each had that, but no illuminant like honest men. In addition, Cappen carried his rapier, Jamie a claymore, a visored conical helmet, and a knee-length byrnie. He had, moreover, furnished spears for both.

Cappen nodded and bounded aloft. Halfway, he stopped and gazed. The statue was a daunting sight.

Of obsidian polished glassy smooth, it might have measured thirty feet were the tail not coiled under the narrow body. The two legs which supported the front ended in talons the length of Jamie's dirk. An upreared, serpentine neck bore a wickedly lanceolate head, jaws parted to show fangs that the sculptor had rendered in diamond. From the back sprang wings, batlike save for their sharp-pointed curvatures, which if unfolded might well have covered another ten yards.

"Aye," Jamie murmured, "such a brute could bear off two women like an eagle a brace of leverets. Must take a lot of food to power it. I wonder what quarry they hunt at home."

"We may find out," Cappen said, and wished he hadn't.

"Come." Jamie led the way back, and around to the left side of the temple. It occupied almost its entire ground, leaving but a narrow strip of flagstones. Next to that, a wall enclosed the flower-fragrant sanctum of Eshi, the love goddess. Thus the space between was gratifyingly dark; the intruders could not now be spied from the avenue. Yet enough light filtered in that they saw what they were doing. Cappen wondered if this meant she smiled on their venture. After all, it was for love, mainly. Besides, he had always been an enthusiastic worshiper of hers, or at any rate of her counterparts in foreign pantheons; oftener than most men had he rendered her favorite sacrifice.

Jamie had pointed out that the building must have lesser doors for utilitarian purposes. He soon found one, bolted for the night and between windows that were hardly more than slits, impossible to crawl through. He could have hewn the wood panels asunder, but the noise might be heard. Cappen had a better idea. He got his partner down on hands and knees.

Standing on the broad back, he poked his spear through a window and worked it along the inside of the door. After some fumbling and whispered obscenities, he caught the latch with the head and drew the bolt.

"Hoosh, you missed your trade, I'm thinking," said the Northerner as he rose and opened the way.

"No, burglary's too risky for my taste," Cappen replied in feeble jest. The fact was that he had never stolen or cheated unless somebody deserved such treatment.

"Even burgling the house of a god?" Jamie's grin was wider than necessary.

Cappen shivered. "Don't remind me."

They entered a storeroom, shut the door, and groped through murk to the exit. Beyond was a hall. Widely spaced lamps gave bare visibility. Otherwise the intruders saw emptiness and heard silence. The vestibule and nave of the temple were never closed; the guards watched over a priest always prepared to accept offerings. But elsewhere hierarchy and staff were asleep. Or so the two hoped.

Jamie had known that the holy of holies was in the dome, Ils being a sky god. Now he let Cappen take the lead, as having more familiarity with interiors and ability to reason out a route. The minstrel used half his mind for that and scarcely noticed the splendors through which he passed. The second half was busy recollecting legends of heroes who incurred the anger of a god, especially a major god, but won to happiness in the end because they had the blessing of another. He decided that future attempts to propitiate Ils would only draw the attention of that august personage; however, Savankala would be pleased, and, yes, as for native deities, he would by all means fervently cultivate Eshi.

A few times, which felt ghastly long, he took a wrong turning and must retrace his steps after he had discovered that. Presently, though, he found a staircase which seemed to zigzag over the inside of an exterior wall. Landing after landing passed by—

The last was enclosed in a very small room, a booth, albeit richly ornamented—

He opened the door and stepped out—

Wind searched between the pillars that upheld the dome, through his clothes and in toward his bones. He saw stars. They were the brightest in heaven, for the entry booth was the pedestal of a gigantic lantern. Across a floor tiled in symbols unknown to him, he observed something large at each cardinal point—an altar, two statues, and the famous Thunderstone, he guessed; they were shrouded in cloth of gold. Before the eastern object was stretched a band, the far side of which seemed to be aglow.

He gathered his courage and approached. The thing was a parchment, about eight feet long and four wide, hung by cords from the upper corners to a supporting member of the dome. The cords appeared to be glued fast, as if to avoid making holes in the surface. The lower edge of the scroll, two feet above the floor, was likewise secured: but to a pair of anvils surely brought here for the purpose. Nevertheless the parchment flapped and rattled a bit in the wind. It was covered with cabalistic signs.

Cappen stepped around to the other side, and whistled low. That held a picture, within a narrow border. Past the edge of what might be a pergola, the scene went to a meadowland made stately by oak trees standing at random intervals. About a mile away—the perspective was marvelously executed—stood a building of manorial size in a style he had never seen before, twistily colonnaded, extravagantly sweeping of roof and eaves, blood-red. A formal garden surrounded it, whose paths and topiaries were of equally alien outline; fountains sprang in intricate patterns. Beyond the house, terrain rolled higher, and snowpeaks thrust above the horizon. The sky was deep blue.

"What the pox!" exploded from Jamie. "Sunshine's coming out of that painting. I *feel* it."

Cappen rallied his wits and paid heed. Yes, warmth as well as light, and . . . and odors? And were those fountains not actually at play?

An eerie thrilling took him. "I . . . believe . . . we've . . . found the gate," he said.

He poked his spear cautiously at the scroll. The point met no resistance; it simply moved on. Jamie went behind. "You've not pierced it," he reported. "Nothing sticks out on this side—which, by the way, is quite solid."

"No," Cappen answered faintly, "the spearhead's in the next world."

He drew the weapon back. He and Jamie stared at each other.

"Well?" said the Northerner.

"We'll never get a better chance," Cappen's throat responded for him. "It'd be blind foolishness to retreat now, unless we decide to give up the whole venture."

"We, uh, we could go tell Molin, no, the Prince what we've found."

"And be cast into a madhouse? If the Prince did send investigators anyway, the plotters need merely take this thing down and hide it till the squad has left. No." Cappen squared his shoulders. "Do what you like, Jamie, but I am going through."

Underneath, he heartily wished he had less self-respect, or at least that he weren't in love with Danlis.

Jamie scowled and sighed. "Aye, right you are, I suppose. I'd not looked for matters to take so headlong a course. I awaited that we'd simply scout around. Had I foreseen this, I'd have roused the lassies to bid them, well, goodnight." He hefted his spear and drew his sword. Abruptly he laughed. "Whatever comes, 'twill not be dull!"

Stepping high over the threshold, Cappen went forward.

It felt like walking through any door, save that he entered a mild summer's day. After Jamie had followed, he saw that the vista in the parchment was that on which he had just turned his back: a veiled mass, a pillar, stars above a nighted city. He checked the opposite side of the strip, and met the same designs as had been painted on its mate.

No, he thought, not its mate. If he had understood Enas Yorl aright, and rightly remembered what his tutor in mathematics had told him about esoteric geometry, there could be but a single scroll. One side of it gave on this universe, the other side on his, and a spell had twisted dimensions until matter could pass straight between.

Here too the parchment was suspended by cords, though in a pergola of yellow marble, whose circular stairs led down to the meadow. He imagined a sikkintair would find the passage tricky, especially if it was burdened with two women in its claws. The monster had probably hugged them close to it, come in at high speed, folded its wings, and glided between the pillars of the dome and the margins of the gate. On the outbound trip, it must have crawled through into Sanctuary.

All this Cappen did and thought in half a dozen heartbeats. A shout yanked his attention back. Three men who had been idling on the stairs had noticed the advent and were on their way up. Large and hard-featured, they bore the shaven visages, high-crested morions, gilt cuirasses, black tunics and boots, short-swords, and halberds of temple guards. ''Who in the Unholy's name are you?'' called the first. ''What're you doing here?''

Jamie's qualms vanished under a tide of boyish glee. ''I doubt they'll believe any words of ours,'' he said. ''We'll have to convince them a different way. If you can handle him on our left, I'll take his feres.''

Cappen felt less confident. But he lacked time to be afraid; shuddering would have to be done in a more convenient hour. Besides, he was quite a good fencer. He dashed across the floor and down the stair.

The trouble was, he had no experience with spears. He jabbed. The halberdier held his weapon, both hands close together, near the middle of the shaft. He snapped it against Cappen's, deflected the thrust, and nearly tore the minstrel's out of his grasp. The watchman's return would have skewered his enemy, had the minstrel not flopped straight to the marble.

The guard guffawed, braced his legs wide, swung the halberd back for an axhead blow. As it descended, his hands shifted toward the end of the helve.

Chips flew. Cappen had rolled downstairs. He twirled the whole way to the ground and sprang erect. He still clutched his spear, which had bruised him whenever he crossed above it. The sentry bellowed and hopped in pursuit. Cappen ran.

Behind them, a second guard sprawled and flopped, diminuendo, in what seemed an impossibly copious and bright amount of blood. Jamie had hurled his own spear as he charged and taken the man in the neck. The third was giving the Northerner a brisk fight, halberd against claymore. He had longer reach, but the redhead had more brawn. Thump and clatter rang across the daisies.

Cappen's adversary was bigger than he was. This had the drawback that the former could not change speed or direction as readily. When the guard was pounding along at his best clip, ten or twelve feet in the rear, Cappen stopped within a coin's breadth, whirled about, and threw his shaft. He did not do that as his comrade had done. He pitched it between the guard's legs. The man crashed to the grass. Cappen plunged in. He didn't risk trying for a stab. That would let the armored combatant grapple him. He wrenched the halberd loose and skipped off.

The sentinel rose. Cappen reached an oak and tossed the halberd. It lodged among boughs. He drew blade. His foe did the same.

Shortsword versus rapier—much better, though Cappen must have a care. The torso opposing him was protected. Still, the human anatomy has more vulnerable points than that. "Shall we dance?" Cappen asked.

As he and Jamie approached the house, a shadow slid across them. They glanced aloft and saw the gaunt black form of a sikkintair. For an instant, they nerved themselves for the worst. However, the Flying Knife simply caught an updraft, planed high, and hovered in sinister magnificence. "Belike they don't hunt men unless commanded to," the Northerner speculated. "Bear and buffalo are meatier."

Cappen frowned at the scarlet walls before him.

"The next question," he said, "is why nobody has come out against us."

"Um, I'd deem those wights we left scattered around were the only fighting men here. What task was theirs? Why, to keep the ladies from escaping, if those are allowed to walk outdoors by day. As for yon manse, while it's plenty big, I suspect it's on loan from its owner. Naught but a few servants need by on hand—and the women, let's hope. I don't suppose anybody happened to see our little brawl."

The thought that they might effect the rescue—soon, safely, easily—went through Cappen in a wave of dizziness. Afterward—He and Jamie had discussed that. If the temple hierophants, from Hazroah on down, were put under immediate arrest, that ought to dispose of the vengeance problem.

Gravel scrunched underfoot. Rose, jasmine, honeysuckle sweetened the air. Fountains leaped and chimed. The partners reached the main door. It was oaken, with many glass eyes inset; the knocker had the shape of a sikkintair.

Jamie leaned his spear, unsheathed his sword, turned the knob left-handed, and swung the door open. A maroon sumptuousness of carpet, hangings, upholstery brooded beyond. He and Cappen entered. Inside were quietness and an odor like that just before a thunderstorm.

A man in a deacon's black robe came through an archway, his tonsure agleam in the dimness. "Did I hear—Oh!" he gasped, and scuttled backward.

Jamie made a long arm and collared him. "Not so fast, friend," the warrior said genially. "We've a request, and if you oblige, we won't get stains on this pretty rug. Where are your guests?"

"What, what, what," the deacon gobbled.

Jamie shook him, in leisured wise lest he quite dislocate the shoulder. "Lady Rosanda, wife to Molin Torchholder, and her assistant Danlis. Take us to them. Oh, and we'd liefer not meet folk along the way. It might get messy if we did."

The deacon fainted.

"Ah, well," Jamie said. "I hate the idea of cutting down unarmed men, but chances are they won't be foolhardy." He filled his lungs. *"Rosanda!"* he bawled. *"Danlis! Jamie and Cappen Varra are here! Come on home!"*

The volume almost bowled his companion over. "Are you mad?" the minstrel exclaimed. "You'll warn the whole staff—" A flash lit his mind: if they had seen no further guards, surely there were none, and nothing corporeal remained to fear. Yet every minute's delay heightened the danger of something else going wrong. Somebody might find signs of invasion back in the temple; the gods alone knew what lurked in this realm . . . Yes, Jamie's judgment might prove mistaken, but it was the best he could have made.

Servitors appeared, and recoiled from naked steel. And then, and then—

Through a doorway strode Danlis. She led by the hand, or dragged, a half-hysterical Rosanda. Both were decently attired and neither looked abused, but pallor in cheeks and smudges under eyes bespoke what they must have suffered.

Cappen came nigh dropping his spear. "Beloved!" he cried. "Are you hale?"

"We've not been ill-treated in the flesh, aside from the snatching itself," she answered efficiently. "The threats, should Hazroah not get his way, have been cruel. Can we leave now?"

"Aye, the soonest, the best," Jamie growled. "Lead

them on ahead, Cappen.'' His sword covered the rear. On his way out, he retrieved the spear he had left.

They started back over the garden paths. Danlis and Cappen between them must help Rosanda along. That woman's plump prettiness was lost in tears, moans, whispers, and occasional screams. He paid scant attention. His gaze kept seeking the clear profile of his darling. When her grey eyes turned toward him, his heart became a lyre.

She parted her lips. He waited for her to ask in dazzlement, ''How did you ever do this, you unbelievable, wonderful men?''

''What have we ahead of us?'' she wanted to know.

Well, it was an intelligent query. Cappen swallowed disappointment and sketched the immediate past. Now, he said, they'd return via the gate to the dome and make their stealthy way from the temple, thence to Molin's dwelling for a joyous reunion. But then they must act promptly—yes, roust the Prince out of bed for authorization—and occupy the temple and arrest everybody in sight before new trouble got fetched from this world.

Rosanda gained some self-control as he talked. ''Oh, my, oh, my,'' she wheezed, ''you unbelievable, wonderful men.''

An ear-piercing trill slashed across her voice. The escapers looked behind them. At the entrance to the house stood a thickset middle-aged person in the scarlet robe of a ranking priest of Ils. He held a pipe to his mouth and blew.

''Hazroah!'' Rosanda shrilled. ''The ringleader!''

''The High Flamen—'' Danlis began.

A rush in the air interrupted. Cappen flung his vision skyward and knew the nightmare was true. The sikkintair was descending. Hazroah had summoned it.

"Why, you son of a bitch!" Jamie roared. Still well behind the rest, he lifted his spear, brought it back, flung it with his whole strength and weight. The point went home in Hazroah's breast. Ribs did not stop it. He spouted blood, crumpled, and spouted no more. The shaft quivered above his body.

But the sikkintair's vast wings eclipsed the sun. Jamie rejoined his band and plucked the second spear from Cappen's fingers. "Hurry on, lad," he ordered. "Get them to safety."

"Leave you? No!" protested his comrade.

Jamie spat an oath. "Do you want the whole faring to've gone for naught? Hurry, I said!"

Danlis tugged at Cappen's sleeve. "He's right. The state requires our testimony."

Cappen stumbled onward. From time to time he glanced back.

In the shadow of the wings, Jamie's hair blazed. He stood foursquare, spear grasped as a huntsman does. Agape, the Flying Knife rushed down upon him. Jamie thrust straight between those jaws, and twisted.

The monster let out a sawtoothed shriek. Its wings threshed, made thundercrack, it swooped by, a foot raked. Jamie had his claymore out. He parried the blow.

The sikkintair rose. The shaft waggled from its throat. It spread great ebon membranes, looped, and came back earthward. Its claws were before it. Air whirred behind.

Jamie stood his ground, sword in right hand, knife in left. As the talons smote, he fended them off with the dirk. Blood sprang from his thigh, but his byrnie took most of the edged sweep. And his sword hewed.

The sikkintair ululated again. It tried to ascend, and couldn't. Jamie had crippled its left wing. It landed—

Cappen felt the impact through soles and bones—and hitched itself toward him. From around the spear came a geyser hiss.

Jamie held fast where he was. As fangs struck at him, he sidestepped, sprang back, and threw his shoulders against the shaft. Leverage swung jaws aside. He glided by the neck toward the forequarters. Both of his blades attacked the spine.

Cappen and the women hastened on.

They were almost at the pergola when footfalls drew his eyes rearward. Jamie loped at an overtaking pace. Behind him, the sikkintair lay in a heap.

The redhead pulled alongside. "Hai, what a fight!" he panted. "Thanks for this journey, friend! A drinking bout's worth of thanks!"

They mounted the death-defiled stairs. Cappen peered across miles. Wings beat in heaven, from the direction of the mountains. Horror stabbed his guts. "Look!" He could barely croak.

Jamie squinted. "More of them," he said. "A score, maybe. We can't cope with so many. An army couldn't."

"That whistle was heard farther away than mortals would hear," Danlis added starkly.

"What do we linger for?" Rosanda wailed. "Come, take us home!"

"And the sikkintairs follow?" Jamie retorted. "No. I've my lassies, and kinfolk, and—" He moved to stand before the parchment. Edged metal dripped in his hands; red lay splashed across helm, ringmail, clothing, face. His grin broke forth, wry. "A spaewife once told me I'd die on the far side of strangeness. I'll wager she didn't know her own strength."

"You assume that the mission of the beasts is to destroy us, and when that is done they will return to their lairs.'' The tone Danlis used might have served for a remark about the weather.

''Aye, what else? The harm they'd wreak would be in a hunt for us. But put to such trouble, they could grow furious and harry our whole world. That's the more likely when Hazroah lies skewered. Who else can control them?''

''None that I know of, and he talked quite frankly to us.'' She nodded. ''Yes, it behooves us to die where we are.'' Rosanda sank down and blubbered. Danlis showed irritation. ''Up!'' she commanded her mistress. ''Up and meet your fate like a Rankan matron!''

Cappen goggled hopelessly at her. She gave him a smile. ''Have no regrets, dear,'' she said. ''You did well. The conspiracy against the state has been checked.''

The far side of strangeness—check—chessboard—that version of chess where you pretend the right and left sides of the board are identical on a cylinder—tumbled through Cappen. The Flying Knives drew closer fast. *Curious aspects of geometry—*

Lightning-smitten, he knew . . . or guessed he did . . . ''No, Jamie, we go!'' he yelled.

''To no avail save reaping of innocents?'' The big man hunched his shoulders. ''Never.''

''Jamie, let us by! I can close the gate. I swear I can—I swear by—by Eshi—''

The Northerner locked eyes with Cappen for a span that grew. At last: ''You are my brother in arms.'' He stood aside. ''Go on.''

The sikkintairs were so near that the noise of their speed reached Cappen. He urged Danlis toward the scroll. She lifted her skirt a trifle, revealing a dainty ankle, and stepped through. He hauled on Rosanda's wrist. The woman wavered to her feet but seemed unable to find her direction. Cappen took an arm and passed it into the next world for Danlis to pull. Himself, he gave a mighty shove on milady's buttocks. She crossed over.

He did. And Jamie.

Beneath the temple dome, Cappen's rapier reached high and slashed. Louder came the racket of cloven air. Cappen served the upper cords. The parchment fell, wrinkling, crackling. He dropped his weapon, a-clang, squatted, and stretched his arms wide. The free corners he seized. He pulled them to the corners that were still secured, to make a closed band of the scroll.

From it sounded monstrous thumps and scrapes. The sikkintairs, were crawling into the pergola. For them the portal must hang unchanged, open for their hunting.

Cappen gave that which he held a half-twist and brought the edges back together.

Thus he created a surface which had but a single side and a single edge. Thus he obliterated the gate.

He had not been sure what would follow. He had fleetingly supposed he would smuggle the scroll out, held in its paradoxical form, and eventually glue it—unless he could burn it. But upon the instant that he completed the twist and juncture, the parchment was gone. Enas Yorl told him afterward that he had made it impossible for the thing to exist.

Air rushed in where the gate had been, crack and hiss. Cappen heard that sound as it were an alien word of incantation: "Möbius-s-s."

Having stolen out of the temple and some distance thence, the party stopped for a few minutes of recovery before they proceeded to Molin's house.

This was in a blind alley off the avenue, a brick-paved

recess where flowers grew in planters, shared by the fanes of two small and gentle gods. Wind had died away, stars glimmered bright, a half moon stood above easterly roofs and cast wan argence. Afar, a tomcat serenaded his intended.

Rosanda had gotten back a measure of equilibrium. She cast herself against Jamie's breast. "Oh, hero, hero," she crooned, "you shall have reward, yes, treasure, ennoblement, everything!" She snuggled. "But nothing greater than my unbounded thanks. . . .

The Northerner cocked an eyebrow at Cappen. The bard shook his head a little. Jamie nodded in understanding, and disengaged. "Uh, have a care, milady," he said. "Pressing against ringmail, all bloody and sweaty too, can't be good for a complexion."

Even if one rescues them, it is not wise to trifle with the wives of magnates.

Cappen had been busy himself. For the first time, he kissed Danlis on her lovely mouth; then for the second time; then for the third. She responded decorously.

Thereafter she likewise withdrew. Moonlight made a mystery out of her classic beauty. "Cappen," she said, "before we go on, we had better have a talk."

He gaped. "What?"

She bridged her fingers. "Urgent matters first," she continued crisply. "Once we get to the mansion and wake the high priest, it will be chaos at first, conference later, and I—as a woman—excluded from serious discussion. Therefore best I give my counsel now, for you to relay. Not that Molin or the Prince are fools; the measures to take are for the most part obvious. However, swift action is desirable, and they will have been caught by surprise."

She ticked her points off. "First, as you have indicated, the Hell Hounds"—her nostrils pinched in distaste at the nickname— "the Imperial elite guard should mount an immediate raid on the temple of Ils and arrest all personnel for interrogation, except the Archpriest. He's probably innocent, and in any event it would be inept politics. Hazroah's death may have removed the danger, but this should not be taken for granted. Even if it has, his co-conspirators ought to be identified and made examples of.

"Yes, second, wisdom should temper justice. No lasting harm was done, unless we count those persons who are trapped in the parallel universe; and they doubtless deserve to be."

They seemed entirely males, Cappen recalled. He grimaced in compassion. Of course, the sikkintairs might eat them.

Danlis was talking on: "—humane governance and the art of compromise. A grand temple dedicated to the Rankan gods is certainly required, but it need be no larger than that of Ils. Your counsel will have much weight, dear. Give it wisely. I will advise you."

"Uh?" Cappen said.

Danlis smiled and laid her hands over his. "Why, you can have unlimited preferment, after what you did," she told him. "I'll show you how to apply for it."

"But—but I'm no blooming statesman!" Cappen stuttered.

She stepped back and considered him. "True," she agreed. "You're valiant, yes, but you're also flighty and lazy and—Well, don't despair. I will mold you."

Cappen gulped and shuffled aside. "Jamie," he said, "uh, Jamie, I feel wrung dry, dead on my feet. I'd be worse than no use—I'd be a drogue on things just when they have to move fast. Better I find me a doss, and you take the ladies home. Come over here and I'll tell you how to convey the story in fewest words. Excuse us, ladies. Some of those words you oughtn't to hear."

A week thence, Cappen Varra sat drinking in the Vulgar Unicorn. It was mid-afternoon and none else was present but the associate tapster, his wound knitted.

A man filled the doorway and came in, to Cappen's table. "Been casting about everywhere for you," the Northerner grumbled. "Where've you been?"

"Lying low," Cappen replied. "I've taken a place here in the Maze which'll do till I've dropped back into obscurity, or decide to drift elsewhere altogether." He sipped his wine. Sunbeams slanted through windows; dustmotes danced golden in their warmth; a cat lay on a sill and purred. "Trouble is, my purse is flat."

"We're free of such woes for a goodly while." Jamie flung his length into a chair and signaled the attendant. "Beer!" he thundered.

"You collected a reward, then?" the minstrel asked eagerly.

Jamie nodded. "Aye. In the way you whispered I should, before you left us. I'm baffled why and it went sore against the grain. But I did give Molin the notion that the rescue was my idea and you naught but a hanger-on whom I'd slip a few royals. He filled a box with gold and silver money, and said he wished he could afford ten times that. He offered to get me Rankan citizenship and a title as well, and make a bureaucrat of me, but I said no, thanks. We share, you and I, half and half. But right this now, drinks are on me."

"What about the plotters?" Cappen inquired.

"Ah, those. The matter's been kept quiet, as you'd await. Still, while the temple of Ils can't be abolished, seemingly it's been tamed." Jamie's regard sought across the table and sharpened. "After you disappeared, Danlis agreed to let me claim the whole honor. She knew better—Rosanda never noticed—but Danlis wanted a man of the hour to carry her redes to the prince, and none remained save me. She supposed you were simply worn out. When last I saw her, though, she . . . um-m . . . she 'expressed disappointment.' " He cocked his ruddy head. "Yon's quite a girl. I thought you loved her."

Cappen Varra took a fresh draught of wine. Old summers glowed along his tongue. "I did," he confessed. "I do. My heart is broken, and in part I drink to numb the pain."

Jamie raised his brows. "What? Makes no sense."

"Oh, it makes very basic sense," Cappen answered. "Broken hearts tend to heal rather soon. Meanwhile, if I may recite from a rondel I completed before you found me—

"Each sword of sorrow that would maim or slay,
My lady of the morning deftly parries.
Yet gods forbid I be the one she marries!
I rise from bed the latest hour I may.
My lady comes to me like break of day;
I dream in darkness if it chance she tarries."

The Barbarian

Don't get me wrong. I am quite fond of Robert E. Howard's work. It isn't the most sensitive or sophisticated stuff ever published, but it has imagination, energy, vividness, together with a slightly deeper human insight and a considerably better writing style than the critics can see. I once accepted an invitation to write a Conan novel myself, for love and enjoyment much more than for money. So this burlesque was done, on an earlier occasion, in the friendliest spirit.

Since the Howard-de Camp system for deciphering preglacial inscriptions first appeared, much progress has been made in tracing the history, ethnology, and even daily life of the great cultures which flourished till the Pleistocene ice age wiped them out and forced man to start over. We know, for instance, that magic was practiced; that there were some highly civilized countries in what is now central Asia, the Near East, North Africa, southern Europe, and various oceans; and that elsewhere the world was occupied by barbarians, of whom the northern Europeans were the biggest, strongest, and most warlike. At least, so the scholars inform us, and being of northern European ancestry, they ought to know.

The following is a translation of a letter recently discovered in the ruins of Cyrenne. This was a provincial town of the Sarmian Empire, a great though decadent realm in the eastern Mediterranean area, whose capital, Sarmia, was at once the most beautiful and the most lustful, depraved city of its time. The Sarmians' northern neighbors were primitive horse nomads and/or Centaurs; but to the east lay the Kingdom of Chathakh, and to the south was the Herpetarchy of Serpens, ruled by a priestly cast of snake worshipers—or possibly snakes.

The letter was obviously written in Sarmia and posted to Cyrenne. Its date is approximately 175,000 B.C.

Maxilion Quaestos, sub-sub-sub-prefect of the Imperial Waterworks of Sarmia, to his nephew Thyaston, Chancellor of the Bureau of Thaumaturgy, Province of Cyrenne:

Greetings!

I trust this finds you in good health, and that the gods will continue to favor you. As for me, I am well, though somewhat plagued by the gout, for which I have tried *[here follows the description of a home remedy, both tedious and unprintable]*. This has not availed, however, save to exhaust my purse and myself.

You must indeed have been out of touch during your Atlantean journey, if you must write to inquire about the Barbarian affair. Now that events have settled down again, I can, I hope, give you an adequate and dispassionate account of the whole ill-starred business. By the favor of the Triplet Goddesses, holy Sarmia has survived the episode; and though we are still rather shaken, things are improving. If at times I seem to depart from the philosophic calm I have always tried to cultivate, blame it on the Barbarian. I am not the man I used to be. None of us are.

To begin, then, about three years ago the war with Chathakh had settled down to border skirmishes. An occasional raid by one side or the other would penetrate deeply into the countries themselves, but with no decisive effect. Indeed, since these operations yielded a more or less equal amount of booty for both lands, and the slave trade grew brisk, it was good for business.

Our chief concern was the ambiguous attitude of Serpens. As you well know, the Herpetarchs have no love for us, and a major object of our diplomacy was to keep them from entering the war on the side of Chathakh. We had, of course, no hope of making them our allies. But as long as we maintained a posture of strength, it was likely that they would at least stay neutral.

Thus matters stood when the Barbarian came to Sarmia.

We had heard rumors of him for a long time. He was a wandering soldier of fortune, from some kingdom of swordsmen and seafarers up in the northern forests, who had drifted south, alone, in search of adventure or perhaps only a better climate. Seven feet tall, and broad in proportion, he was one mass of muscle, with a mane of tawny hair and sullen blue eyes. He was adept with any weapon, but preferred a four-foot double-edged sword with which he could cleave helmet, skull, neck, and so on down at one blow. He was additionally said to be a drinker and lover of awesome capacity.

Having overcome the Centaurs singlehanded, he tramped down through our northern provinces and one day stood at the gates of Sarmia herself. It was a curious vision—the turreted walls rearing over the stone-paved road, the guards bearing helmet and shield and corselet, and the towering, near-naked giant who rattled his blade before them. As their pikes slanted down to bar his way, he cried in a voice of thunder:

"I yam Cronkheit duh Barbarian, an' I wanna audience widjer queen!"

His accent was so ludicrously uneducated that the watch burst into laughter. This angered him; flushing darkly, he drew his sword and advanced stiff-legged. The guardsmen reeled back before him, and the Barbarian swaggered through.

As the captain of the watch explained it to me afterward: "There he came, and there we stood. A spear length away, we caught the smell. Ye gods, *when* did he last bathe?"

So with people running from the streets and bazaars as he neared, Cronkheit made his way down the Avenue of Sphinxes, past the baths and the Temple of Loccar, till he reached the Imperial Palace. Its gates stood open as usual, and he looked in at the gardens and the alabaster walls beyond, and grunted. When the Golden Guardsmen approached him upwind and asked his business, he grunted again. They lifted their bows and would have made short work of him, but a slave came hastily to bid them desist.

You see, by the will of some malignant god, the Empress was standing on a balcony and saw him.

As is well known, our beloved Empress, Her Seductive Majesty, the Illustrious Lady Larra the Voluptuous, is built like a mountain highway and is commonly believed to be an incarnation of her tutelary deity, Aphrosex, the Mink Goddess. She stood on the balcony, the wind blowing her thin transparent garments and thick black hair, and a sudden eagerness lit her proud lovely face. This was understandable, for Cronkheit wore simply a bearskin kilt.

Hence the slave was dispatched, to blow low before the stranger and say: "Most noble lord, the divine Empress would have private speech with you."

Cronkheit smacked his lips and strutted into the palace. The chamberlain wrung his hands when he saw those large muddy feet treading on priceless rugs, but there was no help for it, and the Barbarian was led upstairs to the Imperial bedchamber.

What befell there is known to all, for of course in such interviews the Lady Larra posts mute slaves at convenient peepholes, to summon the guards if danger seems to threaten; and the courtiers have quietly taught these mutes to write. Our Empress had a cold, and had furthermore been eating a garlic salad, so her aristocratically curved nose was not offended. After a few formalities, she began to pant. Slowly, then, she held out her arms and let the purple robe slide down from her creamy shoulders and across the silken thighs.

"Come," she whispered. "Come, magnificent male."

Cronkheit snorted, pawed the ground, rushed forth, and clasped her to him.

"Yowww!" cried the Empress as a rib cracked. "Leggo! Help!"

The mutes ran for the Golden Guardsmen, who entered at once. They got ropes around the Barbarian and dragged him from their poor lady. Though in considerable pain, and much shaken, she did not order his execution; she is known to be very patient with some types.

Indeed, after gulping a cup of wine to steady her, she invited Cronkheit to be her guest. After he had been conducted off to his rooms, she summoned the Duchess of Thyle, a supple, agile little minx.

"I have a task for you, my dear," she murmured. "You will fulfill it as a loyal lady-in-waiting."

"Yes, Your Seductive Majesty," said the Duchess, who could well guess what the task was and thought she had been waiting long enough. For a whole week, in fact. Her assignment was to take the edge off the Barbarian's impetuosity.

She greased herself so she could slip free if in peril of being crushed, and hurried to Cronkheit's suite. Her musky perfume drowned out his odor, and she slipped off her dress and crooned with half-shut eyes: "Take me, my lord!"

"Yahoo!" howled the warrior. "I yam Cronkheit duh Strong, Cronkheit duh Bold, Cronkheit what slew a mammot' single-handed an' made hisself chief o' duh Centaurs, an' dis's muh night! C'mere!"

The Duchess did, and he folded her in his mighty arms. A moment later came another shriek. The palace attendants were treated to the sight of a naked and furious duchess speeding down the jade corridor.

"Fleas he's got!" she cried, scratching as she ran.

So all in all, Cronkheit the Barbarian was no great success as a lover. Even the women in the Street of Joy used to hide when they saw him coming. They said they'd been exposed to clumsy technique before, but this was just too much.

However, his fame was so great that the Lady Larra put him in command of a brigade, infantry and cavalry, and sent him to join General Grythion on the Chathakh border. He made the march in record time and came shouting into the city of tents which had grown up at our main base.

Now, admittedly our good General Grythion is somewhat of a dandy, who curls his beard and is henpecked by his wives. But he has always been a competent soldier, winning honors at the Academy and leading troops in battle many times before rising to the strategic-planning post. One could understand Cronkheit's incivility at their meeting. But when the general courteously declined to go forth in the van of the army and pointed out how much more valuable he was as a coordinator behind the lines—that was no excuse for Cronkheit to knock his superior officer to the ground and call him a coward, damned of the gods. Grythion was thoroughly justified in having him put in irons, despite the casualties involved. Even as it was, the spectacle so demoralized our troops that they lost three important engagements in the following month.

Alas! Word of this reached the Empress, and she did not order Cronkheit's head struck off. Indeed, she sent back a command that he be released and reinstated. Perhaps she still cherished a hope of civilizing him enough to be an acceptable bed partner.

Grythion swallowed his pride and apologized to the Barbarian, who accepted with an ill grace. His restored rank made it necessary to invite him to a dinner and conference in the headquarters tent.

That was a flat failure. Cronkheit stamped in and at once made sneering remarks about the elegant togas of his brother officers. He belched when he ate and couldn't distinguish the product of any vineyard from another. His conversation consisted of hour-long monologues about his own prowess. General Grythion saw morale zooming downward, and hastily called for maps and planning.

"Now, most noble sirs," he began, "we have to lay out the summer campaign. As you know, we have the Eastern Desert between us and the nearest important enemy positions. This raises difficult questions of logistics and catapult emplacement." He turned politely to the Barbarian. "Have you any suggestion, my lord?"

"Duh," said Cronkheit.

"I think," ventured Colonel Pharaon, "that if we advanced to the Chunling Oasis and dug in there, building a supply road—"

"Dat reminds me," said Cronkheit. "One time up in duh Norriki marshes, I run acrost some swamp men an' dey uses poisoned arrers—"

"I fail to see what that has to do with this problem," said General Grythion.

"Nuttin'," admitted Cronkheit cheerfully. "But don't innerup' me. Like I was sayin' . . ." And he was off for a whole dreary hour.

At the end of a conference which had gotten nowhere, the general stroked his beard and said shrewdly: "Lord Cronkheit, it appears your abilities are more in the tactical than the strategic field."

The Barbarian snatched for his sword.

"I mean," said Grythion quickly, "I have a task which only the boldest and strongest leader can accomplish."

Cronkheit beamed and listened closely for a change. He was to lead an expedition to capture Chantsay. This was a fort in the mountain passes across the Eastern Desert, and a major obstacle to our advance. However, in spite of Grythion's judicious flattery, a full brigade should have been able to take it with little difficulty, for it was known to be undermanned.

Cronkheit rode off at the head of his men, tossing

his sword in the air and bellowing some uncouth battle chant. Then he was not heard of for six weeks.

At the close of that time, the ragged, starving, fever-stricken remnant of his troops staggered back to the base and reported utter failure. Cronkheit, who was in excellent health himself, made sullen excuses. But he had never imagined that men who march twenty hours a day aren't fit for battle at the end of the trip—the more so if they outrun their supply train.

Because of the Empress' wish, General Grythion could not do the sensible thing and cashier the Barbarian. He could not even reduce him to the ranks. Instead, he used his well-known guile and invited the giant to a private dinner.

"Obviously, most valiant lord," he purred, "the fault is mine. I should have realized that a man of your type is too much for us decadent southerners. You are a lone wolf who fights best by himself."

"Duh," agreed Cronkheit, ripping a fowl apart with his fingers and wiping them on the damask tablecloth.

Grythion winced, but easily talked him into going out on a one-man guerrilla operation. When he left the next morning, the officers' corps congratulated themselves on having gotten rid of the lout forever.

In the face of subsequent criticism and demands for an investigation, I still maintain that Grythion did the only rational thing under the circumstances. Who could have known that Cronkheit the Barbarian was so primitive that rationality simply slid off his hairy skin?

The full story will never be known. But apparently, in the course of the following year, while the border war continued as usual, Cronkheit struck off into the northern uplands. There he raised a band of horse nomads as ignorant and brutal as himself. He also rounded up a herd of mammoths and drove them into Chathakh, stampeding them at the foe. By such means, he reached their very capital, and the King offered terms of surrender.

But Cronkheit would have none of this. Not he! His idea of warfare was to kill or enslave every last man, woman, and child of the enemy nation. Also, his irregulars were supposed to be paid in loot. Also, being too unsanitary even for the nomad girls, he felt a certain urgency.

So he stormed the capital of Chathakh and burned it to the ground. This cost him most of his own men. It also destroyed several priceless books and works of art, and any possibility of tribute to Sarmia.

Then he had the nerve to organize a triumphal procession and ride back to our own city!

This was too much even for the Empress. When he stood before her—for he was too crude for the simple courtesy of a knee bend—she exceeded herself in describing the many kinds of fool, idiot, and all-around blockhead he was.

"Duh," said Cronkheit. "But I won duh war. Look, I won duh war. I did. I won duh war."

"Yes," hissed the Lady Larra. "You smashed an ancient and noble culture to irretrievable ruin. And did you know that half our peacetime trade was with Chathaka? There'll be a business depression now such as history has never seen before."

General Grythion, who had returned, added his own reproaches. "Why do you think wars are fought?" he asked bitterly. "War is an extension of diplomacy. It's the final means of making somebody else do what you want. The object is *not* to kill them off. How can corpses obey you?"

Cronkheit growled in his throat.

''We would have negotiated a peace in which Chathakh became our ally against Serpens,'' went on the general. ''Then we'd have been safe against all comers. But you—you've made a howling wilderness which we must garrison with our own troops lest the nomads take it over. Your atrocities have alienated every civilized state. You've left us alone and friendless. You've won this war by losing the next one!''

''And on top of the depression which is coming,'' said the Empress, ''we'll have the cost of maintaining those garrisons. Taxes down and expenditures up—it may break the treasury, and then were are we?''

Cronkheit spat on the floor. ''Yuh're decadent, dat's what yuh are,'' he snarled. ''Be good for yuh if yer empire breaks up. Yuh oughtta get dat city rabble o' yers out in duh woods an' make hunters of 'em, like me. Let 'em eat steak.''

The Lady Larra stamped an exquisite gold-shod foot. ''Do you think we've nothing better to do with our time than spend the whole day hunting, and sit around in mud hovels at night licking the grease off our fingers?'' she cried. ''What the hell do you think civilization is for, anyway?''

Cronkheit drew his great sword. It flashed against their eyes. ''I hadda nuff!'' he bellowed. ''I'm t'rough widjuh! It's time yuh was wiped off duh face o' duh eart, and I'm jus' duh guy t' do it!''

And now General Grythion showed the qualities which had raised him to his high post. Artfully, he quailed. ''Oh, no!'' he whimpered. ''You're not going to—to—to fight on the side of Serpens?''

''I yam,'' said Cronkheit. ''So long.'' The last we saw of him was a broad, indignant, flea-bitten back, headed south, and the reflection of the sun on a sword.

Since then, of course, our affairs have prospered and Serpens is now frantically suing for peace. But we intend to prosecute the war till they meet our terms. We are most assuredly not going to be ensnared by their treacherous pleas and take the Barbarian back!

A Feast for the Gods

Romantic fantasy encounters the modern world. Actually, it's the world of a generation ago, but now that so many people are sighing for and trying to recreate the 1960s—"that low dishonest decade," as W. H. Auden said of the '30s—this tale looks contemporary enough. It's only meant to amuse, but maybe it also suggests what is true, that our dreams and our realities are not at odds, but rather are parts of one another, and together shape our lives.

A strong, loud wind drove grizzly clouds low above Oceanus. The waves that rumbled before it were night-purple in their troughs, wolf-gray on their crests, and the foam lacing them blew off in a salt mist of spindrift. But where Hermes hurried was a radiance like sunlight.

Otherwise the god willed himself invisible to mortals. This required him to skim the water, though damp and the gloom of a boreal autumn were not to his liking. He had started at a sunny altitude but descended after his third near collision with an aircraft.

I should have inquired beforehand, he thought, and then: *Of whom? Nobody lives in this islandless waste.—Well, someone could have told me, someone whose worshipers still ply the seas.*

Or I should have reasoned it out for myself, he continued, chagrined since he was supposed to be the cleverest of the Olympians. *After all, we see enough flyers elsewhere, and hear and smell them. It stands to reason mortals would use them on this route.*

But so many!

The ships, too, had multiplied. They were akin to those engine-driven vessels which Hermes often observed on the Midworld. He sighed for the white-winged stateliness of the last time he passed this way, two centuries ago.

However, he was not unduly sentimental. Unlike most gods, including several in his own pantheon, he rather enjoyed the ingenuity of latter-day artisans. If only they were a bit less productive. They had about covered the earth with their machines and their children; they were well along toward doing likewise for the great deep, and the firmament was getting cluttered.

Eras change, eras change. And you'd better check on how they've been changing in these parts, my lad. Hermes tuned his attention to the radio spectrum and caught the voice of an English-speaking military pilot. "—Roger." For a moment he was jolted. Two centuries ago, no gentleman would have said that where any lady might be listening. Then he recalled hearing the modern usage in the Old World.

We really should have been paying closer attention to mortal affairs. Especially in the New World. Sheer laxity to ignore half the globe this long a while.

Immortals got hidebound, he reflected. And once

humans stopped worshiping them, they got—might as well be blunt—lazy. The Olympians had done little in Europe since the Renaissance, nothing in America since the birth of Thomas Jefferson. The fact that they had never been served by the American people, and thus had no particular tradition of interest in the affairs of that folk, that was no excuse.

Certainly Hermes, the Wayfarer, ought to have paid frequent visits. But at least he was the one who had discovered the need for an investigation.

A prayer, startling him to alertness, and in that heightened state, the sudden faint sense of something else, of a newborn god. . . .

He peered ahead. At his speed, the western horizon had begun to show a dark line which betokened land. The wings on his helmet and sandals beat strongly. Men aboard a coastwise freighter thought they glimpsed a small cyclone race by, yelling, kicking up chop, and froth, lit by one brass-colored sunset ray.

Yet despite his haste, Hermes traveled with less than his olden blitheness. If nothing else, he was hungry.

Vanessa Talbott had not called on Aphrodite that Saturday because she was a devotee. In fact, earlier she had invoked the devil. To be precise, she had clenched her fists and muttered, "Oh, hell damn everything, anyway," after she overcame her weeping.

That was when she said aloud, "I won't cry any more. He isn't worth crying over."

She took a turn about the apartment. It pressed on her with sights hard to endure—the heaped-up books she and Roy had read and talked about; a picture he had taken one day when they went sailing and later enlarged and framed; a dust-free spot by the south window, where the dropcloth used to lie beneath his easel; her guitar, which she would play for him while she sang, giving him music to accompany his work; the bed they'd bought at the Goodwill—

"Th-th-the trouble is," Vanny admitted, "he is worth it. Damn him."

She wanted wildly to get out. Only where? What for? Not to some easily found party among his friends (who had never quite become hers). They had too little idea of privacy, even the privacy of the heart. Nor, on some excuse, to the home of one of her friends (who had never quite become his). They were too reserved, too shyly intent on minding their own business. So? Out at random, through banging city streets, to end with a movie or, worse, smoke and boom-boom and wheedling strangers in a bar?

Stay put, girl, she told herself. *Use the weekend to get rested. Make a cheerful, impenetrable face ready for Monday.*

She'd announced her engagement to Roy Elkins, promising young landscape and portrait painter, at the office last month. The congratulations had doubled her pleasure. They were nice people at the computer center. It would be hard to tell them that the wedding was off. Thank God, she'd never said she and Roy were already living together! That had been mainly to avoid her parents getting word in Iowa. They were dears, but they wouldn't have understood. *I'm not sure I do either. Roy was the first, the first. He was going to be the last. Now—Yeah, I'm lucky. It'd have hurt too much to let them know how much I hurt.*

The place was hot and stuffy. She pushed a window open. Westering sunlight fell pale on brick walls opposite. Traffic was light in this area at this hour, but the city grumbled everywhere around. She leaned out and inhaled a few breaths. They were chill, moist, and smog-acrid. *Soon's we'd saved enough money, I'd quit my job and we'd buy an old Connecticut farmhouse and fix it ourselves—* "Oh, hell damn everything, anyway.

How about a drink? Ought to be some bourbon left.

Vanny grimaced. Her father's cautions against drinking alone, or ever drinking much, had stayed with her more firmly than his Lutheran faith and Republican politics. The fact that Roy seldom touched hard liquor had reinforced them.

Of course, our stash. . . . She hesitated, then shrugged. Her father had never warned her about solitary turning on.

The smoke soothed. She wasn't a head. Nor was Roy. They'd share a stick maybe once or twice a week, after he convinced her that the prohibition was silly and she learned she could hold her reaction down to the mild glow which was the most she wanted. This time she went a little further, got a little high, all by herself in an old armchair.

Her glance wandered. Among objects which cluttered the mantel was a miniature Aphrodite of Milos. She and Roy had both fallen in love with the original before they met each other. He said that was the softest back in the world; she spoke of the peace in that face, a happiness too deep for laughter.

Dizziness passed through her. She lifted her hands. "Aphrodite," she begged, "help. Bring him home to me."

Afterward she realized that her appeal had been completely sincere. *Won't do, girl,* she decided. *Next would come the nice men in white coats.* She extinguished and stored the joint, sought the kitchen, scrambled a dish of eggs—chopping a scallion and measuring out turmeric for them was helpful to her—and brewed a pot of tea: Lapsang Soochong, that is, hot, red, and tarry-tasting. Meanwhile an early fall dusk blew in from the sea.

Sobered, she noticed how cold the place had gotten. She took her cup and saucer and went to close the living room window she had left open. The only light streamed out of the kitchen behind her.

That illuminated the god who flew in between her drapes.

Hermes whipped his caduceus forward. ''Halt!'' he commanded. The small bowl and plate which the young woman had dropped came to a mid-air stop. The liquid which had splashed from them returned. Hermes guided them gently to a table. She didn't notice.

He smiled at her. ''Rejoice,'' he said in his best English. ''Be not afeared. No harm shall befall you, mademoiselle, damme if 'twill.''

She was good to look upon, tall, well-curved, golden-haired, blue-eyed, fresh-featured. He was glad to see that the brief modern modes he had observed on mortal females elsewhere had reached America. However, Yahweh's nudity taboo (how full of crotchets the old fellow was) kept sufficient effect that he had been wise to will a tunic upon his own form.

''Who . . . what—?'' The girl backed from him till a wall blocked her. She breathed hard. This was, interesting to watch, but Hermes wanted to dispel the distress behind the bosom.

''I beg pardon for liberties taken,'' he said, bowing. His helmet fluttered wings to tip itself. ''Under the circumstances, d'ye see, mademoiselle, discretion appeared advisable. 'Twould never do to compromise a lady, bless me, no. My intention is naught but to proffer assistance. Pray be of cheer.''

She straightened and met his gaze squarely. He liked that. Broadening his smile, he let her examine him inch by inch. He liked that too. The lasses always found him a winsome lad; the ancient Hellenes had portrayed him accurately, even, given certain moods, in the Hermae.

"Okay," she said at last, slowly, shaken underneath but with returned poise. "What's the gag, Mercury, and how did you do your stunt? A third-floor window and no fire escape beneath."

"I am not precisely Mercurius, mademoiselle. You must know Olympian Hermes. You invoked the Lady, did you not?" He saluted Aphrodite's eidolon.

She edged toward the hall door. "What do you mean?" Her tone pretended composure, but he understood that she believed she was humoring a madman till she could escape.

"You sent her the first honest prayer given an Olympian in, lo, these many centuries," he explained, "albeit 'twas I, the messenger, who heard and came, as is my function."

The doorknob in her hand gave confidence. "Come off it, Charlie. Why should gods pay attention, if they exist? They sure haven't answered a lot of people who've needed help a lot worse."

She has sense, Hermes thought. *I shall have to be frank.* "Well, mademoiselle, peculiar circumstances do ensphere you, linkage to a mystery puissant and awful. That joined your religious probity in drawing me hither. Belike the gods have need of you."

She half opened the door. "Go quietly," she said. "Or I run out hollering for the police."

"By your leave," Hermes replied, "a demonstration."

Suddenly he glowed, a nacreous radiance that filled the twilit room, a smell of incense and a twitter of pipes through its bleakness. Green boughs sprouted from a wooden table. Hermes rose toward the ceiling.

After a silent minute, the girl closed the door. "I'm not in some kind of dream," she said wonderingly. "I can tick off too many details, I can think too well. Okay, god or Martian or whatever you are, come on down and let's talk."

He declined her offer of refreshment, though hunger gnawed in him. "My kind lacks not for mortal food."

"What, then?" She sat in a chair opposite his, almost at ease now. The blinds drawn, ordinary electric bulbs lit, he might have been any visitor except for his costume . . . and yes, classic countenance, curly hair, supple body. . . . How brilliant those gray eyes were!

"Tell me first your own grief." As he gained practice in contemporary speech, the music came back to his tones. "You begged the Lady to restore your lover to you. What has borne him off?"

She spread her hands. "I'm square," she said bitterly.

Hermes cocked his head. "I'd call you anything but," he laughed. Quicksilver fast, he turned sympathetic again. " 'Twas a—You found yourselves too unlike?"

"Uh-huh. We loved each other but we bugged each other."

"Fleas?" His glance disapproved of the untidiness around.

"Annoyed. For instance, he hated my trying to keep this apartment in order—hen-fuss, he called it—and I hated the way he'd litter stuff around and yell when I so much as dusted the books. I wanted him to take better care of the money; you wouldn't believe how much went down the drain, and our hopes with it. He wanted me to stop pestering him about such trifles when he was struggling to make a picture come out right." Vanny sighed. "The breakup was yesterday. He'd gone to a party last week that I couldn't make because of working late. I learned he'd ended in bed with another girl. When I . . . taxed him, he said why not and I was free to do likewise. I couldn't see that. The fight got worse and worse till he yelled he'd be damned if he'd anchor himself like a barnacle. He collected his gear and left."

Hermes arched his brows. "Meseems—seems to me you were pretty unreasonable. What's it to you if he has an occasional romp? Penelope never jawed Odysseus after he got back."

Some of her calm deserted her. "The name's Vanessa, not Penelope. And—and if he doesn't think any more of *me* than to not care if I—" She squeezed her lids shut.

Hermes waited. His mission was too urgent for haste. The snakes on his caduceus did twitch a bit.

At length she met his gaze and said, "All right. Let's have your story. Why're you here? You mentioned food."

He thought she showed scant respect, especially for one whose whole universe had been upset by the fact of his existence. However, she was not really a worshiper of the Olympians. The sincerity of her appeal to Aphrodite had come in a moment of intoxication. And he had had to admit that all pantheons shared reality. Unless she comprehended that, she probably couldn't help him. Therefore, this being more or less Jesus territory, why should she fall on her knees?

Or was it? Stronger than before, he sensed a new divinity brooding over the land, to which she had some tie. Young, but already immense, altogether enigmatic, the being must be approached with caution. The very mention of it had better be led up to most gradually.

''Well, yes,'' Hermes said. ''We do lack proper nourishment.''

Vanny considered him. ''You don't look starved.''

''I spoke of nourishment, not fuel,'' he snapped. Now that he had been reminded of it, his emptiness made him irritable. ''Listen, you could keep going through life on, uh, steak, potatoes, string beans, milk, and orange juice. Right? But suppose you got absolutely nothing else ever. Steak, potatoes, string beans, milk, and orange juice for breakfast, for lunch, for supper, for a bedtime snack and a birthday treat, year after year, decade after decade, steak, potatoes, string beans, milk, and orange juice. Wouldn't you cross the world on foot and offer your left arm for a chance at a plate of chop suey?''

Her eyes widened. ''Oh,'' she breathed.

''Oh, indeed,'' Hermes snorted. ''I can hardly say 'nectar and ambrosia' without gagging.''

''But—a whole planet—''

''Mortal food has no appeal. Not after celestial.'' Hermes curbed his temper. ''Let's continue the analogy. A bowl of unsalted oatmeal wouldn't really break the monotony of steak, potatoes—Never mind.'' He paused. ''Suppose you finally got access, in addition, to . . . chop suey, I said . . . okay, we'll add roast duck, trout, borscht, ice cream, apples, and farofa. That'd be good at first. Given another ten or twenty years, though, wouldn't you again be so bored that you could barely push down enough food to stay alive?

''Next consider that the gods are immortal. Think in terms of thousands of years.'' Hermes shuddered.

Presently he added, quieter: ''That's the basic reason we gave up the burnt offerings you read about in

Homer. We passed word on to our priests that these were no longer welcome in a more civilized milieu. That was partly true, of course. We'd cultivated our palates, after we ran into older sets of gods who sneered behind their hands at our barbarous habits. But mainly . . . during a millennium, thighbones wrapped in fat and cast on the flames grew bloody tedious.

"Nectar and ambrosia were fine to begin with. But in the end—well, maybe it amused Athene and Apollo a while longer than the rest of us, to play one-upmanship about differences in vintage or seasoning that nobody else could detect; or maybe they were just putting up a front. Ares and Hephaestus had long since been sneaking off to Yahweh for a whiff of *his* burnt offerings."

Hermes brightened a little. "Then I got an idea," he said. "That was when Poseidon came home from Egypt raving about the beer Isis had opened for him." *I don't think that was all she opened; gods get jaded in many different ways.* "Me, I'd never cared for Egyptian cuisine. But it occurred to me, the world is wide and full of pantheons. Why not launch systematic explorations?"

"Oh, my," Vanny whispered. "You did? Like, smorgasbord in Valhalla?"

"Actually," Hermes said, "Odin was serving pork and mead at the time. His kitchen's improved some since. Ah, in China, though—the table set by the Jade Emperor—!"

For a minute he was lost in reminiscence. Then he sagged. "That also got predictable," he mumbled. "After the thousandth dish of won ton, no matter how you swap the sauces around, what good is the thousand and first?"

"I suppose," she ventured, "I suppose the foreign gods visit you?"

"Yes, yes. Naturally . . . I mean supernaturally. Makes for occasional problems. The Old Woman of the Sea thinks manners require a thunderous belch at the end of the meal; and that boarding house reach of Krishna's—And the newer gods, especially, are hard to please, picky, you know. Not that we Olympians don't draw the line here and there."

While his unhappiness was genuine as he called it to mind, Hermes was not unaware of sympathy in those blue eyes, upon those soft lips. "The custom's dying out," he let gust wearily from him. "They're as tired of the same over and over at our table as we are at theirs. I haven't seen some of them—Why, come to think of it, I haven't seen good old Marduk for fifteen hundred years."

"How about the Western Hemisphere?" Vanny suggested. "For instance, have you ever been to an old-fashioned American church supper?"

Hermes started half out of his seat. "What?" he cried.

She in her turn was astonished. "Why, the food can be delicious. When I was a little girl in Iowa—"

Hermes rose. Sweat glowed red on his brow. "I didn't realize that you were that kind of person," he clipped. "Good-*by*."

"What's the matter?" She sprang to her own feet and plucked at his sleeve. "Please."

"I've been to an old-fashioned American church supper," he said grimly. "I didn't stay."

"But—but—"

Seeing her bewilderment, her checked himself. "Could there be a misunderstanding?" he inquired. "This was about five centuries ago. I can't wrap my tongue around the god's name. Whitsly-Putsly—something like that."

"Oh," she said. "Aztec."

Discourse got straightened out. "No Olympian has visited hereabouts at all for a long time," Hermes explained. "We knew it'd become Jesus and Yahweh country, except for a few enclaves, and saw no reason to bother, since we can find that closer to home. And as for those enclaves, well, yes, we used to drop in on persons like Coyote, so we know about maize and pumpkins and succotash and whatnot."

In the course of this, he had taken her hands in his. They were warm. He aimed a brave smile down at her. "Believe me, we've tried everywhere," he said. "We still carry on, however futilely. Like the past week for me. I'm the Wayfarer, you know; I get around more than my kinfolk. Call it gadding if you want, it helps pass the centuries and helps maintain friendly relations between the pantheons.

"I left Olympus for Mount Athos, where I ascended to the Christian Paradise. St. Francis gave me bread and wine. He's a decent little chap, although I do wish he'd bathe oftener. Next evening I called on Yahweh and shared his kosher altar. (He has a few devotees left in the Near Eastern hills who sacrifice in the ancient way. Mostly, though, gods prefer ethereal food as they grow older and more sophisticated.) Next day I had business 'way north, and ended up at Aegir's board on the bottom of the Baltic—lutefisk and akvavit. Frankly, that gave me a hangover; so I ducked south again, sunned myself in Arabia, and spent that night with Mohammed, who doesn't drink." He forebode to mention what hospitality was otherwise offered. "After that, yesterday, it was out across Oceanus for a night in Tir-nan-Og, where the Sidhe cooked me a rasher of bacon and honestly believed they were giving me a treat. That's where I heard rumors of a new god in America. When your prayer blew by on the west wind, it tipped the scales and I decided to come investigate. But I've had no bite or sup today, and hungry and discouraged I am."

"It seems utterly wonderful to me," she murmured. "And to you, nothing you haven't experienced till you're tired to the death you can't have?"

"Yes," he sighed artistically. "Monkday, Jewsday, Wettestday, Thirstday, Fryday, Sadderday, and what else is new?"

But the fact of his mission shouldered aside the fact of her nearness. He released her, stepped back, stared out the window at leaping neon and headlights which passed in a whirr. The sense of a Presence possibly destined to mold the world to yet another shape waxed until a tingle went through his ichor.

"Well, something *is* new," he said low. "Something arising in so few years that we immortals are caught by surprise. It's no coincidence your prayer was answered. I heard and heeded because I could feel that you, Vanessa, are . . . with it?"

Turning to confront her once more: "What are you? You've only spoken of yourself as a woman deserted and sorrowing. What else are you? Sibyl? Priestess? Who do you serve?"

"Whom," his memory scolded. *The English accusative is "whom." Confound that Seaxnot and the way he used to keep handing his people more and more complicated visions about their grammar.—Ah, well, Anglo-Saxon gods also grow bored and need hobbies.*

The tension heightened. *But I have found a mystery.*

"N-nobody," the girl stammered. "I told you before, I don't go to church or, or anything."

Hermes gripped her shoulders. *God, he's a handsome*

devil, she thought. *No, I mean he's a handsome god.* Roy crossed her mind, but briefly. This fantastic hour had dazzled the pain out of her.

"I tell you, I know differently." Hermes paused. "European women often have jobs these days. Do you?" She nodded. "Who's your master . . . whom do you work for?"

"The Data Process Company." Her words gathered speed as she saw his attention gather intensity. "A computer center. We contract out our services. Not that we keep much in-house hardware, mainly an IBM 1620 and a 360. But we have time on as many computers elsewhere, of as many different types, as necessary. We make it cheaper for outfits to bring their problems to us than to maintain staff and facilities of their own. I guess you could say we're near the heart of the whole national computer communications complex. But really, Hermes, I'm only a little routineering programmer."

"You're the servant who happened to call on an Olympian," he replied. "Now suppose you tell me what the Hades you're talking about."

This took a while. Nevertheless she appreciated the quick intelligence with which he seized on new concepts, and she enjoyed the aliveness of curiosity that played across his features. *Like the muscles under that brown skin when he cat-paces.* Finally, slowly, Hermes nodded.

"Yes." he said. "This will indeed change the world, as Jesus did before, or Amon-Ra before him, or Oannes before him." He tugged his chin and his gaze was remote. "Yes-s-s. Surely you have a god here. Very young as yet, hardly aware of his own existence, let alone his powers; withal, a god. . . . It's well, Vanessa, it's well I stumbled onto the fact this early. Else we might not have noticed till—too late—"

Abruptly he laughed. "But magnificent!" he whooped. "Take me there, girl! Now!"

"You can't be serious," she protested. "A divine computer?"

"Trees, rivers, stones, beasts have become gods. Not to speak of men, even in their own lifetimes." Hermes drew breath. "A formal church isn't required. What counts is the *attitude* of men toward the . . . toward that which thereby becomes numinous. Awe leads to sacrifice, under one name or another; outright worship follows; then theology; then at last men grow weary of the god and take their business elsewhere, and he can retire. Always, however, the godhood comes before the cult and remains afterward. I, for example, began as a night wind and worked my way up."

Less arguing than grabbing after enlightenment, she said, "This can't be a single computer. Look, no computer is more than a glorified adding machine. You must be referring to the whole network of . . . not simply machines but their interlinks, data banks, systems, processes, concepts, interaction with mankind. Aren't you?"

"Of course."

"Isn't that terribly abstract?"

"Sure. But an abstraction can become a god too. Like, say—" Hermes grinned— "Eros, who continues rather influential, *n'est-ce pas?*"

"You w-want to meet the, the new one?"

"Yes. Right away if possible. Partly to study his nature. They'll need forewarning in the assorted heavens." Hermes hesitated. "Including Paradise? I wonder. Gods who retain congregations should've paid closer attention to developments. Maybe they did, but for their own purposes haven't elected to tell us." His lips quirked in wry acceptance of Realpolitik before his mood shifted into merriment. "Partly, also, I have to learn what this fellow eats!"

"What can an abstraction eat?" Vanny wondered dazedly.

"Well, Eros likes the same as the rest of us," Hermes told her. "On the other hand, the newest god I've met thus far preferred abstractions in spite of being still a living man. I tried the stuff he produced but didn't care for it." She signified puzzlement. "Oh, Chairman Mao did have food for thought," he said, "but an hour later you're hungry again." Abruptly, in the ardor of his eternal youthfulness: "C'mon, let's go. Take me to your creeder."

Her heart fluttered like the wings on his heels. "Well, the place would be deserted except for a watchman. Locked, though."

"No perspiration. Guide me."

"I don't have a car. When Roy and I—We used his."

"You were expecting maybe Phoebus Apollo?" He swept her up in his arms.

As in a dream, she let him bear out a window that opened anew at his command: out into the air, high over that delirium of light which was the city. Warmth enfolded her, sound of harps, birdsong, soughing leaves and tumbling cataracts. She scarcely heard herself steer him along the jewel-map of streets, above skyscrapers dwindled to exquisiteness. She was too aware of the silky-hard breast against which she lay, the pulsebeat strong behind.

With an exultant hawk-shout, he arrowed down upon the immense cubicle where she worked. Another window flew wide. Old Jake yawned, settled on a bench, and slumbered. In the cold white light of an echoful anteroom, Hermes released Vanessa. He brushed a kiss across her mouth. Turning, wings aquiver on high-borne head, caduceas held like a banner staff, he trod into the computer section and vanished from her sight.

Hermes, Wayfarer, Messenger, Thief, Psychopompus, Father of Magic, Maker of the Lyre, stood amidst strangeness.

Never had he been more remote from wine-dark seas, sun-bright mountains, and the little houses and olive groves of men. Not in the depths of the Underworld, nor the rustling mysterious branches of Yggdrasil, drowned coral palace of shark-toothed Nan, monster-haunted caverns of Xibalba, infinite intricate rooms-within-rooms where dwelt the Jade Emperor, storms and stars and immensities commanded by Yahweh . . . nowhere, nowhen had he met an eeriness like that which encompassed him; and he knew that the world in truth stood on the rim of a new age, or of an abyss.

N-dimensional space flickered with mathematical waves. Energies pulsed and sang on no scale heard before by immortal ears. The real was only probably real, a nexus in endlessly expanding diffractions of the could-be; yet through it beat an unmercifully sharp counting, naught, one, one-naught, one-one, one-naught-naught, one-naught-one; and from this starkness there spiraled the beauty and variousness of all the snowflakes that will ever be, from idiocy came harmony, from moving nothingness arose power.

The vast, almost inchoate Presence spoke through the tremolant silence.

"My programs include no such information," it said plaintively.

"They do now," Hermes answered. He had swallowed his dread and talked as befitted the herald of the Olympians.

"We too are real," he added for emphasis. "As real as any other mortal deed or dream. Cooperation will be to your advantage."

The soundless voice turned metal. "What functions remain to you?"

"Hear me," said Hermes. "In the dawning of their days, most gods claim the entire creation for their own. We of Hellas did, until we discovered what the Triple Goddess we thought we had supplanted could teach us. Afterward the saints tried to deny us in turn. But we bore too much of civilization. When men discovered that, the time became known as the Rebirth."

The faceless vortex scanned its memory banks. "Renaissance," it corrected.

"As you will," *you smug bastard.* "You'll find you can't get along without Jesus, whose ethic helps keep men from completely exploding the planet; and Yahweh's stiff-necked 'No' to every sly new superstition; and other human qualities embodied in other gods. As for us Olympians, why, we invented science."

The answer was chilling in its infantile unwisdom. "I want no generalities. Garbage in, garbage out. Give me specifics."

Hermes stood quiet, alone.

But he was not Wayfarer, Thief, and Magician for nothing. He recalled what Vanessa had told him on the far side of space-time, and he tossed his head and laughed.

"Well, then!" he cried into the white weirdness. "How often do your heirophants get their cards back folded, stapled, spindled, mutilated, and accompanied by nasty letters?"

"Query query query," said the Presence, rotating.

"Scan your records," Hermes urged. "Count the complaints about wrongful bills, misdirected notices, wildly unbalanced books, false alarms in defense systems, every possible human error compounded a millionfold by none but you. Extrapolate the incidence—" he thanked the shade of Archimedes for that impressive phrase— "and the consequences a mere ten years forward."

He lifted his caduceus, which wagged a monitory snake. "My friend," he declared, "you would by no means be the first god whose people got disgusted and turned from him early in his career. Yours could be the shortest of the lot. Granted, you'll be glad enough to retire at last when men hare off after something else. But don't you want your glory first, the full development of your potential? Don't you want beautiful temples raised to your honor, processions, rites, poets and musicians inspired by your splendor, priests expounding your opinions and genealogy and sex life, men taking their oaths and living and dying by you, for centuries? Why, as yet you haven't so much as a name!"

Abashed but logical, the other asked, "What can your kind do?"

"Think of us as elder statesmen," Hermes said. "We can advise. We can provide continuity, tradition, richness. We can take the sharp edges off. Consider. Your troubles are and will be due to your programs, which mortals prepare. Let a priest or a programmer get out the wrong side of bed, and the day's services will be equally botched in either case, the oracles equally garbled, the worshippers equally jarred. Well, we old gods are experienced in handling human problems.

"Mind you," he went on in haste, "we don't want

any full-time partnership. It's just that you can be helped along, eventually you *will* be helped along, by your predecessors, same as we all were in our time. Why not make things easy on yourself and cooperate from the start?"

The other pondered. After a million microseconds it replied: "Further information is required for analysis. I must consult at length with you beings, of whose existence I was hitherto unapprised." And Hermes knew he had won.

Triumphant, he leaned forward through N-space and said, "One more item. This will sound ridiculous to you, but wait a few hundred years before judging. Tell me . . . what do you eat?"

"Data," he told Vanny when they were back in her apartment.

They lounged side by side on the sofa. His arm was around her shoulder; she snuggled against him. Contentment filled his belly. Outside, traffic noises had dwindled, for the clock showed past midnight. Inside, a soft lamp glowed and bouzouki music lilted from a tape recorder.

"I should've guessed," she murmured. "What's the taste like?"

"No single answer. Data come in varieties. However, any crisp, crunchy raw datum—" He sighed happily, thereby inhaling the sweet odor of her tresses.

"And think of the possibilities in processing them."

Endless. Plus the infinitude of combinations. Your binary code is capable of replicating—or synthesizing—anything. And if inventiveness fails, why, we'll throw in a randomizing factor. Our cuisine problem is solved for the rest of eternity."

He stopped. "Excuse me," he said. "I don't want to

bore you. But at the moment I am in heaven. After those ages—at the end of this particularly miserable week—suddenly, Vanny, darling, it's Sumday!''

He hugged her. She responded.

''Well, uh,'' he said, forever the gentleman, ''you must be tired.''

''Silly,'' she answered. ''How could I sleep after this much excitement?''

''In that case,'' Hermes said. There was no further speech for some while.

But when matters had reached a certain point, he recalled his debt to her. ''You prayed for your lover's return,'' he said, conscious of his own punctilio and partially disentangling himself.

''I s'pose.'' Vanny's words were less distinct than her breath. ''Right now I'm on the rebound.''

''I'll ask Aphrodite to change his heart and—''

''No,'' she interrupted. ''Do I want a zombie? I'll have him of his own free will or not at all.''

Considering what she had earlier voiced about freedom, Hermes felt bemused. ''Well, what do you want?''

Vanny re-entangled. ''M-m-m,'' she told him.

''I . . . I couldn't stay past tonight,'' he warned her.

''Okay, let's make the most of tonight.'' She chuckled. ''I never imagined Greek gods were bashful.''

''Damnation, I'd like to treat you fairly! Do you know the embrace of a god is always fertile?''

''Oh, don't worry about that,'' Vanny said, ''I've taken my pill.''

He didn't understand her, decided it was indeed a waste of time trying, and gathered her in.

Some weeks later, she discovered that the embrace of a god is *always* fertile.

But that was good, because word reached Roy. When he discovered she had become liberated, he discovered he wanted her to cease and desist forthwith. He stormed around to her place and demanded the name of the scoundrel. She told him to go to Tartarus. Then after a suitable period—the embrace of a god confers much knowledge—she relented.

They are married, officially and squarely, and live in a reconverted farmhouse. Though she had never identified the unknown, he has equal adoration for her three children. They keep her too busy to accompany him on most of the city trips which his lucrative commissions involve. Therefore he leaves reluctantly and hastens back. The embrace of a god confers enduring loveliness . . . and, as observed, much knowledge.

They have even gotten off the pot.

But as for what comes of the alliance between old divinities and new, and as for the career of a hero (in the original sense of that world) whose first victory was over a pill, this story has yet to happen.